The Bystander's Bible

By: Rev. Tom Muzzio *(resigned)*

Territorial Enterprise Foundation
P.O. Box 16
Virginia City, NV 89440

ISBN: 1548520063
ISBN-13: 9781548520069

Library of Congress Information Pending

Cover design by Mark Nerys, art by Caravaggio

Edited by Edith Wacker

THE PREFACE

Wow, when I released my memoir, entitled *God Told Me to Hate You,* last year I wasn't ready for the blowback! After all, I wasn't really trashing the Bible itself–just the literal interpretation which is really dumb. It could be that the Fightin' Fundies are flat-out stupid . . . or maybe that's just an act. Well, for some weird reason, they're in Trump's army even if they wouldn't lift a finger to fight a war themselves. But, no, the original Bible did not fall down out of the sky one day in 1611 and hit King James on the head. It is just a collection of myths and stories–nothing more. People have been editing the "good book" for centuries. All I am doing is adding my two cents and presenting pertinent questions. By the way, this book is meant to make you laugh–not cry or have a conniption fit. Enjoy!

P.S.: Anything in **Boldface** type is a *direct* quote from the Bible (the *New International Version*).

TABLE OF CONTENTS

can fulfill his mission to deliver the Israelites from bondage at the moment God is about to kill him.

12   **Marah,** *maidservant of Zipporah.* (Exodus 15, 16).
On the great Sinai adventure from the beginning: she cares for Moses, Aaron and the mob of Jews who spent forty years trying to get out of the desert.

13   **Toro-Manoro,** *a Hebrew indentured servant with a super big problem.*
(Selections from Exodus, Leviticus, Deuteronomy)
He and his wife face execution for violating a new Jewish law regarding conjugal visits and other new sexual regulations.

14   **Rahab,** *madam of a brothel in Jericho.* (Joshua 1-8).
She saves two of Joshua's spies in exchange for her life and for her working girls and business.

15   **Tingnanmo,** *Joshua's right-hand man at the battle of Aijalon.* (Joshua 10).
He saw an astronomical wonder never seen before (or since). Overwhelmed, he took a name that means "Wow, look at that!"

16   **Delilah,** *Samson's (on-again, off-again) girlfriend.* (Judges 16).
She delivered Samson into the hands of the Philistines by learning the secret of his long hair after he did his trick with the 300 foxes and slayed ten thousand soldiers with the jawbone of an ass.

17   **Mancini,** *Saul's lefthand man.* (I Samuel 9-28).
Endora raised Samuel from the dead and he saw the whole ghoulish event! He couldn't kill Saul in the end, so Saul had to perform ritual seppuku on himself.

18   **Inamorato,** *Jonathan's valet and armor-bearer.* (I Samuel 17-31; II Samuel 1)
Hopelessly in love with Jonathan—he pined, but Jon's heart beat for David. What a sad story. What a tortured sweet guy.

19   **Dahan-Dahan,** *a councilman of The Queen of Sheba.* (I Kings 4-11).
He was responsible for organizing the amazing journey to visit King Solomon. He also turned out to be quite a clever negotiator.

20   **Teensee and Weensee,** *angels in the service of the Lord.* (Book of Job).
These angelic twins retell the story of Job and the bet made between God and Satan (from the heavenly view). And all along Job had no idea what was happening to him and why.

21   **Shadrack,** *a friend of Daniel.* (Book of Daniel).
He tells firsthand of the "fiery" furnace and Daniel in the lions' den. Being close to the "Chief of the Magicians" certainly has its benefits.

22   **Scribner-Jai,** *Jonah's secretary.* (Book of Jonah)
Swallowed whole with Jonah, he took dictation the entire time! Then he accompanied his famous partner on his mission to save Nineveh.

THE OLD TESTAMENT

Chapter 1

The Archangel Explains Creation

Michael's rendition of the Big Bang

If you get your information about how this whole thing began from the blockheads who wrote the Bible, you are certainly out of luck. For one thing, they weren't there. I was. My name is Michael and I am an archangel. That is, I am a really high-up kind of angel, and I was right there when God decided to create the Universe. I had been with the old man for as long as I can remember, along with the heavenly host. God (or Yahweh, as some like to call him) had quite an entourage back then. Of course, there were all sorts of angels and "giants" called Nephelim, and a whole slew of really cool angels who followed the coolest angel of all, Lucifer. He was, like, way cooler than even God himself, but I will let him tell his own story later. Right here I want to stick to my version.

After God got sick of Lucifer and the cool angels upstaging him, he kicked them all out of Heaven. To tell you the truth, after they left, things were really boring around the place, and the heavenly host got tired of singing praises for *ten thousand years* at a time. What a drag!

Then God got the cool idea to create the Universe. He called it "the Heavens and the Earth." I was okay with the idea, but warned him that he should plan things out a bit before just speaking everything into existence. He let me know that—because he was God and all—he didn't need a blueprint. So I just stood back while he puffed up and created out of zero. *Bang*. I was impressed. Well, sort of.

So, I said: "Fine. You created the Heavens, but no stars, planets, nebula or anything interesting. Just a big, empty, dark place with a little dark blob floating around. It is formless and void," I considered aloud. "And

1

all there is down there is water! Like, what's with that?"

"Aha, watch this!" he remarked, and then roared forth . . . **"Let there be light!"** (Genesis 1: 3). And, I will admit, there was light. Impressed again, I wondered where the light was coming from. But, before I could ask, he took to creating again right then and there!

"Let there be an expanse between the waters to separate water from water." (Gen. 1: 6). Wow, I was thinking, this is really awesome. So God created a thing called "sky" with water above it and water below it. Far out. Huh?

"But, your heavenly majesty," I pondered, "why do you need water *above* the sky?"

"Like, where do you suppose the rain is going to come from?" he replied impatiently. "I am going to create a storehouse of rain, snow and ice and keep them above the sky, so that when I want precipitation I can simply turn on the moisture! Keen idea, don't you think?" (See Job 40).

"Well, so far, haven't you created a rather wet place?" I queried him.

"Oh, all right . . . **Let the water *under* the sky be gathered to one place, and let dry ground appear."** (Gen: 1: 9). Lo and behold, it did! So God called the dry ground "land" and gathered together waters, which he called "seas." And saw that it was good.

"Now what?" I went on with my game of twenty questions. "Let's see, we have water above the sky and below the sky and we have dry land and seas. How about creating the sun, the moon and the stars?"

"Oh, you have no imagination, Michael," he said condescendingly. "I will get to that. Meanwhile, watch this!" Poof, flora! (But no corresponding fauna). **Then God said, "Let the land produce vegetation: seed-bearing plants and trees on the land that bear fruit with seeds in it, according to their various kinds."** (Gen. 1: 11-13).

"That is really amazing . . ." I remarked. "But how are all these seed-bearing plants and trees going to make it without a sun? Like, come on. You are not thinking about photosynthesis! Certainly a smart fellow like you must realize that all these plants will need sunlight to survive!"

"Oh, for pity's sake, Mike, I am *omnipotent* already. I can do whatever I want. And I am creating this earth and I get to do it any bloody way I please. But, to satisfy your need for order—poof! There . . . the sun. Are you happy now?"

"Okay, I admit I feel a bit better now, but you still haven't made the moon yet!"

"Here we go again," he said exasperatedly. "Like, abracadabra . . . voila, the moon!

So it came to pass. God made two great lights–the greater to govern the day and the lesser light to govern the night. He also made the stars. (Gen 1: 16).

"Thanks for remembering the stars," I complimented. "I would have created them *first*, but hey . . . they are nice. Of course, the moon isn't really a light. It just reflects light from the sun," I pointed out gingerly.

"Picky, picky, picky," he snorted. And I knew to just stow that observation for now. After all, I felt some more creating coming. And sure enough! What would he think of next? (Fauna, perhaps?) Since he was obviously reading my mind, being omniscient and all, he raised his "mighty" hand and made the first animals! **Livestock!** (Gen 1: 24).

"Wait a minute," I blundered, puzzled, "Why create livestock first? What about **creatures that move along the ground, and wild animals, each according to its kind?**" (Gen 1: 24).

"Alright, alright," he replied testily. "See if I ever invite you to a creation again! Harrumph."

"So, that's it?" I stuttered. "You are just going to leave it at that?"

"Well, what more do you want?" he quizzed. "I kind of like it this way. (Sigh.) Okay, Mr. Smarty, what do you in all your infinite wisdom think we need to add to this real nifty planet?"

"Well, how about people?" I asked. "After all, somebody has to take care of all that livestock! Or didn't you think of that?"

"No need to get snippy," he replied wearily.

"Let us make man in our image, in our likeness, and let them rule over the fish of the sea and the birds of the air, over the livestock, over all the earth, and over all the creatures that move along the ground." (Gen 1: 26).

It's about time, I mused to myself.

So he created human beings. He blessed them and commanded them to **"Be fruitful and multiply: fill the earth and subdue it. Rule over the fish of the sea and the birds of the air and over every living creature that moves on the ground."** (Gen 1: 28).

"Well, you did it," I congratulated him. "A bit bassackwards, to be sure, but it is done."

"Is there anything I have forgotten?" he asked, not expecting a reply.

"Well, are they just going to float around aimlessly or are you going to actually put them somewhere specific?" I asked.

"Okay, okay . . . How about a garden?" he said. "He needs a job anyway, so he can take care of it."

Always thinking ahead, I wondered aloud: "Where shall the garden go?"

"Well, definitely somewhere in the *East*!" he insisted. "Some place with rivers and gold!" (See Gen. 2: 10-11).

"Like maybe in Mesopotamia?" I encouraged.

"Mesopowhat? Where?" he blustered, exhausted. "Heavens and Earth no! That's way too long and hard to remember. How about something short and catchy, like *Iraq*?"

"I like it!" I chirped enthusiastically. "That's enough creation for me. Can I buy you a drink?"

"Naaa," he sighed. "I need a nap."

Thus the heavens and the earth were completed in all their vast array. By the seventh day God had finished the work he had been doing; so on the seventh day he rested from all his work. And God

blessed the seventh day and made it holy, because on it he rested from all the work of creating that he had done. (Gen 2: 1-3).

After all that, I think I'd need a nap too :-)

Chapter 2

All About Eve

Adam's helpmate talks candidly about life in the garden,
her fear of snakes, and her need for sewing lessons

Likely you have heard of me. I have been called the mother of mankind. My story is very important, so pay attention! Like, first of all, here we are in the Garden of Eden. It is okay, but kind of a mess. There are all these animals running hither and yon, pooping all over the place. Adam was assigned by God to "tend" the garden. He didn't have much of a green thumb to begin with, but tending was really a problem since shovels and rakes hadn't been invented yet.

Besides that, Adam kept trying to keep the wildlife from trampling all the flowers by shouting at them. It was really redundant shouting stuff like "Bad animal" and "Get your ass out of there, animal!" and "Quit peeing on the chrysanthemums, you stupid whatever-you-are!" This immediately caught God's attention, so he decided that all those creatures needed *names*.

So God ordered Adam to name them all in their multi-millions. Simple: he just started with Aardvark and went from there. He was doing fine until he began running out of names somewhere around the Dikdik, whereupon he told God that he needed a helpmate. Of course, God (being omniscient and all) already knew that, so I came on the scene to help with the tending and naming. And let me tell you—it was really a hard thing to just keep thinking up new names. Adam thought it would be easier if we could use different languages for, like, the Nilpferd, the Pagpaliwanag, and the Pakibasa. But God thought that it might confuse everybody, and insisted on using *his own* language: King James English. After all, that's God's native tongue. Everybody knows that.

So the man gave names to all the livestock, the birds of the air and all the beasts of the field. But for Adam no suitable helper was found! (Genesis 2: 20). Like, *where* did they look? All those weird animals were no help at all . . . except the donkey. He could talk, but wouldn't speak unless he had something to say! (Numbers 22: 21-39).

So God got back into creation mode and made me out of one of Adam's ribs. Very creative. Adam was so happy to see me that he exclaimed: **"This is now bone of my bones and flesh of my flesh; she shall be called *woman* for she was taken out of man."** (Gen. 2: 21-22). You have to admit that is pretty eloquent for a guy who was just created that day, named all the animals on the Earth, and was facing a major cleanup job to boot!

So we decided to make the best of things. We began tending the garden as ordered. Of course, we were naked, but we didn't have any shame. Come on, you've got to realize that neither of us was more than twenty-four hours old at the time, and that we were exhausted and needing a Pepsi . . . or better yet, a cocktail! We were definitely not in the mood. But then an interesting thing happened. A serpent arrived on the scene. He wasn't some ol' snake like hillbilly preachers say. He was a guy, a superhero, or an angel or something. No matter what he really was, he was hot! He was really good-looking, suave, and—above all—*crafty*.

Now the serpent was more crafty than any of the wild animals the Lord God had made. (Gen. 3: 1-3).

He *beguiled* me! He really did. And I fell for it. First of all, he really laid it on thick about my great body (being naked and all). Then he showed me this really cool tree with all sorts of erotic-looking fruit dangling from its contorted branches. I told him that we were not allowed to eat from that particular tree because it would make us as smart as God himself. He didn't seem to be buying that one bit.

He asked: **"Did God really say, 'You must not eat from any tree in the garden'?"**

So I said: **"We must not eat from the tree that is in the middle of the garden, for if we touch it we will die."** (Gen. 3: 1-3).

"Like, it's the third rail of the garden," he teased. "Oh, come on, just a little nibble. **You will not surely die. For God knows that when you**

eat of it your eyes will be opened, and you will be like God knowing good from evil." (Gen. 3: 4-5).

Well, not only was he crafty, but he was right! Adam and I took a bite and all hell broke loose. I mean, right away we realized that we were butt naked right there in front of God and everyone! I could even hear the heavenly host titter! I was so embarrassed. Then we felt shame! OMG, what are we to do?

"Quick!" I ordered Adam, "Fetch some fig leaves, pronto!"

"Here. What are you going to do with them?" he asked in that dumbass way that only a man who is *one-day-old* can ask.

"Like, duh, I am going to sew us some 'coverings,' you idiot!" I said. What a doofus!

To which he replied rather dully, "But they haven't invented needle and thread yet!" That was a problem, so we just grabbed the leaves and made a dash for some nearby shrubbery.

Around then it was getting dark, the sun orbiting around us and going down out of sight; the garden cooling off. **Then the man and his wife heard the sound of the Lord God as he was walking in the garden, and they hid from him among the trees of the garden.** (Gen. 3: 8).

"Where are you?" he cooed mockingly. Obviously, he didn't need to ask questions since he is omniscient and knows everything already. But he was just toying with us. He knew good and well that we were hiding behind the philodendron. "We're over here, your holiness," Adam blurted out. **"I heard you in the garden, and I was afraid because I was naked; so I hid."** (Gen. 3: 9,10).

I told him later that he should have just kept his mouth shut. But God was obviously pissed. He roared: **"Who told you you were naked?"** (Gen. 3: 11). Like he didn't know. It was Lucifer, that crafty fallen angel/serpent hybrid thing slinking around the garden. And then, "Have you eaten from the tree that I commanded you not to eat from?" Busted!

Then God turned his guns on me: **"What is this you have done?"** (Gen. 3: 13). I knew that he knew that I knew that he knew, but I wasn't about to take the fall for this fiasco, so I pinned it all on the serpent. I mean, like, who else could I lay it on? At least I gave it a shot. At that point God lost it. He got all puffed up and bellowed at the serpent first. "You slithering, slinking, slimy somethingorother! Get your scrawny ass out from behind that sycamore tree, and look me straight in the eye, and tell me what you did!"

"Well, I beguiled her," he boasted. "It was a piece of cake. She fell for the whole thing. She was putty in my hands!"

Well, you won't believe what happened next! I mean—as God is my witness—the serpent's hands and feet disappeared, and he turned into a snake right then and there! I was freaked. **"Cursed are you above all the livestock and all the wild animals! You must crawl on your belly and you will eat the dust all the days of your life."** (Gen. 3: 14).

I couldn't help myself. "Love your scales, Dear," I taunted. But as he slithered away he gave me the evil eye—the Lucifer look, the Satan stare —and hissed: "Just *try* to stay out of my way, my little pretty! I'm going to fuck you over big time. And your little dog too!"

Well, perhaps I shouldn't have been quite so mouthy. God Almighty turned on me next and cursed me with a mighty curse: **"I will greatly increase your pains in childbearing; with pain you will give birth to children."** And if that wasn't bad enough, then came the real sexist putdown of all times: **"Your desire will be for your husband, and he will *rule* over you."** (Gen. 3: 16). What a bitch!

But the All Powerful One was not quite out of curses. He grabbed Adam by the fig leaves and snorted: **"Cursed is the ground because of you; through painful toil you will eat of it all the days of your life."** (Gen. 3: 17). Shit! So Hubby got life at hard labor . . . all over a crummy little piece of fruit. Now, does that seem fair? At this point, BTW, Adam finally got around to giving me an official name. I was no longer referred to as "the woman," but as **Eve, the mother of all the living.** (Gen. 3: 20). I rather liked that. But the final kick in the teeth was when God killed a couple spare animals and made us some Flintstones suits of fur to replace our fig leaf ensemble that he deemed to be *entirely* too tacky.

Then, get this! God kicked us out of the garden right there on the spot! Of course, I didn't say anything right then, but I was ready to split anyway. Adam was kinda worried. Like, where were we to go? What were we going to do? I mean, like, we were out on our fanny. And the creator of the Universe didn't want us sneaking back in either. Nope, **he placed on the east side of the Garden of Eden cherubim and a flaming sword flashing back and forth to guard the way to the tree of life.** (Gen. 3: 24). Well, he gave us a choice that we couldn't refuse. So we hit the road. But all was not lost. The minute we got past the flaming sword and out of the garden we found a cave and realized that the serpent had been right. Our eyes were opened! We ditched the furs, and, well, the Bible puts it this way: **Adam lay with his wife Eve, and she conceived.** (Gen. 4: 1). And that's all I have to say about that.

Chapter 3

Tatlo

Cain's Wife. The third child of Adam and Eve.
This daughter had to become the wife of Cain for the story to work.

Likely you have never heard of me. My name is Tatlo (it means *three*). I was born to famous parents: Adam and Eve. My story is rarely told, since my two older brothers get all the press in the Bible. So let me tell you their *real* story and then it will make sense.

Well, it all started after my folks were unceremoniously kicked out of the Garden of Eden for eating some fruit from God's magic special tree. Well, of course, they had to find some low-cost housing, so they lived in a cave where my eldest brother, Cain, was born. Since God had cursed my dad to a life of hard labor, it was only natural that his firstborn would follow in his footsteps and become a farmer.

My second brother, Abel, branched out from this tradition and became a shepherd. Apparently, Dad and Mom brought some of the livestock with them when they fled Eden. Abel practiced animal husbandry. He preferred hanging with the animals to getting his hands dirty tilling the soil. This arrangement seemed okay to everybody for a while. Then came time for offerings. What? What the hell is an offering—and what are they for? I know, I know—nobody has said anything about offerings yet. Somehow the four people on the planet so far just knew to do offerings by magic or osmosis or something. At any rate, we were supposed to know—even though nobody told us how to do them, or what was okay as a sacrifice and what was not. Bummer. Well, at least it was a *partial* success. The Bible puts it this way: **In the course of time Cain brought some of the fruits of the soil as an offering to the Lord. But Abel brought fat portions from some of the firstborn of his flock. The**

Lord looked with favor on Abel and his offering, but on Cain and his offering he did not look with favor. So Cain was angry and his face was downcast. (Genesis 4: 3,4).

I talked to Cain about this some time later, and he was still pissed that Yahweh had not been more specific. "Like, how was I supposed to know that God didn't want cereal and fruit?" he whined. "He made such a big to-do about one little piece of fruit back in the garden—you would think he really is into fruit. Apparently not. He certainly isn't a vegetarian. Now he tells me! He wants fat!"

Anyhow, God just *assumed* that Cain knew better. **"Why is your face downcast? If you do what is right, will you not be accepted? But if you do not do what is right, sin is crouching at your door: it desires to have you, but you must master it."** (Gen. 4: 6). Poor Cain. He was really bummed out. He had never even heard of sin before. Nobody explained to him that not only was it crouching at his door and wanted to get him, but that he had to master it by doing what is right! Wow, all those deep concepts! Sin, right and wrong, and mastering it. And, above all—the scariest of all—*crouching!*

Anyway, Cain clocked Abel over the head with a charred sheep bone. Then, like-father-like-son, he hid out from God. Of course, God (being omniscient and all) knew exactly where he was all along, but he liked to toy with Cain as he had with his father, Adam.

God cooed, "Hey, Cain . . . like, where's your kid brother, the cute one with the really cool offering? Too bad your offering was squat. You were supposed to give me the best of your harvest!"

"Yeah, but . . ." my brother stumbled, "you didn't tell me that!"

"Well, like, duh! You were supposed to *know!*"

"Oh, sure, like I was supposed to know. Well, I didn't. And, besides, **Am I my brother's keeper?"** (Gen. 4: 9).

Well, God was really pissed at Cain then. The cat-and-mouse game was over. He cursed Cain on the spot. Henceforth nothing would grow for him. His green thumb was gone. To Cain that was a really big deal! **"My punishment is more than I can bear! I will be a restless wanderer on the earth, and whoever finds me will kill me!"** (Gen. 4: 14).

"Oh, get over yourself, Cain . . ." I retorted, "like, who is going to kill you? Aren't we the only people on the planet?" Now, without dear Abel, it's just Dad and Mom and you and me." *Us four and no more.*

But Cain went on . . . "Did you forget, my dear Tatlo: Mom is the mother of all the living! Obviously, we have all sorts of other brothers and sisters out there somewhere, and they are sure to do me in! We need to get out of here right now!" Obviously he had already been thinking about this. "I suggest that we head out East somewhere—maybe near the River of Pishon in the land of Havilah, where there is gold!" (Gen. 2: 12).

"Who's WE?" I asked. "What makes you think I will be your wife? Besides, nobody said that your curse should apply to me too!"

"Well, I've got you beat . . ." he said with a grin. "I've read ahead in the book, and you're pregnant! So you *have* to go with me! So there! Nanner, nanner, nanner. Come on—let's hit the road."

Well, I figured that being the wife of a happy wanderer couldn't be that bad, so we set out for the **Land of Nod, east of Eden**. (Gen. 4: 16). I know that is in Iran, but—you must admit—it has a catchy name. Actually, we *had* to go that way since the flaming sword was still flashing back-and-forth in front of the garden. Really—Nod was our only option. And I was open to new things.

So we lived in Nod for several hundred years and had kids and more kids. We sort of lost track of Mom and Dad back in the cave, but they both lived over 900 years. **Altogether Adam lived 930 years, and then he died.** (Gen. 5: 3). I was pregnant again, so we missed the funeral. Believe me, we did our part fulfilling God's commandment to be fruitful and multiply. Heck, I was still going strong at 800. I was the original "fertile Myrtle."

Then, as if the population boom wasn't enough, the *Nephilim* showed up. They arrived from the sky! Nobody knew who they were at first. Even now, nobody is really sure. But, in any case, they were really awesome and super horny! Some folks called them "Sons of God." Others, "Giants." Still others called them fallen angels, and, still others, "Extra-terrestrials." "ETs" for short.

The Bible puts it this way: **When men began to increase in number on the earth and daughters were born to them, the sons of God saw that**

the daughters of men were beautiful, and they married any of them they chose. (Gen. 6: 1,2). And—take it from me—they really chose a lot. And don't buy the part about them *marrying* any of us. No way. They just fucked us and left. And the Bible still calls the offspring that they left behind the "heroes of old, men of renown." I still kind of wish that those hot guys would come back down here to Earth one of these days. I really miss the sex! But don't tell Cain. He has a temper—as you know. But, other than a few minor indiscretions here and there, now and then, I was a pretty good wife all in all. I put up with Cain all those years, didn't I?

Oddly enough, this whole intergalactic fuckfest really pissed Yahweh off. He was so mad that Earth women were letting these aliens have their way with them that he cut down the life span of everybody on Earth! Well, if he had given us any indication that we weren't supposed to be screwing around with the Nephilim maybe that would have been fair warning. But no . . . he just bellows out a new commandment: **"My spirit will not contend with man forever, for he is mortal: his days will be a hundred twenty years."** (Gen. 6: 3). So there. Take that.

And, just in case you haven't noticed, the human lifespan is now a hundred twenty years. But that wasn't what was really eating at God about all this. It was not that we were all screwing for hundreds of years and having beau-coups children (as he had commanded), but that we were all wicked! What? Wicked! Like, couldn't he at least explain to us what his definition of wickedness was? We were supposed to know already? Just like with Cain, he just *assumed* that we were supposed to know better. He never told us what sin was, what wickedness was, and what evil was. **The Lord saw how great man's wickedness on the earth had become, and that every inclination of the thoughts of his heart was only evil all the time.** (Gen. 6: 5). He just got his knickers in a twist and decided to do something about it.

So what did he do? He *repented!* Yup. **The Lord grieved that he had made man on the earth and his heart was filled with pain. So the Lord said, I will wipe mankind, whom I have created, from the face of the earth—men and animals, and creatures that move along the ground, and birds of the air—for I am grieved that I have made them.** (Gen. 6: 6,7).

The omniperfect god *admitted* that he had made a mistake. Mankind was a flop—a biological error. He decided to blast the whole thing and start all over. He had blown it, so what should he do? Maybe giving some commandments or some rules or something to let mankind know they were sinning? Maybe defining the terms like *sin, evil,* and *wickedness.* It might have really helped. Or he could have forbidden Earthlings from fucking with Nephilim. He is just so angry and out of touch with reality that he wants to lash out and destroy the whole kit-and-kaboodle without even giving anybody a second chance.

So God contemplates how he is going to destroy his creation. You know, the one he called "good!" Of course, as an omnipotent deity, he could simply speak the whole thing out of existence. But that was too final. Obviously, he really didn't want to make it just disappear. No, he wanted to play with his little toys for a while. Make them pay for their sin and debauchery. But how? After all, these things have to be handled delicately. He is thinking . . ."Ah, yes, a flood. That will make them suffer . . . and their little dogs too!"

Chapter 4

Yatbaatsam

Noah's daughter-in-law and the wife of Shem

Hi to everybody out there in the world—or what's left of it. My name is Yatbaatsam, the 183rd child of Adam and Eve. I am the wife of Shem and daughter-in-law of Noah, the famous ark-builder. Actually, I have to make one thing clear right off the bat: Noah did not do any of the actual construction on the boat. My husband, Shem, and his two brothers, Ham and Japheth, actually did the work. Noah dealt with all those animals arriving in pairs at the launch site. Of course, that was no small feat. But he always gets credit for being a super carpenter. Now my hubby was the real brains of the operation, and his two brothers (my brothers-in-law) more or less followed his lead. Not to brag, of course, but you have to admit, it was quite an amazing project that they pulled off—all on their own, as nobody around the neighborhood would lift a finger to help them! Of course, they got theirs in the end. LOL. Glug . . . glug . . . glug!

Well, the whole family was kind of shocked when Noah announced the project over dinner one night. "God told me that he is sick of all these wicked people down here on Earth, and that he is going to destroy them all with a flood." We were kind of freaked-out, because the coming flood was going to kill all the animals on Earth as well. OMG, I thought, that is really some serious news. What are we all supposed to do? Well, God told my father-in-law, Noah, that he was going to bring two of each animal species right here to our house; the boys were to build an ark in the back yard. Of course, we would have to move the lawn furniture first.

The ark—a really big boat like no one had ever seen before or even imagined—was to be made out of gopher wood. Well, my first question was . . ."What the hell is gopher wood? And where in the hell are you going to get all that wood around these parts? And the whole thing is going to have to be covered in *pitch!* Pitch? What kind of trees produce that much pitch, and especially out here in the desert?" Well, Shem gave me one of those looks . . . you know, like, "Shut up you babbling woman. What do you know about ship-building anyway? Just make us some sandwiches and get some tent-making materials ready, because after the flood we are all going to have to have something to live in." So I just shut up as instructed . . . but I had my doubts. I just sort of grumbled under my breath: "And, like, what do *you* know about ship-building, Mr. Smartypants?"

So, Shem called up the local lumberyard and ordered 500 cords of gopher wood and 10,000 gallons of pitch. I mean, they had to do it that way—although it wasn't cheap. They would have gone out themselves to find the wood, cut down the trees and drain the sap; but then Noah dropped the real bombshell. We all had only *six days* to do the whole project, as **Seven days from now I will send rain on the earth for forty days and forty nights, and I will wipe from the face of the earth every living creature that I have made.** (Genesis 6: 13-21). What? How are those three guys going to build an ocean liner out of wood and pitch in six days? On the seventh the animals all have to be inside, as God said it was going to start raining then! Well, I had my doubts.

Then, Ham's wife, Yatbaatsei, quietly asked: "Like, what are all those animals going to eat? And what is going to prevent the carnivores from eating the herbivores? And what about those dinosaurs? I mean, some of them—like the T-Rex—are a nasty lot." Because dinosaurs were still roaming the Earth at that time, we were ever mindful to give them wide berth. Of course, some dinosaurs were quite tame and offered good transportation. Our pet diplodocus, Dinny, (named after Alley Oop's friend and reptilian sidekick) likes it when we saddle him up and take a run around the neighborhood.*

"Just knock off all those stupid, irrelevant questions," snapped Japheth, the third of the brothers. "Nobody else on Earth is going to help us, as they are all out there sinning and being wicked, so we will simply have to use dino-labor. Surely the larger herbivores can help with the heavy lifting!" But then, after all that, God told Noah to exclude the dinosaurs from the ark, so they all perished in the worldwide flood. You can still see their fossils, though, in Wyoming. God never did like them much anyway. Obviously.

Well, hush my mouth! On cue the animals began arriving just like God promised. Noah was all a'twitter. The three boys managed to build the ark in the allotted six days and helped Noah get the animals all assigned their rooms inside the ark by the seventh. The lions, tigers and bears were kept well away from the smaller mammals, rodents and frogs. God instructed Noah how to organize the living arrangements. The pandas from China and the koalas from Australia had thought to bring their own food with them as they had made their way thousands of miles across oceans and over massive mountains and burning deserts to get there. I was amazed. But God had spoken to them and let them know that since food for their exclusive diets did not grow in the "Holy Land" they would have to bring their own.

Then, sure enough, on the seventh day it started to rain. **And the springs of the great deep burst forth!** (Gen. 7: 11). Water just came gushing up from everywhere under the dry land. Wow, how great is that? In no time we began to float, and the ark was launched out into the deep, and we let the shoreline go. Thus began our epic journey. Some of the animals got seasick, but, other than that, they mostly behaved themselves. So we all floated rather aimlessly for the duration of the forty-day downpour. Of course, we were all getting sick of this boat ride from hell, as it was very stinky down with all those animals, and reptiles and amphibians. The birds were restless too. Finally, Noah sent out a dove to check out the scene. It came back empty-beaked. Apparently, God didn't tell Noah that after the forty-day storm, we were going to have to sit and cool our heels in the boat until the water ran off. It took 150 days for all that water to run off the edge of the dry land. So we sat. Noah sent the dove out again and it came back with an olive branch, indicating that it was safe to open the doors of the ark and let all the animals go free. "It's about time," I said to Yatbaatsei. She agreed. But now what? Where were we going to live? Fortunately, the boys had ordered us to bring tent-making materials, so we set to sewing together some real cool tents.

Noah was so jazzed that he immediately went up a bit higher on Mt. Ararat from where we had landed, and built an altar. There he took several clean animals (that we had thought to bring in addition to the other wild creatures and livestock). He sacrificed them and splashed their blood all over the place and lit it with his handy Bic lighter that he thought to bring for such occasions. Everything was still kind of wet, so lighting a fire would have otherwise been tricky. But Noah was really in -tune with the Almighty, who likely forewarned him to "bring fire." Offerings are really important to Yahweh (aka God) as you know.

He was so tickled at Noah's burnt offering that he decided never to wipe out mankind and the animal kingdom with a flood ever again. (Next time it is going to be fire. But that's an upcoming tale.) God was so moved by the whole experience that he put a rainbow in the sky as a sign of a new covenant between him and mankind. I even made a rainbow flag to celebrate the occasion. And it survives to this day!

Well, Noah was a gardener by trade and calling, so he immediately set to planing a vineyard. Since all the plants and trees and other vegetation had been killed by the flood, Noah had thought to bring a few grape plant starts, which he planted right away. All the animals ran, walked, hopped, and/or slithered away to repopulate the planet—and the vineyard grew. After our first year on Mt. Ararat, the vineyard produced its first batch of really quality grapes. We all got into stomping and tromping on them until wine was produced. And what a fine vintage it was! We called it *Ararat 1,* as it was the first year for grape/wine production. It was good stuff . . . and Noah really got into it. We noticed that he was getting "into" his cups a bit too much after a while. Of course, us women couldn't say anything about it, but I did mention to Shem that his dad was kind of tipsy most of the time.

When he drank some of its wine, he became drunk and lay uncovered inside his tent. (Gen. 9: 21). Well, I could tell that Noah's behavior was embarrassing his sons. **Ham, the father of Canaan, saw his father's nakedness and told his two brothers outside. But Shem and Japheth took a garment and laid it across their shoulders; then they walked in backwards and covered their father's nakedness. Their faces were turned the other way so that they would not see their father's nakedness.** (Gen. 9: 22,23). They were very discreet. :-)

Well, we all just went about our normal day jobs while he slept it off. But when he came to, he was massively pissed. I mean, he threw a total fit. I withdrew to our tent as Noah lit into the boys. They had to take it. Yatbabtsei (Ham's wife), Yatbaatwu (Japheth's wife), and I hid in the tent, but watched through the seams and cracks. Noah was on a rage. Apparently, Ham had reentered the tent and somehow "victimized" poor Noah while he was naked and passed-out. Of course, we didn't catch exactly what he actually did to Noah in the tent while he was indisposed, but we guessed that it must have been something really bad—something that Yahweh really doesn't get behind. So he fell into a rant. He began cursing. He cursed a whole lot of stuff, but in the end, he cursed most of all his grandson, Canaan, who was sleeping quietly in his crib at the time.

We all asked ourselves, why in the hell curse *him*? Beats me, but it wasn't just any old curse. He cursed his grandchild into slavery! Slavery —what is that? Since there were only the eight of us from the ark and a few new kids who had been born since we left the boat and took to living in tents on the side of the mountain, who was there to enslave? Well, all of Canaan's descendants, of course! What? Why? And was that fair? I felt sorry for Yatbaatsei. That was a real bummer.

"Cursed be Canaan! The lowest of slaves he will be to his brothers." He also said: **"Blessed be the Lord, the God of Shem! May Canaan be the slave of Shem. May God extend the territory of Japheth; may Japheth live in the tents of Shem, and may Canaan be his slave."** (Gen. 9: 24-27).

Well, it was at this point that Ham and Yatbaatsei decided to split the scene, as being a slave to one's brothers and their kids doesn't exactly appeal. So they left Ararat and headed to Africa, as God had "turned their skin dark" and in true Lamanite fashion, they decided to find their own digs and develop their own neighborhoods.

Meanwhile, Ham and I had a slew of kids, and so did Noah and Mom-Noah. They were likewise producing more babies as well every nine months for another 350 years. I lost track of all their kids—but not ours. I knew all their names (we just numbered them, as I am, likewise, #183). But Noah did name some of his later-born sons, like Cush and above all, Nimrod, who grew to be . . . **a mighty warrior on earth. He was a mighty hunter before the Lord.** (Gen. 10: 9).

Well, Nimrod was a restless child and kind of a juvenile delinquent as a kid growing up. He had serious ADD and finally just couldn't sit still in our town any longer. We had long since left Ararat for the flatlands, become farmers and sheepherders and merchants and stuff like that. By about year 200, Nimrod was just getting out of control, so he decided to blow that pop stand and head out to become a professional hunter. And a mighty warrior on the Earth. He had a real knack for killing things (like animals and people).

He and some of his kids and some of our kids decided to sally forth and find the plain in Shinar. They settled there and founded a really big town. They called it Babel. Nice name, huh? But we heard that under Nimrod's administration, they were going to really knock the socks off the whole world. They were planning to build a tower that would reach clear up to

Heaven, where Yahweh lives. We were skeptical at first, but Nimrod pointed out that it was doable, as his dad, Japheth, and his other two uncles, Ham and Shem, had built an ark half the size of the Titanic out of wood in only six days. He had a point.

*Creationists insist that in order for the stories of Genesis to work, dinosaurs had to cohabitate with man on Earth up until the flood. Dr. Ken Ham's *Museum of Creation* in Nashville, TN is proof :-)

Chapter 5

Teensee (Talks of Babel)

*Come, let's go down and screw with their heads
and fuck up their language!*

A black cloud has just rolled into Heaven. The choirs of angels and all the cherubim and seraphim are quiet today. YHWH, aka Yahweh, or God or Gawd—or whatever you want to call the Almighty—is upset. We here in Heaven have heard "from some quarter" that something bad is happening down on Earth and that the master of the Universe is pissed. He has been in a bad mood all morning because of it, and is preparing to head down there to check it out. He does this from time to time and he even brings one or two of us angels along on his junkets. I really hope he will choose me to go. I like travel, and, besides, it is so crushingly boring up here in Heaven listening to the angelic "heavenly" host constantly singing the Doxology. The first ten thousand years were okay, I guess, but I relish something different now and then.

Oh, BTW, my name is Teensee.* I am a model A-509 series angel. I am not an android or an automaton, but a real sentient, feeling angel created by God himself (along with millions of others like me). I was a very successful design. I have a twin brother, Weensee. He and I hang together during our coffee breaks. We don't have to sing the Doxology all the time, mind you, as there are millions more of the heavenly host who want their turn to have center stage entertaining the creator of Heaven and Earth. We all just take turns—the rotation method. Right in the middle of the Korean Children's Choir's rendition of "Holy Holy Holy" God got the news.

Mankind, down on planet Earth, was building a tower. "What?" God asked in shock. "A tower? Why does he need a tower? And what is it for? I never authorized man to build towers!" In a strange tone of befuzzlement, he ordered several other A-509s to dash right down there to a place called Babel to check it out. They came back with their report.

"Well, it is true, as we heard," they explained confidentially to the Lord. "Man is indeed building a tower. It is planned to reach all the way up here to Heaven!" (And it was well underway by this time.)

"What in the hell do they think they're doing?" demanded Yahweh. "We can't have them building their way clear up here to Heaven. After all, that clown Jack, who climbed the beanstalk up here a few years ago, proved that it *can* be done!" God was worried. "Of course, we turned Jud, one of the giant Nephilim, on him. Haha. That was a hoot, huh? We sure fee-fi-fo-fummed him right back down to where he belonged, didn't we?"

"Yes sir, we surely did," we agreed.

"Well, what are they building it out of?" he demanded to know.

"Bricks and tar," they replied knowingly. (Genesis 11: 2-4).

"Oh, you've got to be kidding!" the Lord exclaimed with a snort. "They can't possibly build a tower that high out of bricks and tar! What a gaggle of idiots! . . . Who is behind this project anyway?"

"Well, it is a guy named Nimrod," they continued; and he i**s a mighty warrior on the Earth. He is a mighty hunter before the Lord!** (Gen. 10: 9). Then they explained to his Majesty that he was one of the many other sons of Noah. (Though not a party to the ark-building mission of some years earlier.)

"Oh yeah, him," the Lord sighed in a most off-the-cuff manner. "What a show-off! You know, I should just let him go ahead with his stupid tower project and watch it fall down under its own weight like when that dunce Snafoo tried that retarded pyramid idea of his down there in Egypt. These jerks just haven't grasped the basic laws of physics yet. Well, sooner or later they will, and then they will likely fly a space probe clear up here into Heaven and disturb all the praising and glorifying of moi."

So God got up out of his "mercy seat" and ordered Weensee and me to get ready to accompany him down to Babel on the express mission of screwing with mankind one more time. Sounded fun.

"Oh yeah. And let's bring Jesus with us. After all, his big effort to save mankind is still years out, but he probably should get a feel for the place —Earth, that is. He'll be down there on his own soon enough!" So we rounded up Jesus who was enjoying all the praise and adoration of the Congolese Christian Gospel Band at the time. The rest of the *praise-a-thon* would have to be postponed while he and Yahweh and us Alpha-509 angels went down to Babel for a look-see.

Then . . . **The Lord came down to see the city and the tower that the men were building. The Lord said, "If as one people speaking the same language they have begun to do this, then nothing they plan to do will be impossible for them. Come, let us go down and confuse their language so they will not understand each other.** (Gen. 11: 5-7). Sounded kind of mean to me. But, hey, I got to get away from Heaven (and all that endless praising) for a spell, so I just went along with it.

Well, the tower was kind of a sad and puny thing—totally wimpy. I couldn't really understand why this ugly black-tar-covered thing bothered the Holy One so much. But it did. So he cursed all mankind to endless misunderstandings by confusing their languages. Now, some folks got ticked off right away and headed out east of the Plain of Shinar. They took to calling themselves Chinese, traveling a far piece until they found the Yellow River and settled around those parts.

Shem and his kin wandered around and found India (or some other place around there). Ham and his kids were in Africa, of course, where Noah had condemned them all to slavery. And some others headed off in the direction of Europe where they would build some more towers and the like; but they at least learned that mud and tar just didn't do the trick. They began building with stone and mortar instead.

Jesus and God got tired of Earth right away and went back up to Heaven for more never-ending celestial tunes. Weensee and I hung around Babel and the Middle East a bit longer looking for the famous fiery sword at the entrance to the Garden of Eden where God had put it years ago to keep Adam and his descendants out. **On the east side of the garden God put cherubim and a flaming sword flashing back and forth to guard the way to the tree of life.** (Gen. 3: 24). But we never found it.

* Teensee (Tin-Sih) means "angel" (heavenly helper :-)

Chapter 6

Fagar

The sister of the servant of Abraham and Sarah

Hello world. Greetings and salutations. I'm Fagar. My twin sister, Hagar, and I were born in Egypt where we ended up as servants in the court of Pharaoh the Great. It was an okay gig since job opportunities for girls like us were kind of limited in Egypt at the time. Our other sisters, Magar and Bagar, were the good-looking ones, so they got sold off to work in the Pharaoh's harem. Hagar and I were what is referred to as maidservants. Actually, we are really slaves, but that particular word isn't quite PC these days. Anyway, whatever you call us—we were working around His Majesty's palace—doing as little as possible, but always trying to look busy.

Well, there was a famine up north in the land of Canaan. Abram went down to Egypt to live there for a while because the famine was severe. **As he was about to enter Egypt he said to his wife Sarai, "I know what a beautiful woman you are. When the Egyptians see you they will say, 'This is his wife.' Then they will kill me but will let you live. Say you are my sister so that I will be treated well for your sake and my life will be spared because of you."** (Genesis 12: 11). So, sure enough, when Pharaoh laid eyes on Sarai, he just had to have her and added her to his collection of foreign beauties. Hagar and I were assigned to attend her in the harem. It was okay work if you could get it. And Sarai was not bad as kept women go, I guess. But Pharaoh didn't let Abram go unrewarded. **Pharaoh treated Abram well for her** (Sarai's) **sake, and Abram acquired sheep and cattle, male and female donkeys, menservants and maidservants, and camels.** (Gen. 12: 16). He really cleaned up, huh?

Well, it may appear to you that everything was just hunky dory . . . Meanwhile: **But the Lord inflicted serious diseases on Pharaoh and his household because of Abram's wife, Sarai.** (Gen. 12: 17). Obviously, the jig was up and Abram was caught in a lie. So Pharaoh unceremoniously kicked them both out of the country. **"Now then, here is your wife. Take her and go!" Then Pharaoh gave orders about Abram to his men, and they sent him on his way with his wife and everything he had.** (Including Hagar and me.) (Gen. 12: 19). I meant to tell you, they really made out like bandits—those two. I didn't mind going with them since Hagar and I were kept together as a team to attend to Sarai who was getting up in years.

We overheard Abram talking to Sarai about their dilemma—namely that they didn't have any kids, which was a real bummer around those parts back then. So Abram went off to talk to Yahweh (God) about their predicament. God assured Abe that he was going to sire a great and mighty nation. When he told Sarai she just laughed. But she had a plan up her sleeve . . . **"The Lord has kept me from having children. Go, sleep with my maidservant; perhaps I can build a family through her."** (Gen. 16: 2-4). Well, I figured that they were talking about *me* as I am far more attractive than Hagar. It was obvious. But Sarah chose my sister because she was kind of dumpy and therefore was no real competition. I understood her reasoning, but from the minute Hagar became pregnant she turned into a total bitch and treated Sarah like trash. Well, she got what she deserved, I guess. Should have chosen me. So, I just kept mum and watched the show.

So Hagar bore Abram a son, and Abram gave the name Ishmael to the son she had born. Abram was eighty-six years old when Hagar bore him Ishmael. (Gen. 16: 15,16).

He turned out to be a kind of sassy child—spoiled rotten. In fact, Abram and Sarai were bummed because Ishmael was rather taciturn and dull as children go. So Abram went off again and had a powwow with the Almighty. He came back and relayed to Sarai what God had told him during their campout together: **"I will confirm my covenant between me and you and will greatly increase your numbers."** (Gen. 17: 2). Thereupon, God changed their names to Abraham and Sarah. Better, huh? I thought so too.

Well, thirteen years went by and Ishmael just didn't seem to be working out. One day God showed up down on Earth with two angels in tow.

(Probably Teensee and Weensee. LOL.) Anyway, he had a chat with Abraham, and then YHWH just out of the clear blue sky asked where Abraham's wife, Sarah, was. To which Abraham replied: **"In the tent."**

Then the Lord said, "I will surely return to you about this time next year, and Sarah your wife will have a son." (Gen. 18: 9,10).

Sarah overheard the dialogue and snickered: **"After I am worn out and my master is old, will I now have this pleasure?"** (Gen. 18: 12).

But God heard her as well and left with this rejoinder: "Well, you'll see!" And he left in a purple puff of smoke. **Now Sarah became pregnant and bore a son to Abraham in his old age at the very time God had promised him. Abraham gave the name Isaac to the son Sarah bore him. When his son Isaac was eight days old, Abraham circumcised him as God commanded him. Abraham was a hundred-years-old when his son Isaac was born to him.** (Gen. 21: 1-5).

Well, the tables were turned. Actually I didn't feel sorry for Hagar all that much. She had been so mean to Sarah during her pregnancy. And, let me tell you, at that age it was a difficult pregnancy. And I was the one to take care of her because Hagar was so "busy" raising Ishmael and all. I didn't buy that last part one bit, but I could see what was coming.

Sarah was mighty sick of both Hagar and Ishmael. So she got Abe in a good mood and then dropped the bomb on him. She demanded: **"Get rid of that slave woman and her son, for that slave woman's son will never share in the inheritance with my son Isaac."** (Gen. 21: 10). To tell you the truth, that kinda freaked me out. Wow. I was curious to know what Abe was going to do with that one. But he decided to take another walk and talk with the Lord. Good idea, that!

Then God said to him, "Do not be distressed about the boy and your maidservant. Listen to whatever Sarah tells you, because it is through Isaac that your offspring will be reckoned. I will make the son of the maidservant into a nation also, because he is your offspring." (Gen. 21: 11-13). But it wasn't going to be easy, I surmised. So he, just following God's orders, dumped both Hagar and Ishmael out in the desert somewhere the next day. Well, that was definitely not the end of that story. Hah! God really never liked that kid much. Of course, he was just a case of undiagnosed ADD. But no matter. God summed him up thusly: **He will be a wild donkey of a man; his hand will be**

against everyone and everyone's hand against him, and he will live in hostility toward all his brothers. (Gen. 16: 12). Brothers? I never found out about them, nor Hagar. She and Ishmael moved to Arabia somewhere and started a new life for themselves.

Abraham went on to another adventure, however, as I should mention. It seems that God was unsure (after all that) that Abraham loved him best. He knew that Abe really doted on Isaac, so God ordered Abraham to kill the boy as proof. That really bummed ol' Abe out, but he dutifully took Isaac up to a *very windy* mountain called Moriah. There God commanded Abraham to sacrifice the lad with a knife that they had brought for the occasion. Once God was sure that the old man was about to off the kid, an angel of the Lord prevented him in the nick of time. Good thing, huh, as he was the only son and Sarah was not up to providing a replacement under any circumstances by then. So they both came down from Mt. Moriah together. God made a promise to Abraham at that time, and I remember it to this day: **"I will surely bless you and make your descendants as numerous as the stars in the sky and as the sand on the seashore."** Oh sure.

Well, after that, we all packed up and moved to Beersheba where Sarah died at age 127! Not bad for an old lady with a bad hip and tennis elbow, huh? Anyway, after that Abraham took another wife, Keturah. But we never got along, so she fired me. I moved to a little suburb of Havilah near Shur and retired. Hear tell, Abraham lived on to 175 and Isaac headed back to Canaan in search of a wife. But that's the last I heard of him. Hope he thinks to dress warm.

Chapter 7

Lotta and Gotta Lot

*The daughters of Lot who survived the destruction of Sodom
and lived to tell about it*

Hi, y'all. My name is Lotta Lot. My elder sister, Gotta, and I lived and grew up in Sodom, a town on the Plain of Shinar. Nothing much ever happened there until one evening, when our dad, Lot, was sitting outside by the front gate of the city, some visitors arrived rather unexpectedly. He wasn't sure if they were men, or angels, so to be sure . . . **When he saw them, he got up to meet them and bowed down with his face to the ground.** (Gen. 19: 1). Of course, Dad was always kind to strangers, since he had himself always relied on the kindness of strangers.

Now, he did not know who they were, or what they were doing there, but he didn't ask. He just invited them over to spend the night with us. Actually, (we found our later), they were on a reconnaissance mission for God, who was planning to nuke the whole town. The back story is that up in Heaven, God heard rumors that evil was afoot in Sodom. He wasn't sure what it was, but it must have been pretty bad, as he sent two angels in disguise to check the town out. God had already decided to level the place with fire and brimstone, but after a fuss with his old friend, Abraham, he agreed to send his trusted duo, Teensee and Weensee, to town to find out if there were any inhabitants here worth saving.

I'm not sure how they happened to know about us, but when Lot invited them home they declined, offering to stay in the town square for the night. I could have told them that it was a bad idea. But Dad was adamant . . . **he insisted so strongly that they did go with him and entered his house. He prepared a meal for them, baking bread without years, and they ate.** (Gen. 19: 3). Dad was quite a chef, actually, and went on to win the Pillsbury Bake-off years later. Mom probably should have done the baking herself, but she was busy attending to the "fleshpots" at the stove over the fire.

Then all hell broke loose. Suddenly there came a loud pounding on our front door. **All the men of Sodom—both young and old—surrounded the house. They called to Lot, "Where are the men who came to you tonight?"** We were totally freaked. I grabbed Gotta and we hid in the bedroom with our two fiances, Mortimer and Mumford. They were pledged to marry us in a few months, but we had never had sex with them. (Well, that was our story, that is. What Lot doesn't know can't hurt him, can it? Besides, that was a crucial element to what happened next.) Gotta and I could hardly believe our ears! **Lot went outside to meet them and shut the door behind him and said, "No, my friends. Don't do this wicked thing. Look, I have two daughters who have *never* slept with a man. Let me bring them to you, and you can do what you want with them."** (Gen. 19: 6-8). What? Dad was so concerned about the two guys—who were perfect strangers—that he offered *us* to the mob! I was furious. Gotta just cried. And our husbands-to-be didn't even stand up for us! Get that!

Anyway, the crowd was definitely getting out of control. They obviously really wanted those two guys in the worst way. And they didn't even want Gotta and me! Now that hurt. I mean, come on . . . we ain't beauty queens or nothin', but what do those two guys have that we don't? (Other than dicks, I mean.) But then they tipped their hand. They were not just *any* men—strangers—they were angels from on high, as they exhibited super-powers, by blinding the whole lot of them outside. Haha. That really fixed 'em, huh? Well, they pulled Lot back inside and it was clearly time for a serious talk. **Then the two men said to Lot, "Do you have anyone else here—sons-in-law, or daughters, or anyone else in the city who belongs to you? Get them out of here, because we are going to destroy this place. The outcry is so great that he has sent us to destroy it."** (Gen. 19: 12,13). Discussion followed.

"Well, Mort and Mum, this is your chance to get out of here with us," Lot stated authoritatively, "This place is going to burn, baby, burn. Are you in?" What a couple of wusses! They both looked at each other and then looked at us. "Ya know, I think we'll give that a pass," they said timidly. "You don't really think they are going to bomb the whole city do you? Probably just this place, or maybe just the neighborhood. Besides, this place is no great shakes any way, so maybe we'll just hit the road for

Gomorrah. That should be a safe distance." So they left! We were shocked. Of course, their strategy of getting out of Sodom really didn't work out well for them, as God flattened Gomorrah too. LOL. Too bad for them. Well, there are plenty of men in Zoar, so who needs those losers anyway?

The next morning the two angels got up early and urged us to get ourselves together right away. Things were about to happen. **"Hurry! Take your wife and your two daughters who are here or you will be swept away when the city is punished."** (Gen. 19: 15). There was no time to lose. We hurried out of the place, but Mom forgot to turn off the stove, and the fleshpots might burn, so about halfway up the first hill, and still within sight of the city—which was now engulfed in flames— she turned around to go back to her "fleshpots" and was turned immediately into a pillar of salt. Now that's something you don't see every day!

Well, we had no time to whine as acid rain began to fall. Dad insisted that we press upward to get as far out of bombing range as possible. The sky grew dark and was a terrible fright. Fortunately, we found a cave. I wasn't too impressed with the place, though. Compared to Sodom it was a total dump, but Dad insisted that we stay.

"But why don't we just go on to Zoar?" Gotta whined. "There are no men here. And, besides, Mort and Mum aren't likely to have survived that fiasco back in Sodom, so who is going to impregnate us? Who?" She had a point, but I just kept quiet. Then she came up with a totally cool idea: "Why go all the way to Zoar?" she reasoned . . .**"Our father is old, and there is no man around here to lie with us. Let's get our father to drink wine and then lie with him and preserve our family line through our father."** (Gen. 19: 13,32). So **both of Lot's daughters became pregnant by their father. The older daughter had a son, and she named him Moab; he is the father of the Moabites of today. The younger daughter also had a son, and she named him Ben-Ammi; he is the father of the Amorites of today.** (Gen. 19: 36-38).

That was quite a story, huh? What ever happened to Moab and Ben-Ammi, you ask? Well, those stories are coming up!

Chapter 8

Fratello Due

*Second son of Jacob—one of eleven elder brothers
of Joseph, the dreamer*

Hello, out there in Egypt and around the World. My name is Fratello Due, one of the elder brothers of Joseph, the singer and dream-interpreter of our family. We are from Canaan. Our Dad is the famous Israel that you have likely heard about, being the grandson of Abraham-the-Great and son of Isaac. Well, we all got together one day to discuss our situation. Heck, there were eleven of us, and that little brat, Joe, made twelve. We only had one flock of sheep among us and cutting everything up twelve ways just wasn't very efficient or practical.

"We need to get a new gig," stated Judah, our eldest brother flatly. "I propose forming a band." We all kinda liked the idea, but then Levi pointed out that the only one of the bunch of us that could actually carry a tune was Joe, the youngest. And what a drag it would be to have to put up with that little snot all the time on the road—touring with the band and all, that is. Well, before telling "Little Joe" our idea, we ran it past our dad, Jacob (aka Israel). He was pumped. "Great idea, guys. And Joe can sing lead. I have heard the rest of y'all and, well, you could sing backup, of course. In fact, I'll have your mom sew up an outfit for him. A sort of 'coat of many colors' (with decorations). It will be totally fab. You'll see!"

Meanwhile, Joe was going on and on—as usual—about a dream he had had recently. It was about him being a sheaf of grain, and all us other "sheafs" bowing down to him. Talk about cheek, huh!? Well, we were all pissed. And that cape of many colors—that was the last straw. I mean, it was totally over the top. I wouldn't be caught dead in that gaudy thing.

32

But the kid loved it; prancing around like the queen of . . . well, somewhere. Suffice it to say, it was definitely a "queeny" poncho.

So we all lit out for Shechem, not far from Schrechlich—in that neighborhood. Joe stayed back to get his new cape fitted, promising to catch up when it was ready. Well, we didn't stop in Shechem as planned, but went on to Dothan (not far from Wetumka) to try to lose him, but he found us anyway.

"Here comes that dreamer!" they said to each other. "Come now, let's kill him and throw him into one of these cisterns and say that a ferocious animal devoured him. So when Joseph came to his brothers, they stripped him of his robe—the richly ornamented robe he was wearing—and they took him and threw him into the cistern. Now that cistern was empty; there was no water in it. (Gen. 37: 23,24). (Imagine that—an *empty* cistern with no water in it!) Duh. Well, they tossed him in anyway. I tried to stop them, of course. But then we all took the cape—which looked very *Liberace* to me—and dragged it around on the ground and we dumped some animal blood on it for effect.

Well, the cistern idea wasn't working—like, it was empty, remember? So, we came up with Plan B. A Midianite caravan bound for Egypt came by just at the right time, so we pulled the little monster up out of the pit, kicking and screaming. We got twenty shekels for him, and it seemed like a good deal (at the time). Dad was distraught, but got over it. Meanwhile, those Midianites sold Joseph into slavery in Egypt. He was bought by a guy named Potiphar, a bigwig in the current pharaoh's administration. He did okay for a few years and then caught a big break. Seems Pharaoh had a weird dream and nobody could interpret it—except Joe, that is. Actually, I think he may have made the interpretation up to ingratiate himself to Pharaoh. (But that's just a guess. LOL.)

Anyway, it worked! To make a long dream short, Pharaoh saw in his dream fourteen cattle coming up out of the Nile river. The first seven were fat and happy. The rest were skinny and unhappy. What was that all about? Well, Pharaoh demanded an interpretation; whereupon Joseph, the demure little fellow that he was, said: **"I cannot do it, but God will give Pharaoh the answer he desires."** (Gen. 41: 16). Well, so, he simply told the old man that the seven fat cows represented seven years of good harvests ahead, and that he should begin immediately filling the Pyramids (the ones at Giza) to the brim with grain because the skinny cows that came up out of the river last represented seven years of famine to follow. Pharaoh took the interpretation and warning seriously. So he ordered the Pyramids to be filled with grain posthaste. **Joseph stored up huge quantities of grain, like the sand of the sea; it was so much that he stopped keeping records because it was beyond measure.** (Gen. 41: 49). Pharaoh was happy, and Joseph was promoted to CEO of the empire. Can you believe the luck of some people? Hell, I could have made up an interpretation as good as that! Well, anyway, sure enough, after seven years famine struck. But, not only was Egypt hit; we in Canaan were also out of grain as well. It was the pits. We were all hungry, and there wasn't even enough to feed the sheep, cattle, and other livestock. We were in quite a pickle. But down in Egypt, Joseph was selling grain like crazy to the highest bidder. **All the countries came to Egypt to buy grain from Joseph, because the famine was severe in all the world.** (Gen. 41: 57).

Well, when Dad caught wind of that, he sent the ten of us to Egypt right away to buy some of that grain. He didn't let the youngest, Benjamin, go, as he felt he was too young and cute, and was afraid that the Egyptians might like him a bit too much in the wrong way (if you get my drift). **So when Joseph's brothers arrived, they bowed down to him with their faces to the ground. As soon as Joseph saw his brothers, he recognized them, but he pretended to be a stranger and spoke to them. Although Joseph recognized his brothers, they did not recognize him.** (Gen. 42: 6,8). And can you believe it . . . he faked us out, pretending not to know us. He remembered that little incident back at the well in Dothan. Well, I told them not to do it—sell the little bugger, that is. But did they listen to me? No! Anyway, now we were in a bad way, as he got testy and called us spies! Come on, we just wanted to buy grain.

Then that little bitch began playing cat-and-mouse with us. He separated us for individual interrogations so that we did not have a chance to coordinate our stories. He found out that we had a younger brother named Ben and that he was Dad's new favorite (after the untimely death of the *previous* favorite, Joseph, who was eaten by a bear or something). So, dear Brother Joe then ordered us to go back and get Ben. And, to make sure we would come back, he had his thugs grab Simeon, tie him, and cart him off to jail. He told us that he would keep him there until we got back with that cute little kid, Ben, that he had heard about.

Well, what were we supposed to do? We trudged back to Canaan. But Dad was pissed because we had mentioned Ben to Pharaoh. Of course, we pointed out that we were all interrogated in different interview rooms and didn't have a chance to get our stories straight. Well, Dad was totally distraught and refused to let us take little Ben to Egypt. Finally, when we ate up all the grain we had brought from Egypt, he relented and let us take the kid back down with us. Hell, Judah even promised to take *full* responsibility to bring Ben and Simeon back—or else! "Or else what?" We all begged to know. Judah was famous for blabbing and acting out before thinking (typical ADD brain that he was). We all knew that, but Dad bought it and we finally set out for Egypt again with Ben in tow . . .

When we got back, Joseph wined us and dined us, and sent us on our way. But, secretly, he had one of his henchmen stick *his* golden goblet into Benjamin's bag. When we were about fifty or so miles out of town, he sent his troops after us. Well, they caught up with us and "discovered" the cup. Bad news. Of course, we knew that it was a plant, but what could we do? We went back with them and had to face Joseph. He asked us more stuff about our Pa, and threatened to keep Ben with him in Egypt. Finally, Judah threw himself on a bed of nails and whined that he had *personally* guaranteed the boy's safe return. So he volunteered to stay behind as a slave. After all, going back to Canaan and facing Dad would have been such a loss of face (after bragging that he would be responsible for the kid's safety) that remaining as a slave in Egypt couldn't be as bad as that!

Well, that must have done the trick because Joseph was so moved that he broke down and blurted out: **"I am Joseph! I am your brother, the one you sold into Egypt!** I mean to tell you—we were totally flabbergasted and flamboozled! Of course, we were scared shitless as well because he could have had us all killed right then and there. But he shocked the hell out of us, saying: **"And now, do not be distressed and do not be angry with yourselves for selling me here, because it was to save lives that God sent me ahead of you."** (Gen. 45: 4,5). So, to let bygones be bygones, Joseph invited the whole family to leave Canaan and come down and live in Egypt. It would be really cool to have the whole family together. We were all totally jazzed. Not only were we getting out of that dump, Canaan (with the worst drought in decades), but Joseph was setting us up in a nice, cushy part of Egypt called *Goshen*. Wow, just the sound of it was marvy. Land-o-Goshen! We could hardly wait.

So, when we got back to Canaan and finally convinced Dad that his son Joseph was not only still alive but was a big wheel in Egypt, he was all hot-to-trot to get the whole family moved out of there and on our way to our new home in lovely downtown Goshen. Actually, it worked out fine at first. We all gathered up our wives and kids (70 of us all together) and headed out for Goshen. But gradually things began to get a bit sour. **There was no food in the whole region; in both Egypt and Canaan.** (Gen. 47: 13). Bad news all around, huh? And our dear little brother had become Pharaoh's tax collector! We paid until there was nothing left. So the IRS sent him out on behalf of the administration and we offered to trade our *livestock* for food. Heck, what else were we to do? I mean, Joseph probably could have given us some free stuff, cut us some slack, or fudged a bit—but either he didn't or couldn't. So the next year, as the famine was still raging, and there was nothing in either Egypt or Canaan left, we finally sold them all our land for food. When *that* food ran out, we had no other choice. We had to sell ourselves. We all made little signs that read: *"Will work for food!"* So, when Joseph came to collect the taxes, we sold ourselves to him. Total bummer, huh?

Judah was royally pissed about the arrangement. He even remarked that we should have left the little brat in that dry well in Dothan after all. All we got out of selling him was twenty shekels of silver and a life of drudgery in Goshen. Some Promised Land! "Well," I pointed out, "Joseph never promised us a *rose garden*." We just had to stick it out as slaves. We didn't own any land now, didn't have any cattle of our own or anything—not even our houses. "Hey, guys," Simeon pointed out one day, "Don't look now, but we are trapped here. We are slaves."

Chapter 9

Tamar

The fiancee of three brothers. Oh, what a tangled web we weave,
and what a mess we may conceive.

You're not going to believe my story. I am Paliparan, manservant to Judah, one of the true patriarchs and heroes of Biblical infamy. My master is the fourth son of Jacob—married to the daughter of Shua of Adullam. Actually, I was kind of a wedding present from good Ol' Shua when he threw quite the party to celebrate the nuptials of his daughter, Walang-Pangalan, to Judah. Now, I have been a friend of some of Shua's other slaves and servants, so I've been dragged to all sorts of parties and wingdings where we all serve the punch and hors d'oeuvres, and park the camels. The wedding at Canaan was great. Even the slaves got smashed.

Well, Judah and W.P. had three boys, Er, which actually means *two*. But their first pregnancy was a false alarm. The second son, Onan, was a very fretful child—given to tantrums and stubbornness. I knew the female slaves who took care of him. Hear tell, he was a holy little terror, never being cooperative, and always contrary. The third son, Shelah, was a sweet little kid. But when the whole story broke, he was too young to know what was going on. So here is the story . . . and I was there!

Well, this all happened in Kezib. Judah found a bride for Er there. (Or somewhere near there anyway :-) Anyway, the bride-to-be was named Tamar (kind of a pushy broad), and she was totally into the whole wedding thing, having planned it right down to the matching outfits for us servants. She had been organizing her big fat Kezib wedding for years —since she was a teenager! No joke. Oh, I might add that those matching outfits: "hi-de-ous!" But what could we say? She really could have used a "queer-eye," but she never thought to ask any of us mere servants for our opinions (so we had to actually wear those getups). But we did it for Er.

Well, Er, the groom, was a real party animal, but weddings aren't really his kind of fun (if you get my drift). The party was awesome. Well, he got drunk and out-of-hand at his bachelor party and . . . **was wicked in the Lord's sight; so the Lord put him to death.** (Genesis 38: 7). Well, of course we were shocked about that, but he was really getting rowdy and choked on a pretzel, and nothing could be done. God took him right there on the eve of his wedding ceremony! Of course, we servants were freaked out. After all, what were we ever going to do with those cool matching outfits for the wedding? LOL. But, of course, Tamar and her dad knew what had to be done. It is a tradition that if the eldest brother cannot fulfill the duties and responsibilities of his position, his runner-up, the second brother, had to take his place and impregnate his wife *for* him to maintain the family line. It is tradition! So . . . Onan's turn!

Then Judah said to Onan, "Lie with your brother's wife and fulfill your duty to her as a brother-in-law to produce offspring for your brother." (Gen. 38: 8). We all cracked up over that one! Ha! "I'll lay odds that Onan won't do it!" whispered my friend, Okularus, in my ear. "He is way too self-centered and difficult to cooperate in *that* old ritual." So we took bets and waited for the report. And as expected, Tamar had a fallback plan. According to Hebrew tradition (from Deuteronomy 25) she had to marry Onan. But Onan was having none of that.

Onan knew that the offspring would not be his; so whenever he lay with his brother's wife, he spilled his seed on the ground to keep from producing offspring for his brother. (Gen. 38: 9). "What a bastard!" we all thought. But would he get away with that for long? Not likely. Well, nobody would have been any the wiser, but somebody had to clean up after coitus, huh? And, of course, it would have to be a slave for that job. Anyway, word got out. Like, duh! Judah was pissed. So was Shua . . . but not as pissed as Tamar. She was livid. "Like, how could that arrogant bastard make such a fool out of me?" she demanded (right in front of everybody). But that's not all.

She wanted to get out of this whole mess and find a man elsewhere. But tradition prevented that. Here's what she was required to do: **His widow** (Tamar) **must not marry outside the family. Her husband's brother shall take and marry her and fulfill the duty of a brother-in-law to her.** (Deut. 25: 5). And if that doesn't work out, as in the case of Onan, she shall go up to him in the presence of the elders, take off one of his sandals, spit in his face and say, "This is what is done to the man who will not build up his brother's line. That man's line shall be known as the Family of the Unsandaled." (Deut. 25: 9,10). Wow, that's a serious situation, huh? You bet. Well, we thought so too!

Well, Onan just laughed at that. Like, what is anybody really going to do about it? Are they going to stand by and *make* him impregnate Tamar? Obviously, the slap with the sandal and the spitting was rude, but it didn't sway that dude Onan one bit. Okularus won that bet hands down. But that's not how this whole part of the story came out . . . Here's more. Onan got his.

What he did was wicked in the Lord's sight; so he put him to death also. (Gen. 38: 10). OMG! Another pretzel? No, Onan just keeled over right on the spot. "Well, he got what was coming to him," claimed one of the maidservants. "Yeah!" exclaimed another. "He was such a brat; he deserved it." But we could all see what a problem this had created. What, with both elder sons now dead, the "responsibility" fell on poor little Shelah . . . and he hadn't even pubed yet! He was a scrawny, wimpy little kid, and hardly a match for that overbearing Tamar. "This is going to be interesting," Okularus predicted sotto voce. It was.

Now, as I said, Tamar was technically engaged to Shelah by default. She was stuck. And she was not happy about it one bit; so Judah struck a bargain with her. **"Live as a widow in your father's house until my son Shelah grows up."** For he thought, **"He may die too, just like his brothers."** So Tamar went to live in her father's house. (Gen. 38: 11). But she was not a happy camper.

After a long time Judah's wife (that would be Walang-Pangalan), **the daughter of Shua, died. When Judah had recovered from his grief, he went up to Timnah. When Tamar was told, "Your father-in-law is on his way to Timnah, she took off her widow's clothes, covered herself with a veil to disguise herself, and then sat down at the entrance to Enaim, which is on the road to Timnah. For she saw that though Shelah had now grown up, she had not been given to him as his wife.** (Gen. 38: 13,14). Well, that's not fair is it?

I was coming to Timnah with Judah as usual (carrying his shit) when we encountered (what we thought to be) a hooker at the entrance to Enaim. She was clad in scarlet and purple (a very poor fashion choice). But

Judah was hot for her right away. She spoke and came on to him, and I knew right away that it was Tamar—that clever bitch! I was amazed that Judah couldn't see through her lame disguise. It was not my place to say anything, so I just kept mum. Then . . .

Not realizing that she was his daughter-in-law, he went over to her by the roadside and said, "Come now, let me sleep with you." (Gen. 38: 15). Pardon me, but that is not exactly what he actually said. It was more like: "How much for a quick fuck? I'm in a hurry." To which she replied crooningly, **"And what will you give me to sleep with you?"** (Well, that wasn't right either, but I think you get the gist). **"I'll send you a young goat from my flock," he said.** (Wow, a young goat! I was impressed! I knew she wouldn't fall for that.) **"Will you give me something as a pledge until you send it?"** she asked. Were they negotiating? Always.

He said, "What pledge should I give you?" To which she quickly demanded: **"Your seal and its cord, and the staff in your hand," she answered.** (Gen. 38: 16-18). Well, let's cut to the chase. They "did it" in the bushes alongside the road, and both got dressed and went their separate ways. Of course, Tamar changed back into her widow-garb and went back home to Shua's. But then the plot really thickens!

Meanwhile, Judah sent the young goat by his friend the Adullamite in order to get his pledge back from the woman, but he did not find her. Hmmm. Uh-oh. Somebody's in trouble. So Judah said: **"Let her keep what she has, or we will become a laughing-stock. After all, I did send her this young goat, but you couldn't find her.** (Gen: 38: 20,21). Actually, I gave the goat to Okularus later and he kept the goat, as he knew what was coming next.

About three months later Judah was told, "Your daughter-in-law Tamar is guilty of prostitution, and as a result she is now pregnant." OMG, Judah was incensed. He was flabbergasted, he was pissed-off. In fact, he was in a full-blown holy fit! **Judah said, "Bring her out and have her burned to death!"** (Gen. 38: 22-24).

Standing in front of the whole motley crew of the elders of Enaim, Judah was blustering on about the decline of morals in the town, and in Timnah, and, yea, even unto the uttermost parts of Canaan. He was really preaching. He was on a totally righteous rant. So they dragged Tamar out —kicking and screaming—and threw her down in front of him. He began going off on her when she simply said: **"I am pregnant by the man who owns these."** (Whereupon she produced the stuff that Judah had given her for sex by the roadside, including his *seal* with the cord still attached). Hmmm. And she added, **"See if you recognize whose seal and cord and staff these are."** (Gen. 38: 25). At that point Okularus arrived with the goat . . . Checkmate.

But it was too late. Judah was embarrassed, but kept his cool. Finally, he regained his composure. He promised never to sleep with her again :-) He never did. **When the time came for her to give birth, there were twin boys in her womb. As she was giving birth, one of them put out his hand, so the midwife took a scarlet thread and tied it on his wrist and said, "This one came out first."** (Gen. 38: 27,28). He was named Zerah, and his twin brother was Perez.

Well, of the two, Perez became the more famous, as he carried Judah's line up unto the time of King David and then on to Jesus, the Son of God. But that is another story. So when the twins were just kids, they went to Egypt with their Dad, Judah, and his other brothers, their wives, and the cousins and all. They all settled in the Land of Goshen, a cool place that their uncle Joseph had arranged for them. They all (including Okularus, who had likewise been sold to Judah as part of the deal with Tamar) joined us on the road to Goshen. And what a trip that was!

Chapter 10

Eslutina

Potiphar's wife who hit on Joseph.
As told by Oholibamah, her maidservant.

Hello out there in Bible Land! My name is Oholibamah-Rama, daughter of Rama Lama-Dingdong. I was named after the daughter of Anah and the granddaughter of Zibeon the Hivite. Cool, huh? Too bad I am a slave. I was sold to a guy named Potiphar down here in Egypt as a birthday present for his wife, Eslutina. I am writing this for her, as she is presently indisposed—doing time in Pharaoh's jail for fraud, , and perjury.

Ya know, one thing I just don't get is how rich folks say the damnedest things right in front of us servants . . . like we don't have ears or something? Now, don't get me wrong—Eslutina was always good to me. No complaints. And she was *especially* nice to the manservants. She did have good taste, and had the hot-looking guys in to her bedchamber quite often to change a lightbulb, or fix the Venetian blinds, or straighten the rugs. She was one horny bitch. And, believe me, Potiphar never knew about any of that. He was a big-time civil servant in the current administration, and just couldn't be bothered with the mundane goings-on around the house. That was what the servants were for.

One day, Potiphar bought this very handsome slave from Canaan, sold to our master by Midianite slavers. His name is Joseph, and—the way he tells it—his big brothers threw him in a well and then decided to sell him. So he ended up here in Master Potiphar's well-appointed home. He is a quite agreeable fellow and is very helpful to Mr. P. and his lovely wife, Eslutina. He's always ready to lend a helping hand to the staff here at the mansion as well. He is one of those people who always seem to land on their feet—and even rise to the top wherever they end up.

The Lord was with Joseph and he prospered, and he lived in the house of his Egyptian master. When his master saw that the Lord was with him and that the Lord gave him success in everything he did, Joseph found favor in his eyes and became his attendant. Potiphar put him in charge of his household, and he entrusted to his care everything he owned. (Genesis 39: 2-4). Things were running smoothly around the place. Joseph was a natural-born administrator so Potiphar just left him in charge when he was away. Well, being the hunk that he was something untoward was bound to happen. It did. **Now Joseph was well built and handsome, and after a while his masters' wife took notice of Joseph and said, "Come to bed with me!"** (Gen. 39: 7). Well, Joseph was way too smart to fall for that. After all, he could get all the sex he wanted with any of the other man and maidservants (willingly). But Mrs. P.? That couldn't come out well, and Joseph knew it . . . let me tell you.

At first, he tried to reason with her. He didn't want to hurt her feelings or anything, but he realized that his job could be at stake if he even thought about playing around with Eslutina. He was no dummy. He replied as politely and firmly as decorum would allow, saying: **"No one is greater in this house than I am. My master has withheld nothing from me except you, because you are his wife."** (Gen. 39: 9). I mean, how much more clear could he make it? But she didn't give up so easily. She took it as sort of a challenge—or so it seemed. Every day she managed to concoct some project that she needed him to attend to—usually in her private chambers. Of course Joseph could see through it and made every attempt to steer clear of her. She really got pissed when he sent another man slave to fix some little thing in her bathroom. Somehow her sink was clogged, and she just needed Joseph—and *him* only—to unclog it.

And though she spoke to Joseph day after day, he refused to go to bed with her or even be with her. (Gen. 39: 10). You have to give him credit, he really tried to avoid her. But then . . .

One day he went into the house to attend to his duties, and none of the household servants was inside. (Gen. 39: 11). Well, this isn't *exactly* true, as several of us were behind one of the coromandel screens and were quietly listening to the whole conversation. "Get over here and fuck me now!" she commanded. It was all we could do not to gasp. Then she shamelessly threw herself at him, ripping at his clothes! We were shocked! (Not really. It was just like in the movies!) But he pulled away and fled. Of course, she had managed to hold onto his cloak. (People were still wearing cloaks back then.) Anyway, this is her rendition of what happened . . .

When she saw that he had left his cloak in her hand and had run out of the house, she called her household servants. "Look," she said to them, "this Hebrew has been brought to us to make sport of us! He came in here to sleep with me, but I screamed." (Gen. 39: 13,14). Don't believe it! We saw the whole thing, but of course we had to play along. After all, we had our own jobs to consider. And besides, if she actually accused him, he could do jail time, and we had to think of our own skins. So we lied for her, saying that, indeed, Joseph came on to her —and not the other way around. Well, she tattled to the master the minute he walked through the door after a hard day's work!

"That Heb you bought for me is a monster!" she whined. "He tried to rape me right in my own room!" Potiphar was outraged. "What?" he shouted. "How dare he—especially after all the nice things I've done for him!" Then . . . **Joseph's master took him and put him in prison, the place where the king's prisoners were confined.** (Gen. 39: 20).

Well, that seemed very unfair to him. We were all really on Joseph's side, so we met to come up with a plan to get back at Eslutina. Of course, the really big deal was that Potiphar whisked him away to prison without a trial—or even a hearing. But, as usual, Joseph—despite managing to fall into shit—came up smelling like a rose. Do you know people like that? Well, one of the manservants on the staff had a friend who worked as a guard at the prison, so he got a lot of juicy news from there. After all, not a lot of interesting stuff happens in our neighborhood, as it is not in a very chic neighborhood of Giza. Having a prison nearby has kept the property values down since they built it years ago. **So the warden put Joseph in charge of all those held in the prison, and he was made responsible for all that was done there. The warden paid no attention to anything under Joseph's care, because the Lord was with Joseph and gave him success in whatever he did.** (Gen. 39: 22,23).

*****

Let me take over from Oho. I am Knoydijai, the current warden of our federal prison in South Giza. Some time ago Oho's master, a certain Potiphar, brought his head slave into our lovely facility. I know Potiphar only slightly, as he has had other slaves that he has brought in to us. And all of them are here for the same thing (trying to rape his wife). Actually, I have it on good authority that Mrs. Potiphar *should be told to keep her window shades all pulled completely down* (if you know what I mean). Anyway, apparently Potiphar, Pharaoh's go-to guy, is out on assignment a lot—so he doesn't pay an appropriate amount of attention to Mrs. P., who has an eye for the hot young male slaves. I have seen this before. But what gets me is that a guy like Mr. P. can just drag a guy like this—Joseph—into our jail and dump him off here (without a trial or anything). Bummer, huh? Well, he bought this guy as a slave from Midianite traders fare and square, so he can do whatever he wants to with him. I think Mr. P. really could have just beaten Joseph to death if he had wanted to, but my suspicion is that he kinda doubted Mrs. P's story. My guess is that the old man had to put the Hebrew slave in here to save face. After all, he certainly could not have failed to notice what was happening around the house when he was away. In any case, Joseph is here and is a very bright fellow so I have promoted him to be my assistant. You never know when it might be handy to have a guy like that around.

Six months pass. Joseph interprets dreams for the other inmates as a hobby. Kind of like fortune telling, Joe has a way of telling a story. It caught my attention so I mentioned it around town, especially where one of Pharaoh's staff might pick up on it. Sure enough! A few days later we got a call from the West Wing of the palace asking us to send the dream-reader over. We did and he made a big hit. But you have already heard that story, haven't you? His brothers and dad came back down to Egypt because Joe wanted to shock them all. Well, that was a groovy story—how he got all his brothers together in front of dear Ol' Dad and revealed himself as being the little brother that they threw down the well. Of course, the story had a happy ending. (Or did it?) Last I heard, Joe and his whole family are now living in Goshen, a flat, marshy place in the Nile Delta. Plenty of mosquitoes and all out there. Last I heard, as well, they were making bricks of mud and straw for Pharaoh's latest pyramid or some other building project. Sounds like they are doing fine. I guess it all worked out well, huh?

Oh wait . . . Just in from CNN: There is unrest in Goshen. The Hebrew slaves are demanding more pay and better hours and working conditions. Pharaoh is not negotiating with them and has increased their workload. There is talk of expecting a deliverer any day. But I am not so sure. Oh well, I will stay tuned and see how that comes out. My experience is that you just don't tangle with Pharaoh. Those who do rarely come out well.

Chapter 11

Zipporah

Wife of Moses

Good evening to all my fans out there in TV Land. My name is Zipporah, and I am proud to say that I am the long-suffering wife of Moses, one of the real heroes of Biblical renown. I didn't know Moses as a child, nor as an adolescent or a young man, but I heard his whole story over and over from his old friends back in Egypt, so I think I can relate the events of his past with a fair amount of accuracy.

Moses was born at a bad time and in a bad place. During those days, the Hebrews living in Egypt were slaves of the pharaoh, who was the top dog of the Egyptian empire back then. Their lives were total shit, and they were really stuck there. But they were breeding like rabbits—at least according to the Egyptian census taker, Maraming-tao. He showed Pharaoh the numbers and birth rates, and the population projections for the region called Goshen where the Hebrew minority had gradually been taking over. Afraid of having a hostile group like that so close to the capital, Pharoah needed a solution. So he prayed about it and came up with an idea that would slow down the Jewish population growth curve.

He decreed: **"Every boy that is born you must throw into the river, but let every girl live."** (Exodus 1: 22). That was a good idea. At least he thought so. Well, Moses' mom, Manangahila, gave birth to him right in the midst of the crisis. Egyptian soldiers were going from house to house rounding up all the male babies and tossing them into the Nile River. Manangahila hid Moses for three months before it got too hot and she couldn't keep him concealed from the authorities any longer. So she put him in a basket and floated him out into the putrid, disease-ridden waters of the Nile.

It just happened that one of Pharaoh's daughters, Umatilla, was bathing in the river that day. I know, what kind of a stupid thing to do is that? Not only was the water polluted and totally unsuited for bathing, but there were crocodiles! OMG, but that particular daughter was headstrong and stubborn. She had been informed that she was infertile, so finding a child floating right there in her bathwater was an obvious sign from some god or goddess somewhere that her problems were over. She simply had her servants retrieve the basket, take the child out, and wrap it up in appropriate attire; and they all headed back to the palace like that was totally normal.

Well, Pharaoh wanted to know where this new addition to his household had come from, upon which Tingnanmo proudly proclaimed that it was a gift from the goddess Hindiko-Alam-E. Of course, Pharaoh didn't buy that for an instant as he was quite skeptical by nature. But, hey, keeping peace around the palace had its rewards. The wives were all enamored with babies, and that left the concubines free for much more fun of a sexual nature (of course).

Moses was a good kid, and did well learning from his tutors. Of course, that stutter of his was rather annoying, but he did manage to learn his way around the palace—with its intrigues, plots and subplots. He was quite interested in his "Dad's" building projects—the pyramids in particular. He went out on site daily and watched as the Hebrew slaves made bricks and hauled them to where the regular Egyptian engineers and workers were doing the actual construction. He was a bit put off by the way the Egyptian overseers treated the slaves.

One day he saw one of those overseers abusing one of the slaves. He looked around and, with nobody watching, he killed the Egyptian (and hid the body). Of course, in Egypt in those days nothing was really in secret, and some other slaves happened to take in the whole event. Hmmm. The next day or so, Moses observed two Hebrew slaves fighting (over some young girl slave) and he tried to break it up. Well, they let loose on Moses (basically telling him to mind his own business).

"Who made you ruler and judge over us? Are you thinking of killing me as you killed the Egyptian?" OMG! Busted. That sure put Moses in a very compromising position, huh? And then Moses thought to himself, **"What I did must have become known."** (Ex. 2: 14). No shit, Sherlock. So what to do? Stick around for the trial or get out of Dodge?

"Fuck this," he was heard to say . . . "I think I'll go heard sheep." And he did! He went out into the Sinai Desert and stayed there for forty years. That's a long time to be alone with a bunch of sheep, huh? Well, he spent some time in Midian, where he met me! My dad, Reuel, was a Midianite priest who liked Moses and gave me to him in marriage. I was okay with that. I got pregnant right awa,y and we called the boy Gershom. Nice simple name, that, eh? Well, we left (with the sheep) and ended up back at Mt. Horeb in the Sinai. I was never very fond of that place—too dry and desolate—but Moses seemed to take to it. He liked to climb up the mountain. One day he had quite an encounter up there. He had what you might call a "spiritual" experience. And I hasten to add that he wasn't doing drugs of any kind. Apparently there was a bush up there. Now I have been up that mountain and never saw a shrub of any kind. It was just growing right out of the rocks. But that's not all—it was on fire! Well, Moses just had to go over and see what was going on. I'll be darned. God and Jesus appeared right there in the burning bush. Totally cool. Anyway, they told M. that they were sending him on a mission to deliver the Hebrews out of slavery in Egypt.

I thought it was quite an honor, but—shy guy that he is—Moses declined the honor, feigning insufficient training in such matters. He really had no experience as a deliverer, and nothing in his background in sheep husbandry had prepared him for such an assignment. God insisted. He told Moses that it was a groovy gig, and that he would totally wow the whole Egyptian royal court and free the slaves in the process. He called it the "Emancipation Proclamation Extravaganza." Moses wasn't buying it, so finally God got fed up with all his whining and stuttering (which got worse when he got nervous). God said: **"What about your brother, Aaron the Levite? I know he can speak well."** (Ex. 4: 14). Whoa! Neither Moses nor I knew anything of him having a brother—especially a Levite priest! How he survived the murder of all the male children back in Egypt, and grew up as a Hebrew (Levite) priest just blew our minds. How is that possible? But from the burning bush we heard a comforting cliché: "With God, all things are possible!" We felt so much better. Then God said:

"He is on his way to meet you, and his heart will be glad when he sees you. You shall speak to him and put words in his mouth; I will help both of you speak and will teach you what to do. But take this staff in your hand so you can perform miraculous signs with it." (Ex. 4: 15-17). So we came down the mountain "on faith," heading out toward Egypt . . . trembling all the way. Then a most peculiar thing happened.

At a lodging place on the way, the Lord met Moses and was about to kill him. But Zipporah took a flint knife, cut off her son's foreskin and touched Moses' feet with it. "Surely you are a bridegroom of blood to me," she said. So the Lord let him alone. (Ex. 4: 25). Huh? We never knew what that was all about, but somehow I knew what to do. I received a "word of knowledge" and was sure that we had to circumcise Gershom right then and there. I perceived it "in the spirit."

Then we ran into Aaron and his troupe coming toward us. He, being a priest and all, had a following in tow and a small Gospel band as well. They were pretty good, but could have used a bit more practice. Of course, that was not going to be the draw when we arrived at Pharaoh's court. They would just play back up for the brothers. Moses demonstrated his magic tricks that the Lord had taught him up on Mt. Horeb, and Aaron hummed along until he got into the theme of their upcoming presentation. He was pumped. And Moses felt better with Aaron there. It was like they already knew each other—but of course they could not have. When we arrived, we knocked on the big green gate only to be turned away by a guard with a phony mustache. I whined and cried and he relented, letting us into the Land of Oz—er, I mean Iz, the magnificent world of Pharaoh, the great and mighty. Totally awesome place, that!

They did their schtick for Pharaoh and the court. Our Gospel band played accompaniment and ended the spectacle with a rousing version of the *Hallelujah Chorus*, but Pharaoh didn't even crack a smile. He had a hard heart. It wasn't for lack of trying, as Moses and Aaron did all the tricks that God had taught them, but that the damned Pharaoh just increased the workload—the brick-output quota for the Hebrew slaves. They all went ballistic on poor Moses. I tried to comfort him, but he went off and had another encounter with the Almighty. He recounted the whole tale to Yahweh, and was the Almighty ever pissed!

"Now you will see what I will do to Pharaoh: Because of my mighty hand he will let them go; because of my mighty hand he will drive them out of his country." (Ex. 6: 1). Yikes! And he meant business. So they scheduled a follow-up interview with Pharaoh and his wizards, magicians and sundry wise-guys, and once again threatened mondo-disaster unless all the Hebrew slaves were immediately released and allowed to leave the country. Fat chance. So Moses pulled the first of several backup tricks that he had in his magic hat. He stretched out his staff and the Nile River turned to blood. OMG, was that ever awful and gross! But not only was there blood in the river, but it got into all the wells, the pots, cisterns, and buckets as well. It was a bloody mess. But the Egyptians figured out that they could simply dig nearby to find fresh water, so the trick bombed.

The second trick was bound to be better, they reasoned. They called down the plague of frogs and those amphibians got into everything. That made Pharaoh "hoppin' mad," but he would not relent. So Moses went for the third trick, and turned the dust of the ground in Egypt into gnats. Actually, I would have reversed the order of the tricks, creating the gnats first, and then the frogs so they could eat the gnats. Anyway, still a bust and Pharaoh was not budging. No way was he going to release his cheap labor force. Somehow somebody had to make the bricks, and the Jews were so handy. Just perfect they were for the job.

Well, as I watched my husband in total wonder, he called down the plague on the livestock, and all of the cattle, sheep, goats, and pigs (livestock) croaked. There was nothing left. Every animal was dead. Now that was a really stinky mess as well. Pharaoh still was unrelenting. So God sent hail! But not without a holy warning! **"Bring your livestock and everything you have in the field to a place of shelter, because the hail will fall on every man and animal that has not been brought in and is still out in the field, and they will die.** (Ex. 9: 19). What? Even I—a poor, uneducated woman—could see what a stupid order that was! Like, duh. All the livestock had died the day before. I think God was getting rattled at this point. Obviously.

God tried locusts next, followed by boils (which only afflicted the Egyptians). Then God sent darkness on the land for three days. Nobody could see their own hand in front of their face. But the Hebrews had light in their homes. Alakazam and shazam! Beat that, you stupid Ol' Pharaoh! But when Pharaoh stuck to his guns on that one as well, God was fed up. He didn't want to do it, but to accomplish a "mighty work" he sent his secret weapon, "the Death Angel," down to Egypt on special assignment. "Go down and go throughout Egypt," was the prime directive. **Every firstborn son in Egypt will die, from the firstborn son of Pharaoh who sits of the throne, to the firstborn of the slave girl, who is at her hand mill, and all the firstborn of the cattle as well.** (Ex. 11: 4,5). I saw a problem with that order right off the bat. Somebody forgot to remind God, the omniscient, that he had already killed all the cattle a couple days earlier in the "plague of the livestock." Oops. Well, obviously, God was getting weary. And gods, they do get weary.

But *that* finally did the trick. Pharaoh, upon hearing of the loss of his own firstborn, relented and gave a decree that the Jews could leave Egypt. Then he got pissed (because he assumed that they were really behind all this mayhem in the first place) and changed the order to: I expel all the Jews from Goshen and throughout all of Egypt as well. They are ordered to leave. They are *commanded* to do so. And their little dogs too! So there.

Well, the chosen people made haste to get the hell out of Dodge. *I watched the whole thing.* Of course, as predicted, they "plundered" the Egyptians on the way out. **There were about six hundred thousand men on foot, besides women and children. Many other people went up with them, as well as both flocks and herds.** (Ex. 12: 37,38). Moses stood in front of the vast array of people. He led in prayer. And before we headed out on our marvelous adventure, he asked in a loud voice: "Now has everybody gone to the bathroom?"

So we all started out—both men and women, great and small; plus camels, donkeys, cattle, horses, sheep and goats (livestock), and flocks of geese, chickens and ducks. Why leave them behind? And, of course, loads of "plunder" from the Egyptians. I knew the terrain that we were going to be heading into, and wondered if it was such a good idea to bring all those silver, gold, and iron candlesticks and other doodads that we had ripped off from the Egyptians. That stuff would surely slow us down. It did. But not as much as those stupid chickens, geese, and ducks did. OMG, what a parade that was! We got to the Red Sea and had to wait all night to cross. The wind had to dry a pathway across the water first. So we waited on the Egyptian side of the border.

Well, wouldn't you know it: Pharaoh changed his mind! Apparently his CPAs and his labor commissioner got together and convinced him that by expelling their free slave labor base, he would actually have to pay Egyptian workers union wages to do the same jobs that we all were doing for free. So Pharoah sent his mighty armies out after us. They would have caught us too, but God intervened, turning himself into a pillar of fire to hold the armed forces of Egypt back. It worked swell, and the sea parted on cue and we all ran full tilt across the path of dry land to safety on the other side (the Sinai Desert side that is). Of course, the ducks and chickens really slowed us down (sigh).

Anyway, finally we all made it to safety in the Sinai Desert just as the pillar of fire went away and the armies of Pharaoh began charging through the gap in the sea. Well, you know the story. The sea crashed back into place, drowning the whole Egyptian army—men, horses, and all. We just stood on the other side and laughed, "Ha Ha Ha. Take that, you lousy uncircumcised scum." We were safe. We cheered. Moses had really pulled it off. We were free and everything looked rosy. So Moses called out: "Let's hit it!" And we all began to march.

Chapter 12

Marah

Zipporah's maidservant and confidant
(They named a lake after her.)

Well, let me take over the story from my Lady Zipporah (affectionately known as Zippa). We were standing on the East side of the Red Sea. Or was it the Reed Sea? Anyway, we had just escaped from Egypt. The Egyptian armies were chasing us, but Dear Yahweh intervened (as a pillar of fire) and kept the soldiers and chariots at bay. When he saw that we had all managed to get over to this side, he disappeared into a cloud of smoke, and the soldiers rushed right in on the same dry-land path that we had taken. Once they were all on their way, we were standing on the other side watching; and the waters came crashing back, and all those guys and all their horses were drowned. What a sight!

It was such carnage. I really didn't have anything against the guys in the army, to tell you the truth. But, hear tell, God loves drowning stuff. Anyway, we turned around en mass and faced south by southwest. Nothing but the Desert of Shur. Oh, sure. And Moses held up his staff and said in a loud voice: "Praise the Lord! Forward march." So we began our epic journey. Zipporah, as the leader's wife (his first, that is) got a camel to ride on. I walked alongside as that is fittin'.

For three days they traveled in the desert without finding water. When they came to Marah, they could not drink its water because it was bitter. So the people grumbled against Moses, saying, "What are we to drink?" (Exodus 15: 22). Now let me point out here that this lake that we came to did not have a name when we arrived. But, as the water was alkali—a natural sink—the water was pure brine—as you would expect in a place like that. Since there is almost no rainfall at all ever in the Sinai, we were lucky to even find that brine-lake. But like most such lakes, the water was bitter. Duh.

Well, everybody was pissed, grumpy, and tired . . . not to mention thirsty. The livestock were all in quite a state. The horses and donkeys were all a'twitter, and the ducks and geese—well, need I say more? It had been three days since any of us had a thing to drink. I will say that the camels were okay with this, though. We had been tromping through the hot sand for three days, and Moses just kept singing: "I'm heading on the upward way, new heights I'm gaining every day" . . . or something like that. It was fine at first—very encouraging. But after the first day or so, it got on my nerves. Well, we finally arrived at this brine-lake and we just couldn't go any further, so we voted to strike. Moses was freaked and went away to talk to God on his own. **Then Moses cried out to the Lord, and the Lord showed him a piece of wood. He threw it into the water, and the water became sweet.** (Ex. 15: 25). Hallelujah, what a guy! So we named the place Marah, which in Egyptian means: *Where da hell are we?* (or something like that).

Well, I mentioned to Zipporah that maybe hanging around here in Marah might be a good idea for a while. After all, now that we had a real honest-to-god water source, everybody was feeling better again. Besides, we really could use some downtime—all of us, including the animals. But everybody was grumbling. Hungry again? Yup. So, as we started out, stomachs growling, Moses assured us that he was going to put in a good word for us with God, and that maybe he would figure out how to feed us. Of course, I quietly mentioned to Zipporah that we might eat some of the sheep, or the cattle, or at least the chickens or ducks. "Shhh!" she shushed me. "That's too obvious . . . too easy. Let the men figure it out. Moses is off talking to Yahweh even as we speak, and they will provide. You'll see." I shut up, but meanwhile everybody around camp was saying: **"If only we had died by the Lord's hand in Egypt! There we sat around pots of meat and ate all the food we wanted, but you have brought us out into this desert to starve this entire assembly to death."** (Ex. 16: 3). Ah, yes, those marvelous "fleshpots" back in Egypt. We had only been delivered from slavery for four or five days at this point, and most of the clods in the crowd were homesick for Egypt already. Talk about a bunch of ingrates! Hell, even I could see that we were better off out here in the sticks than back baking bricks in the hot sun. What was wrong with these people? BTW, Zippa named me Marah after the lake.

Moses finally returned with a big smile on his face. He had been out there somewhere communing with the Almighty, pleading our case. God was definitely getting tired of all the whining, so he promised Moses he would fix the problem. He was going to actually "send" food to us in camp—and on a regular basis. Kewl, huh? **"I will rain down bread from heaven for you. You will know that it was the Lord when he gives you meat in the evening and all the bread you want in the morning."** (Ex. 16: 4,8,15).

That night we heard a giant sucking sound. Then a fluttering sound as thousands of quail flew into the camp. It was quite a scene. Have you ever tried to catch a quail? It's not as easy as you might think. But anyway, despite the fact that all those little birds upset the horses and donkeys something fierce, we did in fact get dinner out of the deal. Then we slept. Moses assured us that in the morning we would get a "surprise." I could hardly sleep. Wow, a surprise! **In the morning there was a layer of dew around the camp. When the dew was gone, thin flakes like frost on the ground appeared on the desert floor. When the Israelites saw it they said to each other, 'What is it?' for they did not know what it was. Moses said to them, "It is the bread that the Lord has given you to eat."** What a marvie-poo surprise! Little did we know that it was going to be our steady diet for years to come.

Well, Moses told us that it was called manna and that it would miraculously fall every night, and we got to go out every morning and pick some up for breakfast. Just like "Sugar-Frosted Flakes" (only without the sugar :-(But Moses and God ran into a problem with the manna a few days later. Sabbath came around and we were not supposed to do any work. Like, how much work is picking up free breakfast— really? But Moses was a stickler for protocol and decorum. The Sabbath is a day of rest, and we were not allowed to pick up any manna on every seventh day. Well, we all reasoned, that's no insurmountable problem. We can just go out the day before and save it for consumption on Sunday. Piece of cake. But, nothing on this journey could be easy!

Each morning everyone gathered as much as he needed, and when the sun grew hot, it melted away. Moses said to them, "No one is to keep any of it until morning." However some of them paid no attention to Moses; they kept part of it until morning, but it was full of maggots and began to smell. (Ex. 16: 20,21). We learned quickly that the shelf-life of manna is 24 hours. Fortunately for us, God made a "special" rule. Manna could be eaten even after its expiration date to accommodate the Sabbath issue. Problem solved! On the day before the Sabbath everybody got into the habit of collecting a double portion. I was amazed. Zipporah was amazed. Hell, everybody was amazed. So Moses said to his brother, Aaron: **"Take a jar and put an omer of manna in it. Then place it before the Lord to be kept for the generations to come."** (Ex. 16: 32). I was quite concerned about this assignment. I heard tell that Aaron did as instructed, collecting an omer of manna and saving it for generations to come. But it apparently got lost in the shuffle and nobody to this day knows where that omer of manna actually is. That really bums me out.

Well, years passed and life became rather boring and predictable. Living in the desert and eating manna and quail all the time got to be a real drag. Then we finally ran out of water again. What? Nobody thought to remind Moses to bring the magic piece of driftwood from Marah? What's wrong with this picture? I mentioned it to Zipporah. Is your husband getting senile? Is it early-onset Alzheimer's? Not only did he and the "men" lose the jar of manna (for future generations), but now you tell me they lost the magic chunk of wood as well? I mean, really. If only the women had a say in the packing and organizing, things likely would have turned out better. But, obviously, God was testing us. I was getting rather turned-off by all these divine "tests." But—Moses to the rescue.

We and all the animals were getting faint—lacking water. In fact, everybody was badly dehydrated when Moses approached this biggish rock and smacked it with his staff. Fortunately, he had remembered to bring that with him from Egypt. Zipporah mentioned to me later that she had made a special effort to keep track of it for Moses, lest he lose that as well. Anyway, water gushed from the rock and we were saved once again. Praise the Lord!

Now you would think that the people would be satisfied, but nooo. They took to bitching and moaning again—sick of quail. So what did God do? Did he alter the menu? Did he give us a variation on the diet plan? No. He sent a total infestation of quail into the camp, and everybody ate themselves disgustingly full. But he got the last laugh, as all those gluttons got food poisoning and died in droves! I could have warned them. So we buried the whole lot of them at the "Graves of Greed" and moved on.

Maybe it was just me, but Zipporah did revisit the notion (in our private girl-to-girl talks) that Moses was "getting up there in years" and was a bit delusional at times. He was approaching his 120th birthday at that point, and he was getting lost a lot. Of course, we had to follow him. I could have done a better job leading that expedition myself. But I am just a woman and a servant at that, so I had learned to keep my mouth shut years ago. We ambled around for forty years, but were getting closer to the "Promised Land" that Moses had been talking about all these years.

Oh, but one more thing I need to say about Moses (before he croaked). He finally got some real serious commands and decrees from the Lord. Well, you have certainly heard about the Ten Commandments. Well, everybody knows about those, so big deal. But Moses continued on with his "little chats with God" over the years, and during that time he presented us all with tons of other rules of which most people are not even aware. I remembered them and passed them on to my hubby and kids. I will have him tell you all about them shortly, but I want to end my version of the story here.

Then Moses climbed Mt. Nebo. God showed him the whole land from Gilead to Dan. "This is the land I promised on oath to Abraham, Isaac and Jacob when I said, 'I will give it to your descendants.' I have let you see it with your eyes, but you will not cross over into it." (Deuteronomy 34: 1,4). **Moses was one hundred twenty years old when he died, yet his eyes were not weak nor his strength gone.** (Deut. 34: 8). It may be true that he didn't need glasses, but when you hear folks nowadays go on and on about how his "strength" was not gone—well, Zipporah tells a different story. But she had been complaining about Moses' waning "strength" for years. I just ignored the whole thing. It's basically just gossip :-)

Chapter 13

Toro-Manoro

A Hebrew indentured servant with a super big problem

Well, this is not a particularly happy way to introduce myself. My name is Toro-Manoro, and I am living under the new set of Jewish laws that Moses lately received from YHWH during one of his frequent chats with the Almighty. You have already met my wife, Marah, after whom a brine lake was named in the Sinai desert where we have been living for almost forty years now. She is an Egyptian slave and I am an indentured servant belonging to Aaron, the brother of Moses, our fearless leader.

I have to work for Aaron for seven years because he bought me fair and square. I am in year six of my obligation. Here's the rule: **"If you buy a Hebrew servant, he is to serve you for six years, but in the seventh year, he shall go free. If he comes alone, he is to go free alone. If his master gives him a wife and she bears him sons or daughters, the woman and her children shall belong to her master, and only the man shall go free."** (Exodus 21: 2,3).

Well, Marah and I get together now and then for "conjugal visits," which is actually a good thing for us, but it also benefits Aaron, as our kids then belong to him. We are kind of like slave producers. Of course, we love the kids, but they could be sold off at a moment's notice. I wish Yahweh would not have made that law up. It is really a bummer in terms of "family values."

Actually, Aaron is not too bad as far as masters go. He is going to release me on time, and he was even going to let me keep my bull, Ferdinand, whom I was planning to rent out for stud fees. I mean, after a servant is released from his indenture, what exactly is he supposed to do to earn a living out here in the wilderness? But the stud fee idea fell through when Ferdinand gored the slaves of some guy in the encampment. And now that there are all these new rules from God, I have to stone him and Aaron has to pay the guy thirty shekels of silver for *each* slave that was gored. And let me tell you, Aaron was not too happy about that!

But rules are rules. **If a man's bull gores a male or female slave, the owner must pay thirty shekels of silver to the master of the slave, and the bull must be stoned.** (Ex. 21: 32). It's the law. Aaron ragged all over me about not keeping the bull penned up. But, like, how was I supposed to do that out here in the treeless wasteland of the Sinai? There is no wood to build a proper pen with in the first place. And if we could find some wood, the campers would have surely found it and used it to build fires. I wonder sometimes exactly how they manage to get those fires going so we can cook our dinners of quail that fly into the camp every night to get caught and barbecued.

Living out here in the wilderness is like one miracle after another. I mean, to tell you the truth, this place is desolate! Nothing grows here, but somehow our cattle, horses, camels, sheep, goats, and chickens never seem to get hungry. It is amazing. But we, the people—both masters and slaves—do get hungry and *thirsty*. But God provides (now and then). We have learned that if we gripe and bitch enough at Moses, he goes off for a powwow with God, and then the big guy does a magic trick (like with the piece of wood back at Marah where the brine lake became sweet). Total marvel, that.

But I wanted to tell you some more of the new rules. **If a man schemes and kills another man deliberately, take him away from my altar and put him to death.** (Ex. 21: 14). That is referred to as "premeditated" and makes sense to me. But if a man kills a mere slave, that's okay. (But he has to pay a fine of around 50 bucks). However, the problem for me is that now, without Ferdinand—my proposed source of future income—I am SOL. (Shit out of luck, and I mean it.) But nobody's sure to whom the fine should be paid. God's instructions on that are unclear :-(

Well, another really horrible thing happened lately, and we (Marah and I) are in big trouble with the Judges. Those are the guys that God and Moses appointed to make up all these new rules. Seems that Marah and I were fucking in my tent one day on one of our semi-supervised conjugal visits. Totally okay, mind you. But suddenly we discovered, to our horror and dismay, that she was menstruating! OMG, no, not that! She cried out. But although I tried to stop her, our chaperone, Lilly—who was waiting outside the tent—heard her and barged in. Seeing the blood, she freaked. Oh no! We had broken one of the new laws! It is forbidden to fuck a woman (even if she is your wife) while she is on her period! I mean, we knew that, but it was kind of an accident! But Lilly was such a stickler for rules. She immediately tattled on us to the Judges, and now we are under "house-arrest" because we weren't allowed out on bail. Oh, just so you know, here is the official rule: **If a man lies with a woman during her monthly period and has sexual relations with her, he has exposed the source of her flow, and she has also uncovered it. Both must be cut off from their people."** (Leviticus 20: 18). Oh, shit, no! Cut off! That means that we have to be shunned, banished—kicked out! And, like, where are we supposed to go out here in the howling wilderness of the Sinai? We wouldn't last a day out there on our own—without the tribe. And especially without the regular food (quail and manna) that we expect daily from God! Oh woe, woe, woe.

Like, are we going to get a trial or a hearing or anything from the Judges? Dunno. But, now that there are all these new rules, everybody is uptight. We just aren't used to shit like this. It reminds me of all those rules back in Egypt under the pharaoh. We never knew when we were doing something wrong, and just about anybody in power could simply accuse us of anything, and, poof, we were in prison—or worse: we would just disappear. Bad news, huh?

Anyway, while Marah and I are sitting here in the sheriff's holding tent, there are some others here with us. We have shared our stories. Another couple, Maximilian and Karlotta, are here because he is accusing her of not being a virgin. They married last week and she apparently did not please him on their wedding bed so he has asked for an annulment. Their situation falls under the new laws as well.

If a man takes a wife, and after lying with her, dislikes her and slanders her and gives her a bad name, saying, "I married this woman but when I approached her, I did not find proof of her virginity," then the girl's father and mother shall bring proof that she was a virgin. (Deuteronomy 22: 20)

If it can be proved that she was indeed a virgin (by her parents displaying a cloth before the elders) the man must be fined. On the other hand . . . **If, however, the charge is true, and no proof of the girl's virginity can be found, she shall be brought to the door of her**

father's house (tent) and the men shall stone her to death. (Deut. 22: 21). Well, it has been kind of tense around here in this makeshift jail, as those two are not speaking to each other, and her parents have not arrived yet with the bloody sheet—the proof of her virginity. Of course, Maximilian is only going to be out a fine if he is wrong, but he isn't sweating it all that much, as there is no money out here in the desert with which to pay it anyway. Haha. So too bad for Karlotta. Bummer, huh?

Two other lawbreakers are here with us as well in this holding cell. It's a rape case. The guy, a local tough named Cloven, has been around raping women before, but always got out of it on a technicality. The law is clear: **If a man happens to meet a virgin pledged to be married (betrothed) and he sleeps with her, you shall take them both out and stone them to death—the girl because she did not scream for help, and the man because he violated another man's wife.** (Deut. 22: 23,24). Well, that case ended up a simple matter of "he said—she said" because she claimed that in fact she DID cry out, but nobody heard her. Likely story. Cloven claimed that she was asking for it and loved it. But in the end, the case turned on the fact that she was betrothed to *another guy*, namely a dude called Gommert, who was pissed off that Cloven had violated (used) his property and now she was deflowered and worthless. But in the end he took her anyway so Cloven got away with it.

This time he has been accused of rape again. However, the circumstances are different because he nailed a *single* girl with no immediate marriage possibilities. Her name is Xin-Loi. And she also claimed to have cried out; but this time she was heard and Cloven was busted. Caught in the act. So here they are waiting trial. The law is very clear on this, too. **If a man happens to meet a virgin who is not pledged to be married and rapes her and they are discovered, he shall pay the girl's father fifty shekels of silver. He must marry the girl, for he has violated her. He can never divorce her as long as he lives.** (Deut. 22: 28,29). This case turns on the issue of the appropriate fine. Her father, Mr. Pakatapos, argues that the fine should be much higher as he planned to get over 200 shekels for her. But the law that Moses got straight from God himself specifies that the fine is 50 bucks and that's it no matter what. So, what to do? It is obviously up to the Judges, and they are dealing with other cases at present.

So, Xin-Loi is stuck here with Cloven. She has no say in the matter at all. She is just a dumb uneducated eighteen-year-old girl, and she is going to have to marry Cloven whether she wants to or not. It is not hers to decide. You can tell she hates his guts, yet is resigned to her fate. She is condemned to be wedded to her rapist for the rest of her life. I wonder sometimes why God would make up such an unfair law. But it is obviously just a case of "trust and obey" (there's no other way).

Marah has had a chance to talk to Xin-Loi. She is bummed out and suicidal. "I just don't get it," she told Marah confidentially. "I was just walking home minding my own business when that thug attacked me, threw me down, and ripped my clothes off. He held me down but I screamed out—as I am supposed to do in such cases—as the law dictates." She really needed to talk. "But he was too strong and heavy for me. Fortunately, a certain Mr. and Mrs. Palohpoh were walking by and heard me scream. Mrs. P. was totally shocked and outraged, and hit him with her purse. He withdrew, but they had recognized him and reported him to the Judges." Marah can be a very good listener. Xin-Loi likes to sit next to Marah for comfort. But she isn't facing stoning like we are for the *sex-on-your-period* incident. Although she considers her sentence— being married to Cloven forever—to be a fate worse than death.

The only others here in the holding cell awaiting judgment are two soldiers in the Lord's Army. We are getting mighty near the border with Canaan, and the new commander, Joshua, is getting ready for us to enter the *Promised Land*. And we need all the soldiers we can get. But these two have committed an abomination before the Lord. They were caught having sex. Oh, and does that ever piss YHWH off big time. **If a man lies with a man as one lies with a woman, both of them have done what is detestable. They must be put to death.** (Lev: 20: 13). So, their fate is sealed (like me and Marah). They are both going to be executed— probably at the same time as we are. After all, "all of Israel" is going to witness our demise, so I guess we are going to be in good company. They say that by making examples out of us, it will be a good lesson for everybody. I still think it is a ripoff all around.

Anyway, I guess that now that Moses is somewhere in the great beyond with YHWH, and Joshua is in charge, the others will finally escape this hellhole called Sinai. I wish I could say that it has been fun. But it has been the pits. I am so sick of eating manna and quail that I am ready to dash my brains out with rocks. There is this big promise of "milk and honey" over there in the "Holy Land," but I hear tell we are going to have to "ethnically cleanse" all the folks who are living there now. God promised Moses that we would "inherit" the land. But sounds to me like it is going to be a bloody fight for us to get it. Too bad I'll miss it.

Chapter 14

Rahab

Just looking out for her girls

Hey, my name is Rahab, and I am the madam of a brothel here in New Jericho. I run a classy joint, and we do a good business . . . mostly Hittites, Amorites, and Jebusites (with an occasional Moabite now and then). They all come to my place and, hey, I'm not prejudiced one way or the other. Their cash is all the same to me. One dick is about the same as the next, I always say. Well, there *are* exceptions. And that reminds me of a story!

One day—a sort of slow day—two soldiers from Shittim checked in to my brothel in Old Jericho. Actually, they said that they were from there, but I didn't believe it. Hey, what do I care if they say they are from somewhere else? It is rather common in this profession. Guys don't like other people knowing they are here, and we are, above all, discreet. But these two guys were somehow "different." Who cares? They each made a choice, and the girls took them upstairs. Nothing unusual here. But then one of the gals, Bertha, sneaked back down and whispered: "I think those two are Jewish spies!"

"How do you figure?" I asked, feigning stupidity.

"Well, when the guy got naked, I noticed that he is cut."

"Like circumcised?" I queried.

"Yup," she added with certainty. "That is kind of a dead giveaway around these parts, huh?"

"Sure is," I replied, thinking . . . Is this a big deal or a big so-what?

"What shall we do?" she wailed. "You have surely heard what they did to Sihon and Og, the two kings of the Amorites east of Jordan?"

"Of course I know what they did!" I snapped. "I read the papers!"

"I'm sure they are here to spy out the land." I observed. "Go back up and do your thing like normal, and let me think what to do." She went back upstairs with a certain air of importance. I took to thinking. Ever since the Jews under their big-time new commander, Joshua, had invaded Canaan, all the various small tribes have been kicked around by his Israelite army. They had beat the shit out of the Amorites, and we appeared to be next on their list. I had to think fast. Well, my mom always said that the best defense was a strong offense, so I decided to play it tough and take them head on.

So I dashed upstairs and barged in on Bertha and the spy. I told her to beat it and talked to the guy directly.

"Look, Mr. Jewish Spy, the jig is up. We know who you and your buddy are, and I have a messenger standing by to run to the king's palace and turn y'all in!" He was obviously stunned and freaked out.

"Hey," he said, rather charmingly, "We aren't looking for trouble. We just needed to get laid."

"Likely story," I countered, "My guess is that Joshua himself sent you, and your mission is to spy out the land. Am I right?"

"Well, yeah, sort of," he confessed. "But the part about getting laid was true. We are all kind of horny out there with Joshua and the Jewish military organization. We don't get any chance to—well, you know."

"You should know we have a problem here," I said flatly. **"We have heard how the Lord dried up the water of the Red Sea for you when you came out of Egypt, and what you did to Sihon and Og, the two kings of the Amorites whom you completely destroyed. When we heard of it our hearts sank and everyone's courage failed because of you, for the Lord your God is God in heaven above and on the earth below!"** (Joshua 2: 10,11).

"Yeah, we're a whole herd of badasses out there," he boasted. "And you guys all should be scared of us."

"Oh, we *are* scared enough," I confessed. "But at the moment, I might point out that it is *you two* who now are in enemy territory, and with your pants down. So let's look at this situation realistically. You two aren't very good spies. Everybody in Jericho saw you come into town and check in here. And those Groucho glasses, noses, and mustaches were really not fooling anyone. So let's talk about how to save you."

"First of all, we'll have to hide you two and get rid of the king's men when they come looking for you. I will give them some cock-and-bull story about how you split already or something."

"Great. Sounds like a plan to me!" he sputtered enthusiastically. "Where do we hide?"

"Not so fast!" I insisted. "What's in it for me and my girls?"

"I don't know," he stumbled. "Joshua just told us to go into Jericho and check things out. He really didn't tell us what to do if we were caught." (Duh). "What's your idea?"

"Well, how 'bout this . . . I hide you now and help you escape. And when you sweep into the city and kill all the inhabitants, you spare me and my girls? I mean, really, what does it cost you? Besides, your pals out there on bivouac are going to need our services sooner or later, huh? And let me assure you that my girls have all sorts of talents that your boring Jewish wives couldn't imagine."

That knowing look spread over his face, and I knew we had a deal. **"Our lives are your lives!"** he assured me. **"If you don't tell what we are doing, we will treat you kindly and faithfully when the Lord gives us the land."** (Joshua 2: 14). We both knew we had made a good deal for all parties involved. However, questions and issues remained.

"What are we going to do while your army is ransacking the town? How will your soldiers know which house not to destroy when you begin your raping and pillaging of Jericho?" I asked.

"Good question," he said thoughtfully. "How 'bout this? Here, take this scarlet cord and tie it in your window! It is a bit cliché and formula, I know, but I'm a sucker for symbolism. It represents the blood on the lintels and door posts in Egypt from when the angel of death passed over the homes of the Hebrews when he killed the firstborn male children throughout the country. And, likewise, we will pass over your home (establishment) . . . The best little whorehouse in Jericho!" We shook on it, and it was a deal.

Now Jericho was tightly shut up because of the Israelites. No one went out and no one came in. Then the Lord said to Joshua, "See, I have delivered Jericho into your hands, along with its king and its fighting men. March around the city once with all the armed men. Do this for six days. Have seven priests carry trumpets of rams' horns in front of the ark. On the seventh day, march around the city seven times, with the priests blowing the trumpets. When you hear them sound a long blast on the trumpets, have all the people give a loud shout; then the wall of the city will collapse and the people will go up, every man straight in." (Joshua 6: 1-5).

Well, for six days me and my girls watched them march around the city. We were all scared shitless. Everybody was totally stressed out. Finally on the seventh day we woke to the sound of the rams' horns. Then everybody outside the walls began shouting like a bunch of banshees and an earthquake followed. Sure enough, the walls came tumblin' down just as predicted! I was impressed. Then the host of the armies of the Lord began pouring in. I double-checked to make sure that the scarlet cord was prominently displayed in my window upstairs.

So every man charged straight in, and they took the city. They devoted the city to the Lord and destroyed with the sword every living thing in it—men and women, young and old, cattle and sheep and donkeys. (Joshua 6: 21). It was a total turkey-shoot! Blood and guts, murder and mayhem. The Israelites swarmed in and began killing everybody in sight. They tossed babies out of windows, dashing their heads on the pavement. They dragged old men and pregnant women outside and cut their throats. They butchered perfectly good cattle, sheep, goats, and chickens. They systematically went from house to house, killing every living thing inside. But they left my brothel alone. The magic cord had done the trick! Amazing. By nightfall there was not a living thing still standing in Jericho. My family, my employees, and I huddled there in the darkness listening to them sing praises to their God. Then Joshua sent for me.

Joshua said to the two men who had spied out the land, "Go into the prostitute's house and bring her out and all who belong to her, in accordance with your oath to her." (Joshua 6: 22). So they took us to their camp and torched the town. By morning it was a smoldering pile of ashes. Of course they looted the place first. Joshua had commanded that all the gold, silver, and bronze articles (even iron pots) be brought to the Lord's storehouse. Then Joshua cursed Jericho. **"Cursed before the Lord is the man who undertakes to rebuild the city, Jericho: At the cost of his firstborn son will he lay its foundations; at the cost of his youngest will he set up its gates."** (Joshua 6: 26).

Well, there we were—the sole survivors of the Battle of Jericho with only the clothes on our backs. Joshua thanked us and sent us on our way. But where in the hell were we supposed to go? After all, our house had burned with the rest of the city. But I guess we should thank our lucky stars we got out with our lives and with an in-demand commodity.

So I got the whole lot of us settled in this little place a few miles from Old Jericho. They call it New Jericho, and it is really growing. Contrary to Joshua's curse, the town rebuilt and now it is quite a bit bigger than ever! But something happened during the looting process. Some of the plunder was stolen! And this is how it was told to me . . .

Shortly thereafter God noticed that some of the *objects d'arte* were missing. Obviously, he was paying attention to detail. Somebody had ripped off some of those cool gold and silver articles from the treasury, and God was royally pissed. So much so in fact that it was effecting the new war—the campaign against the town of Ai. Joshua was in a total tizzy. The battle for Ai was going very wrong. So, Joshua throws himself down on the ground and grovels before the Lord: "Why is Ai beating the shit out of us?" he asks God—weeping and wailing.

So God tells him that somebody has stolen some of his bling. The battle, then underway, will flop unless the missing doodads are found and returned to the storehouse. God roars out: **He who is caught with the devoted things shall be destroyed by fire, along with all that belongs to him. He has violated the covenant of the Lord and has done a disgraceful thing in Israel.** (Josh. 1: 15). Aha! The reason that things are not going well in Ai is that somebody has had his fingers in the till. They caught the culprit, a certain Achan, son of Carmi (son of Zimri, son of Zerah of the tribe of Judah), who saw in the plunder a beautiful robe from Babylon, 200 shekels of silver, and a wedge of gold weighing fifty shekels. Yo! So he just had to have it all. He ripped them off, and buried them under his tent. When Joshua grilled him, he confessed. Then Joshua screamed and yelled at him: **"Why have you brought this disaster on us? The Lord will bring disaster on you today."** (Josh. 7: 25). Whereupon they stoned him and his family and cremated them, thus fulfilling God's curse of fire. God was incensed that someone took a robe that belonged to him! (And it fit so well!) But once they threw rocks at Achan and his family and killed them all, everything was okay. Ai was destroyed, and Israel was ready for its next victim.

Joshua burned Ai and made it a permanent heap of ruins, a desolate place to this day. He hung the king of Ai on a tree and left him there until evening. At sunset, Joshua ordered them to take the body from the tree and throw it down at the entrance of the city gate. And they raised a large pile of rocks over it, which remains to this day. (Josh. 8: 28). Really? To *this* day? Where is it? Hmmm. I have lived quite a few years now since the burning of Jericho incident, and am getting ready to retire from the brothel biz. But I've still never ever even seen that pile of rocks. Sigh.

Chapter 15

Tingnanmo

Joshua's righthand man at the battle of Aijalon

Joshua is my superhero. My name is Tingnanmo and I attend to his horse, wash his clothes, polish his armor, and bring him his dinner when he is on duty. Actually, that is most of the time since he is a great general and all so he keeps me busy. I don't mind. I just love being with the troops. I really support the troops.

Well, after the fall of Jericho, we Jews really began to kick pagan butt. Everybody was scared of us, so they got together and decided to take us on as kind of an anti-Jewish team. The kings of Jerusalem and Hebron got together with the kings of Jarmuth, Lachish, and Eglon. Together they planned the "mother of all battles" in the Valley of Aijalon. Joshua was stoked. He was never one to back down from a fight, and since he had defeated the Amorites, he got the troops all pumped up, telling them that they were unstoppable.

I was all jazzed about the upcoming scrap as well. Of course, I was too young to participate, but sure wished I could. I did work extra hard to make sure all of the General's shit was together. It was! Of course, the troops were still totally pumped about their extravagant invasion and destruction of the town on Jericho some time earlier. They really trashed the placed and killed everybody in the whole town . . . right down to the kids and dogs. But they deserved it. After all, they don't worship YHWH, the one true God, like we Jews do, so fuck 'em.

Well, we were camped at Gilgal. I've always liked that place. That's when we heard that the five kings were massing near Gibeon. The shit was obviously about to start. **The Lord said to Joshua, "Do not be**

afraid of them; I have given them into your hand. Not one of them will be able to withstand you." That was reassuring :-)

So we marched all night and took them by surprise. **The Lord threw them into confusion before Israel, who defeated them in a great victory at Gibeon.** (Joshua 10: 8,9). They all ran through the briars, and they ran through the brambles, and they ran through the places where the rabbits wouldn't go. They ran like hell down the road going to Beth Horon, and we cut them down all the way to Azekah and Makkedah. It was absolute chaos. I mean, it was totally cool. Those pussies were, like, doing it in their pants. God was so definitely on our side that day. Then, to top it all off, on the route, **As they fled before Israel on the road, the Lord hurled large hailstones down on them from the sky, and more of them died from the hailstones than were killed by the swords of the Israelites.** (Josh. 10: 11).

One thing I have learned about YHWH, when he really gets pissed at somebody (or their army), he sends down hailstones on them, and they die in droves. But then the most amazing thing happened. I mean, it was like nothing you could imagine. Joshua (my boss) yelled out to Heaven:

"O sun stand still over Gibeon, O moon over the Valley of Aijalon." And it did! Holy shit! It did! **So the sun stood still and the moon stopped, till the nation avenged itself on its enemies. The sun stopped in the middle of the sky and delayed going down about a full day. There has never been a day like it before or since, a day when the Lord listened to a man. Surely the Lord was fighting for Israel!** (Josh. 10: 12-14). All of us "servants and other onlookers" just stood there in awe, looking up in the sky yelling, "tingnan mo!" (Look at that!) I decided right then and there to take that as my new name. I was tired of being called Walter anyway. Tingnanmo is way cooler, don't you think? Totally awesome! *There has never been a day like it before or since.*

Talk about being on the "God Squad" . . . Nothing could stop us now. After we hung those pesky kings and dumped their headless bodies in a ditch, we just kept on going. We were so on a roll. Well, we just kept conquering everybody around us, taking over their lands, killing all the people and animals, and trashing their cities. It was a blast.

Well, after we had pretty much ethnically cleansed the entire region, Joshua took to sort of being a king himself, adjudicating various squabbles and petty quarrels among the Jews. Life got kinda boring so I drifted away. Joshua didn't really miss me, as he was wrapped up being kind of a judge all the time. Later, I heard that he divided the land up, and the folks voted to appoint real judges to deal with all those issues and doing all the ceremonial shit as well. Boring.

I bumbled my way back to Jericho and married an older woman there named Rahab. She told me that she had met Joshua some years ago. He had spared her and her working girls from the destruction that he rained down on the town when the Lord's armies took it. She always had a soft spot for him after that.

The town was kind of in a building boom when I got there even though God had forbidden such a project. **"Cursed before the Lord is the man who undertakes to rebuild this city, Jericho. At the cost of his firstborn son will he lay its foundations; at the cost of his youngest will he set up its gates."** (Josh. 6: 26). Oooh.

Actually, nobody had the guts to start the rebuilding operation until Rahab, the only survivor of the original massacre (and a few of her girls), decided to circumvent the curse by initiating the reconstruction project *herself.* And since she was a woman and the curse specifically forbade *men* from breaking ground, she declared herself mayor of Jericho and kicked off a fundraising drive to start laying new foundations and new gates. It was a smashing success, and Jericho is here today to prove that a woman with a brain and balls can just about do anything! Hey, I'm cool with that ;-)

Chapter 16

Delilah

Samson's (on-again, off-again) girlfriend

Hey, y'all, my name is Delilah. It's pronounced Duh-lah-luh 'round these parts—in the Valley of Sorek. Well, some time back I was shacking up with this Jewish guy named Samson. He had been the leader of the Israelites for twenty years even though they were under Philistine administration at the time. He was a total thug, but I get off on the "bad boy" type, so I fell for him (sort of). It was kind of one of those "doomed to failure" affairs, but it was fun while it lasted.

See, Samson was a Nazarite. That's a Jewish thing. He had these really weird things he was not allowed to do, like drink booze, touch dead bodies, or cut his hair. Makes sense, I guess . . . sort of. We met in a most peculiar way. He had been enjoying the benefits of a whorehouse in Gaza when the Philistine constabulary tried to capture him with his pants down. It almost worked—or so I hear—but he managed to escape, and en route back to Jerusalem he passed through Sorek. We got it on right away, and he forgot about going home for a while. He was a "Total Gym" bodybuilder type, and was hopelessly in love with himself, but we had some laughs. Of course, I didn't bother to tell him that, actually, I was an employee of the Philistine administration. The leaders came to me with a proposal when they caught wind that Samson was in town and staying with me.

"See if you can lure him into showing you the secret of his great strength and how we can overpower him so we may tie him up and subdue him. Each of us will give you eleven hundred shekels of silver." (Judges 16: 5,6). Well, that would be a real haul for me, and the leaders really wanted to capture him as he was the top dog of the Jews and had been for twenty years. The very idea that he was here in their midst and so vulnerable was just too tempting for them. They had to capture him. But these things have to be handled delicately. My assignment was to get him to reveal the source of his great strength. At first, when I stroked his muscles, he told me that it was a special herbal milkshake or some such bullshit. I knew it had to be more than that since lots of the Philistine bodybuilders drank those power drinks, but none was as buff as Samson. Obviously, there was something more. So I plied him with wine and purred: **"Tell me the secret of your great strength and how you can be tied up and subdued."** (Judges 16: 6,7). Well, I should have known that it wasn't going to be that easy. He told me that if he were to be tied up with seven fresh thongs (undried) that he would be as weak as a kitten. Well, I fell for it and told the elders. They gave me the thongs and I tied him up while he was passed out from the wine. When he woke with a start, he easily broke the thongs, giving me that look like "Come on, you didn't think I would really tell you, did you?"

Well, I really needed the money, so I tried again. That flopped, and I was pissed. At this point I was bound and determined to make him talk. The third time failed as well, so I really turned it on big time: **"How can you say 'I love you' when you won't confide in me? . . . With such nagging she prodded him day after day until he was tired to death.** (Judges 16: 14,15). You know, I never quite got why they didn't just send a platoon of Marines in and arrest him. It would have been easier. But finally I had success. Finally he spilled the beans.

"No razor has ever been used on my head," he said, "because I have been a Nazarite set apart to God since birth. If my head were shaved, my strength would leave me, and I would become as weak as any other man." (Judges 16: 17). Well, that did the trick. I let him sleep with his head on my lap while the soldiers came in and we shaved his head quietly. Then they clamped on some bronze shackles and carted him off to prison (where they gouged out both his eyes). I got my silver, and that was the end of the story as far as I was concerned.

I didn't stick around after that, preferring to just take the money and run. I bought a nice condo in Gaza and decided to stay. Well, my sister still lived back in Sorek, so I kept up with the Samson saga from what she told me. Obviously, his hair grew back while he was in the clink. But, dummies that they were, nobody thought about that when they decided to humiliate him in public during the celebration of their god, Dagon.

They said: **"Our god has delivered our enemy into our hands, the one who laid waste our land and multiplied our slain."** (Judges 16: 24). Well, while they were all totally smashed, drinking too much at the festival, they got the cool idea to bring Samson out of prison to "entertain" them. So they did! Big mistake. I could have warned them not to do that. But they thought it would be great fun. So they dragged him out and put him on display right up in front of everybody. Well, according to the press release, there were over 3,000 men standing on the roof of the temple. (Judges 16: 27). With a weight load like that, I doubt that the building could hold them. There were all manner of others around the courtyard and on the platform when they brought him out. He couldn't see, so he asked them to put his hands on the pillars that held the place up. Then he shouted out:

"O sovereign Lord, remember me. O God, please strengthen me just once more, and let me with one blow get revenge on the Philistines for my two eyes." (Judges 16: 28). He put one hand on each pillar and cried out: **"Let me die with the Philistines!"** And then he pushed the pillars apart, bringing the whole place crashing down. Total suicide, but wow, was that ever a crushing way to go out. Wish I had been there to see it. Of course, the papers the next day said that it was due to the extra weight on the roof, but we all knew it was really our boy Samson. **Thus he killed more in death than while he lived.** (Judges 16: 29).

Then his brothers and his father's whole family went down to get him. They brought him back and buried him between Zorah and Eshtaol in the tomb of Manoah, his father. (Judges 16: 31). Of course, my sister told me on the QT that they weren't absolutely sure if it was Samson or not as there were thousands of bodies that were all rather flat.

Chapter 17

Mancini

Saul's lefthand man

I want to tell y'all a story 'bout a man named Saul, super King of Israel who took a fall. My name is Mancini and I was King Saul's lefthand man for many years. His story begins with the prophet Samuel. I never actually saw the prophet alive. However, I did have a chance to meet him . . . but that comes later. Let me fill you in on the actual situation from the beginning of the saga. You see, since Moses and Joshua croaked, the nation of Israel (a group of tribes really) had been administered by a collection of "Judges" and the occasional prophet sent by God to stir things up a bit now and then.

Samuel ministered unto the Lord under Eli. In those days the word of the Lord was rare; there were not many visions. (1 Samuel 3: 1). What a bummer. Well, for years we Jews have been fussing and fighting with those pesky Philistines—as you know. Well, sometimes we win, sometimes we lose. It is kind of dependent on the whim of Yahweh. He keeps telling us that we are sinning too much, which pisses him off. So he lets the Philistines clobber us now and again. When we repent and promise to do better, he lets us win. It's been going on for generations now, so ho-hum. But when there are no visions and cool stuff like that coming down the pike, we are kind of on our own. However, now and then we get an awesome prophet like Samuel and he keeps us straight.

But there was this one particular battle some time back when the Philistines whooped our asses and we lost 30,000 men. Damn. But what was worse—we lost the Ark of the Covenant. That was a bloody big fuckin' deal, let me tell you. Actually, when Eli heard about it he dropped dead on the spot. That's serious.

Well, the joke was on the Philistines. That thing brought them nothing but bad luck, and they were sorry that they even took it in the first place. They really didn't need it, but just to rub our noses in it, they took it and it caused them all sorts of grief. Haha. Too bad. Now God was none too happy with us, mind you, but he really hated having his sacred thing in the hands of those uncircumcised fools. So he fixed them. He sent plagues of rats into their fields and, worse, he gave them all a totally crappy affliction. **The Lord's hand was heavy upon them, and he brought devastation upon them, and afflicted them with tumors. And he smote the men of the city, both great and small, and they had emrods (hemorrhoids) in their secret parts.** (1 Sam. 5: 8,9). Well, they got sick of that fast enough. So lacking any Prep H, they decided to send the damned thing back to us Jews on a cart. Now, we were delighted to get it back; but true to form, we couldn't just accept it with our thanks, could we? No, we had to negotiate to take it off their hands.

So we made them pay a tribute—a fine. Five golden hemorrhoids and five golden rats. How symbolic, huh? Well, as Jews, we are not allowed to make graven images, but there's nothing in the Law of Moses that forbids us to have the pagans make them for us, is there? So they smelted some groovy tumors and rat statuettes for us and we called it good.

But the underlying issue here was not so much the quality of the final offering. No, it was way bigger. We looked around and noticed that all the other kingdoms around us had kings. Duh, they were called *kingdoms*. Like, wow. But we were technically a theocracy, as we had all these doofy, old judges and the occasional prophet. But we didn't have a real bonafide king like all the tribes around us in every direction. We wanted a king. We *needed* a king. Well, Samuel told us that YHWH was totally down on that idea, because HE was supposed to be our king. We didn't need an earthly king like those other stupid tribes. We had him. Oooh. How cool. What a concept! But the people kept bitching and complaining. How come they get a king and we don't? That's not fair. I just kept my mouth shut about this, as I really didn't care one way or the other. Saul was my master, and I was supposed to look out for him. And I did.

But apparently Samuel and God were talking in private, as a peculiar thing happened one day when Saul was sent on a mission by his father-in-law, Kish. **The asses of Kish were lost.** (I Sam. 9: 3). OMG, that's terrible. We were dispatched immediately to find them. So I suggested that we go consult a "seer" in the Land of Zuph. (Actually, she was an aunt of mine and she was quite adroit at finding missing stuff.) So off we went to the Land of Zuph. But we didn't get that far in our search for the straying ungulates; instead we ran into Samuel! How weird is that? I picked up right away that Samuel was in a bad mood—and for sure he didn't like Saul. I just stood there while they talked.

"Hey, Sam," Saul said in anticipation. "Can you tell me where to look for the lost asses of Kish? Like, you are a famous prophet and all that, so no doubt you can tell me right off the top of your head." Well, Samuel (obviously chaffing) replied:

"No, I can't tell you where those goddamned donkeys are. How should I know? Besides, I have a message for you from God Almighty."

"Who me?" Saul stuttered in amazement.

"Yes, you, you dingbat." His voice was dripping with contempt. "God has chosen you to be the king of Israel."

"Oh, that can't be right," Saul stammered. "I have no specialized training in government or even basic civics."

"Well," Samuel continued, "I guess you don't need a college degree to be a king, and, like it or not (and I don't), God has told me to tell you that you are indeed nominated and elected to be the new (first) king of the twelve tribes of Israel. Congratulations." You could feel the tension in the air.

"Well, I'm not sure I'm up to it," he said demurely. "I'm so unqualified." I could tell that he was warming up to the idea, though. Finally, Samuel blew up at him and roared:

"Oh, for God's sake take the crown!" So my master became the king of Israel on that day. I took pix. Saul thus began his career as a monarch. And he rather liked it. He immediately decided to go into battle with the Philistines—logical choice. So he attacked a remote garrison and we wiped them out. **"Let the Hebrews hear!" So all Israel heard the news. "Saul has attacked the Philistine outpost, and now Israel has become a stench to the Philistines."** (I Sam. 13: 3,4). It was not really such a big deal but Saul was broadcasting all over how he had kicked Philistine ass every way from Sunday. I kind of thought that he was overblowing it a bit, but he loved to toot his own horn. It was, after all, just an outpost, a remote garrison. But the Philistines caught wind of it and decided to put him in his place.

So they responded. The Philistines assembled to fight Israel, with three thousand chariots, and six thousand charioteers, and soldiers as numerous as sands on the seashore. They went up and camped at Micmash. (I Sam. 13: 5). Well, Saul was freaked! OMG, we had never seen anything like it. Saul was shitting his pants. His men could tell that he had no idea at all what to do, let alone how to command an army—and against those odds? Fat chance. So the men hid and then slithered away, leaving Saul holding the bag. He was totally befuddled. He didn't know what to do, so he made a burnt offering to the Lord. Too bad God wasn't accepting offerings that day (I guess, because Saul didn't get any help from on high). Then Samuel arrived unannounced. And he was hopping mad.

I wasn't sure what he was so mad about, but he told Saul in no uncertain terms that he was not going to be king for long unless he got with the program and (ignoring the Philistines for now) knocked out the dreaded Amalekites once and for all. Now God was still pissed at the Amalekites for harassing the Hebrews fleeing Egypt. God was sick, sick, sick of those people and wanted them gone permanently. He was going to give Saul one last chance to eliminate the Amalekites for good. God's orders were clear.

Now, go, attack the Amalekites and destroy everything that belongs to them. Do not spare them; put to death men and women, children and infants, cattle and sheep, camels and donkeys. (I Sam. 15: 2,3). Well, okay, I was a bit squeamish myself about killing all those little kids and babies, but Saul launched right out and went for it. He attacked them with the full force of the Israelite armies and did, in fact, kill everybody of the Amalekite tribe. I mean, we wiped them all out. Every living soul. Then we started on the animals. But Saul yelled out: "Wait a minute! Hold your horses. Let's not get too hasty. There are some pretty good livestock here. Perhaps we shouldn't slaughter *everything*. Let's hold back some of the prime animals . . . for sacrifice to the Lord, of course!"

So he failed to kill everything with breath in its nostrils as he had been instructed. Bad move. I really couldn't say anything about it, of course, being a mere servant. But I felt a cold chill as they led all the best beasts away, leaving the rest bleeding all over the ground. Well, as suspected, God was pissed off right away, saying: **"I am grieved that I have made**

Saul king, because he has turned away from me and has not carried out my instructions." (I Sam. 15: 10). I'll say. In fact, he kept the best for himself; after all, he was the king of Israel.

God was definitely not going to let Saul off the hook. He was "disobedient" by not killing all the animals, and God decided to simply shun him. He turned his back on Saul and wouldn't pay any further attention to him. He was definitely on God's blacklist. Then, once Samuel caught wind of this, he was spittin' mad. He confronted Saul with some disheartening information: he was going to be replaced. Then, after giving Saul the bad news, the old prophet dropped dead. He simply checked out without telling Saul who the new king was going to be. **Now the spirit of the Lord had departed from Saul, and an evil spirit from the Lord tormented him.** (I Sam. 16: 14). That was a real downer. He went into kind of a super funk. Nothing was going right for him, and he was diagnosed with severe clinical depression. Then, to make things worse, the Philistines showed up again. They were amassing a huge army at Shenem to fight against Saul. The king was freaked. He was really off his game and was unsure if he and his army could beat the combined Philistine army arrayed against them. So what did he do?

He inquired of the Lord but the Lord did not answer him, either by dreams or Urim or prophets. (I Sam. 28: 6). God was *so* ignoring him. But he needed advice. So I quietly recommended we visit a "seer." He liked my idea, but there weren't too many folks with such powers of perception around Shenem at the time, so we had to go all the way to Endor to find one. We encountered a witch when we got there. Her name was Endora. She was very old, having lived other lifetimes and in other places. I heard later that she got her own TV show years later with her daughter, Samantha. It was a real hit.

Well, Saul was in disguise when we first spoke with Endora. He didn't want her to recognize that the king was crawling to a mere witch to help him out with his Philistine issue. But soon enough she recognized him when he asked her to bring Samuel the prophet up from the dead for him. She was scared to death, but he assured her that he would not kill her if she would grant his request. So she did!

The king said to her, "Don't be afraid. What do you see?" The woman said, "I see a spirit coming up out of the ground." (I Sam. 28: 13). I've got to tell you, I was shaking in my boots at that point. It was Samuel alright, and Saul lost it and toppled over in a dead faint. But I revived him with some smelling salts that I always carry for such occasions. When he came to, he threw himself prostrate on the ground in front of the ghost of the crotchety old man. Obviously, Samuel was annoyed. **"Why have you disturbed me by bringing me up?"** he growled. **"I am in great distress."** Saul blubbered: **"The Philistines are fighting against me, and God has turned away from me. He no longer answers me, either by prophets or dreams. So I have called on you to tell me what to do."** (I Sam. 28: 15).

Well, Ol' Samuel lit right into Saul who was groveling like a slave, shaking in fear and despair. The old prophet had always had nothing but contempt for Saul (I always knew that). And he just couldn't help but rub the king's face in the dirt. He explained why God had abandoned him: **"Why do you consult me, now that the Lord has done what he predicted through me? The Lord has torn the kingdom out of your hands and given it to one of your neighbors—to David. Because you did not obey the Lord or carry out his fierce wrath against the Amalekites, the Lord has done this to you today."** (I Sam. 28: 16-18).

Well, the cat was out of the bag. Saul was losing his kingship because he didn't finish off the Amalekites. Actually, he *did* kill all the people, only keeping a few cows for himself. But God was not pleased. He obviously knew that Saul had not used those heifers for sacrifices. What a lie. God saw right through his ruse. Now to add insult to injury, he had appointed his son-in-law, David, to replace him.

I was well aware that the king had kind of grown angry with David, as he was such a talented young guy. Everybody loved David and that pissed the king off. Now he was being informed that David was going to take over his job. He was mad. And did he just give up right then and there? Hell no. He decided to fight to keep his tenure. I knew that was probably not going to work out. But he wasn't the kind of guy who was going to go quietly. And he didn't. Take it from me.

Chapter 18

Inamorato

Unrequited love is such a bummer

Hello, all, my name is Inamorato. I am the valet and armor-bearer for Jonathan, son of Saul, the king of Israel. I am, like, totally in love with Jonathan, but he doesn't even know I exist. It's so sad, but I live in hope. Actually, my master only has eyes for David, son of Jesse, who will undoubtedly be king of Israel himself someday soon. I have been loyal and faithful to Jonathan for years now, and practically worship the ground he walks on. I wish he would take me in his arms and kiss me passionately—like he does with David. I just have to stand outside and guard the door while they make love. Wish they would invite me to join in. A three-way with them would be so hot. But that is just a fantasy, I realize. Sigh.

Anyway, David was well-known to everyone around these parts from the time he was a kid and clobbered Goliath the Philistine with a rock to the head back in Socoh in the Valley of Elah. One lucky shot with his sling and he was famous. Of course, I shouldn't be jealous. He was obviously born under a lucky star. After killing that giant, Goliath, he whacked off his head with a sword and all of Israel went wild for him. Oh, and did I mention that he was a talented musician as well? Yeah, he could play the harp like a pro—and he wrote his own stuff too. He calls them "psalms," but they just sound like mood music to me. Well, anyway, what do I know about music and poetry? I am just a poor kid from Gob. Actually, I was lucky to get the gig with Jonathan. I bring him stuff to eat, make his bed, carry his gear, and occasionally give him a back rub. Wish it could be more. But he is the son of the king and a big time fighter—a man of combat. Oh, I just love a man in uniform.

David married the daughter of King Saul, so he spends time hanging around the court when he is not out fightin' with the Philistines, the Amorites, the Amalekites, and all those troublesome dudes around and about Israel. Jonathan has his own wives and kids, too, so they have to make special arrangements to get together for sex. I help facilitate those connections. It is an unofficial part of my job description.

Their story started back when Saul hired David to be his therapist. Actually, it was not really a shrink that the king wanted, as he was big into music therapy, and David could really soothe his jangled nerves with his harpsmanship. It really chilled the king out, and relaxed him after a hard day at battle. It was during that time that David and Jonathan met and began a lifelong friendship—and more. It was definitely a case of "love at first sight." I know. I was there. **And Jonathan made a covenant with David because he loved him as himself. Jonathan took off the robe he was wearing and gave it to David, along with his tunic, and even his sword, his bow and his belt.** (I Samuel 18: 3,4). David did likewise, and the rest is history. They always enjoyed undressing each other—especially after winning a big battle. Of course, that was the beginning of their troubles.

King Saul sort of picked up on the boys' "special" relationship. He did not approve, of course, but kind of ignored it at first. But then things began to change gradually. He kept sending them off to war, and they succeeded swimmingly. David took command, and Jonathan was quite willing to be his second. David was a natural top and Jonathan loved to bottom for him any time. David was getting quite a reputation as a field commander. He just kept winning battles and Saul got jealous. After all, he fancied himself as a fierce fighting man himself. And David just kept upstaging him. Saul was pissed.

"Saul has slain his thousands, and David his tens of thousands." (I Sam. 18: 7). OMG, how Saul hated that song. Of course, David never sang it in his presence, but the crowds around the countryside sang it all the time and it really got under the King's skin. **And from that time on Saul kept a jealous eye on David.** (I Sam. 18: 9). See the problem? I sure did. Saul kept sending David out on various suicide missions, and David won every time. He was really on a roll. **In everything he did he had great success, because the Lord was with him.** (I Sam. 18: 14).

Oh, I should include here the story of how David got the opportunity to marry the daughter of the King in the first place. It was totally cool. After David beat the shit out of the Philistines yet another time, Saul offered one of his daughters, Merab, to David. But the *other* daughter, Michal, really wanted David for herself. The king saw an opportunity to tease David, who wanted Michal as well. So he offered her up on one condition. He said: **The king wants no other price for the bride than a hundred Philistine foreskins, to take revenge on his enemies. Saul's plan was to have David fall by the hands of the Philistines.** (I Sam. 18: 25). Devious plan, huh? Well did it work? Hell no. David just sallied forth and whomped on a bunch of Philistines and brought back (get this) *two* hundred bloody foreskins! The king about lost it; but a deal is a deal, and David got Michal in the end. But his heart really beat for my master, Jonathan. I could relate.

Well, finally the king had had enough of David. He was sick of hearing of all his successes in battle. He told Jonathan and his guards to kill him. Of course, that was stupid. My master immediately warned David who fled the scene. Jonathan tried to reason with the king. **"Let not the king do wrong to his servant David; he has not wronged you, and what he has done has benefited you greatly."** (I Sam. 19: 4). I mean, come on, Dad, why are you so pissed off? David is an asset to you. Why off him? He wins battles for you and you don't even thank him. **"Why, then, would you do wrong to an innocent man like David by killing him for no reason?"** (I Sam. 19: 5). Why indeed? So Jonathan managed to patch things up between the king and David, but that only lasted a while until the next skirmish with the Philistines. **Once more war broke out, and David went out and fought the Philistines. He struck them with such force that they fled before him.** (I Sam. 19: 8).

This gave Saul a migraine and he took to his bed. He was really losing it. Getting totally paranoid and delusional, he called for David to play the harp and calm him down. (This was before Valium). But during the harp solo, Saul got so agitated and worked up that he threw a spear at David. He missed, but David got the picture—hey, this guy is out to get me. He withdrew. In fact, he got out of Dodge and made his way to Ramah. He hid out there. But Saul sent out a posse to find him and get rid of him once and for all. They bumbled all around Judah trying to find him, with no success.

But Jonathan found him first. Of course, he knew where to look. They had a secret spot in Ramah near Nob where they met for a magic interlude now and then. I kept lookout, so I knew the place and was sure David would be found there. They embraced. After about an hour together ;-) **Jonathan said to David, "Go in peace, for we have sworn friendship with each other in the name of the Lord." Then David left, and Jonathan went back to the town.** (I Sam. 20: 42).

Anyway, Saul's praetorian guards ran all over trying to catch David. Things were getting too hot in Nob, so David snuck away and made his way to Gath. That didn't work out either, as the King of Gath, Achish, figured to kidnap him. He faked being insane there and wriggled out of that one as well. Finally, he ended up in Mizpah (in Moab). That is a lovely place, actually. They even named a famous hotel after it in the region of Tonapah. Well, he wanted to stay, but the Philistines were attacking a nearby town called Keilah and David just couldn't resist a good scrap. So he and his 600 men (wherever they came from) ran right for it and into the fray. Great fun. After that, he headed out into the desert of Ziph where he held out a spell. Meanwhile, Saul and his entourage were still trying to track him down. David moved into a cave in the Desert of En Gedi. **So Saul took three thousand chosen men from all Israel and set out to look for David and his men near the Crags of the Wild Goats. He came to the sheep pens along the way; a cave was there, and Saul went in to relieve himself.** (I Sam. 24: 1,2).

Little did he know that David and his men were way back inside the cave. While he was taking a leak, David snuck up behind him. He could have killed him right then and there, but he hesitated. (I was not there for this episode, but some of his men watched the whole thing from the darkness and I heard about it later through the grapevine). After all this chasing around when David finally gets the upper hand on Saul, he just couldn't bring himself to do it. He spared the king's life. Saul actually got the picture. He knew that his reign was essentially over. All but the shouting . . . so he said to David: **"You are more righteous than I. You have treated me well, but I have treated you badly. The Lord delivered me into your hands, but you did not kill me. May the Lord reward you well for the way you treated me today. I know that you will surely be king and that the kingdom of Israel will be established in your hands."** (I Sam. 24: 17-20). How cool is that?

More battles ensued. The Amalekites were wasted, but the Philistines just kept coming. Then . . . I guess it was bound to happen sooner or later: my beloved master and secret love, Jonathan, was killed in battle. I was devastated and so was his dad, Saul. But we didn't have a chance to grieve right then and there as the Philistine army was bearing down on us and the king didn't want to be captured by those horrible fucks. He would rather kill himself than get captured. He called over to me to pick up his armor and said: **"Draw your sword and run me through, or these uncircumcised fellows will come and run me through and abuse me."** (I Sam. 31: 4). I just couldn't do it! **So Saul took his own sword and fell**

on it. (I Sam. 31: 5). He committed a kind of ritual seppuku—Hara-kiri. The king was dead, but so was my dear Jonathan.

David cried when he heard of it. There was nothing I could say to comfort him. He had no idea that I felt the same way. I just kept my mouth shut and cried inside. Then in true David fashion, he wrote a soliloquy for Jonathan. It was a lament, and he ordered all his men to to sing it. I sang it too.

How the mighty have fallen in battle! Jonathan lies slain on your heights. I grieve for you, Jonathan my brother; you are very dear to me. Your love for me was wonderful, more wonderful than that of women. (II Samuel 1: 26). I knew what he was talking about. He certainly had a point of comparison.

Well, I was kind of at loose ends when Jonathan was killed, so David took me on as one of his male valets, but it wasn't quite the same. We did battles and all that all the time, of course, but as we all got older the thrill was gone. I retired and moved into a small condo near the palace where David wrote psalms and lots of sonnets and proverbs. He still played the harp. Then he and one of his wives had a son that he really took to. His name was Solomon.

Solomon was kind of like his dad—smart, talented, and driven (in many ways). So I observed from afar after that. But I still had friends in the palace, and we shared the occasional bit of gossip. Solomon grew into quite the politician, and, as David got older, he more or less took over as the new king of Israel. David had a near-forty-year run as king. But to tell you the truth, I think he was glad when he could hand the whole thing over to Solomon. The kingdom was definitely in capable hands as they embarked on a super-big building construction project . . . The Temple. It was definitely going to be huge!

Chapter 19 (Part 1)

Dahan-Dahan

A Councilman of the Queen of Sheba

Greetings to all from the grand court of Sheba, Queen of Ethiopia. In 964 BC, we took a little trip up to Israel from here in the wilds of East Africa. Now, the queen had heard that there was this totally cool king named Solomon who lived up there in a kingdom far, far away. Rumor had it that this king was, like, the greatest king on Earth. All the other kings on the planet came to bring him bling. The queen and her court had heard: **King Solomon was greater in riches and wisdom than all of the other kings of the earth. The whole world sought audience with Solomon to hear the wisdom that God had put in his heart. Year after year, everyone who came brought a gift—articles of silver and gold, robes, weapons and spices, and horses and mules. Solomon accumulated chariots, and twelve thousand horses, which he kept in the chariot cities and also with him in Jerusalem.** (I Kings 10: 23-26).

Well, the queen was in a dither about all this, as she felt right away that, since *all* the other monarchs in the world were making their way to Jerusalem with tribute for Solomon, she had to do likewise. But, of course, she was in a quandary as to what kind of a gift would be appropriate for such a magnificent ruler. Well, her accountants at the court—and those of us in the government—pointed out to her that Ethiopia is a very poor country, so we couldn't possibly come up with a gift as grand as, say, the Emperor of China or the Shogun of Japan. Besides, China had learned to produce silk a thousand years before Solomon, and could bring him all sorts of fancy robes that he liked so much. What could we possibly produce to equal that? And without bankrupting the treasury as well. What a pickle!

So she called us all together for a cabinet meeting, and we discussed the various possibilities. I mean, we had to come up with something fitting the greatest and smartest king on the planet, but what? Goats were suggested. We have lots of goats in Ethiopia. Camels? Maybe we could capture a lion or two. What a conundrum. "How about gold?" suggested the Chancellor of the Exchequer. "We have mines, and could likely come up with a fairly impressive stash of bullion." That did the trick! "Excellent suggestion!" expressed the queen joyfully, "Let's get on it right away. There is no time to lose. Kick up the production in the mines immediately. Make the slaves work extra hours if necessary." So gold production at the Sheba Mines and Minerals Inc. went into high gear. "I want to bring at least 400 tons with me when we arrive in Jerusalem. That much ought to get their attention, huh?"

"Four hundred tons?" shrieked the finance minister. "Do you realize how much that is?" We all stood still in stunned silence. How could anybody speak to the queen in that sharp tone of voice? "It would totally bankrupt the entire country." he stated flatly. We were all shaking as we awaited the queen's response. "Well then, how much *can* we afford? After all, we have to make a good show of it."

"How about 150 tons?" the minister proffered. "That's an insult to one so high and exalted as King Solomon," the queen sputtered. "We will simply have to do better than that. Tell you what. You guys all go home and sleep on it and come back tomorrow with a concrete proposal." So we all left. I didn't sleep a wink, but couldn't think of a thing. So we got together again the next day. It was intense. When the queen arrived, we all rose and held our collective breath.

Finally the chairman of the Office of Management and Budget (the OMB) stepped forward with a plan. "I suggest we scrape together 200 tons for *actual* delivery to Solomon, and give the rest to him as a pledge. We could pledge an additional 200 tons at a future date. We could therefore call it a 'future'—sort of like a stock future." The queen was delighted. So we wrote a promissory note to the King of Israel to present along with the gold bars that we would pack onto camels and lug all the way from Africa to Jerusalem. Of course, there is no easy way to get there except through Egypt, so we would have to bribe the guards at the border and then pass through hundreds of miles of Pharaoh's territory with upwards of, like, $200 million in hard cold cash. Piece of cake. What could possibly go wrong?

So the queen charged us with getting the caravan together while she went to get her hair done. She would need an entirely new wardrobe for the trip, of course. She didn't want to look dowdy in front of all those Chinese ladies with all their la-la silk robes, you know. Certainly something suitable could be produced by the mills and factories of Africa. She had to look her best.

We calculated that each camel could carry around 900 lbs. So, to just get the gold moving we would need 440 camels. One of the accountants figured that we should just requisition 500, as the other sixty would be needed to carry the queen's stuff. So we hit the road. Well, actually there wasn't a real road until we got past Sudan and into Egypt. The travel planners figured that the distance between the queen's palace in Central Ethiopia to Jerusalem is around 3,000 miles. If we could make five miles a day, it would only take us 600 days to get to Jerusalem via the Suez Canal (which hadn't been built yet :-). Of course, that is, if we didn't stop. So when the chefs calculated the amount of food we would need for all that entourage and the animals, we just figured a cool *two years* to make the trip.

Two years later we arrived in Jerusalem. It was everything we had heard about and more! King Solomon was indeed magnificent, and the queen really fell for him. She gave him the gold and a really cool certificate with an embossed seal as a promise of the rest. Solomon's CPAs were a bit skeptical so they went into a conclave with our accountants. While the king and queen were "doing it" in Solomon's playroom (he had 700 other wives), the financial gurus pounded out a final draft which the royal couple really liked. Since all 200 tons of the remaining tribute due the king were still in the ground in Ethiopia, he would have a quick claim to the mines, and, henceforth, the Royal Mines of Ethiopia would be called *King Solomon's Mines*. Everybody was happy.

Chapter 19 (Part 2)

The Temple Builder

Finally the Jews get a cool place for the Ark of the Covenant

Good morning, and salutations from the Temple Mount in Jerusalem. I am Templeton, an architect once in the employ of the King of Israel, Solomon the Great. After the Queen of Sheba and that mondo collection of Africans left Jerusalem, God had a talk with Solomon and told him that he, YHWH, wanted the king to begin construction of a totally awesome new temple for him to hang out in when he was visiting Earth.

For 500 years we Jews had been wandering around dragging with us this really cool thing from God called the *Ark of the Covenant*. It was kind of a big, golden box with two angel images on top. Since God forbade us from making graven images, we always were amazed that he broke his own rule when he ordered Moses and Aaron to build the bloody thing. Anyway, it contained the stone tablets with the *Ten Commandments* inscribed on them, Aaron's rod, and—most importantly—that golden jar with an omer of manna inside. Like, totally wet-your-pants cool stuff, huh? Anyway, we dragged that dumb thing around for years and covered it in a crappy-looking tent that we called a *Tabernacle*. It got all dusty from road trips, and banged up in battles, but it was our good luck charm. Of course, it didn't always work, so it got captured now and then. Once we finally got it back from the Philistines, it was clearly time to put it in its place in the new temple for ever and for always.

I was tasked as the chief architect to build Solomon's Temple, and I did my job with all my heart and soul. I could go into all sorts of details, but that would likely bore you. It was huge, awesome, and totally fab. Let me tell you—I was proud, Solomon was proud, and God was proud. It was one groovy place! But all was not well in Yahweh-land. Solomon, son of David the Beloved, sinned in the eyes of the Lord, and we all saw trouble coming. It was Solomon's real weakness: women. Hell, the king could have any woman he wanted, and when he conquered other tribes, he usually got a wife or two as tribute. Nobody actually knows how many wives the king was keeping in his harem, but it is rumored to be over 700. Of course, there were at least 300 lesser women, called concubines, kept in that forbidden abode as well. But Solomon just couldn't get enough pussy.

King Solomon, however, loved many foreign women besides Pharaoh's daughter—Sidonians, Moabites, Edomites, Hittites (and Samsonites :-). But *they* brought a lot of baggage with them—or so I hear. **They were from the nations about which the Lord told the Israelites, "You must not intermarry with them, because they will surely turn your hearts after their gods."** (I Kings 11: 1-3). Well, just as God had warned, Solomon began getting into new and rather exotic different religions because he liked to play sex games with his various wives, as many were of weird sects that appealed to Solomon's kinkier side (if you know what I mean).

As Solomon grew old, his wives turned his heart after other gods, and his heart was not fully devoted to the Lord, his God, as the heart of David his father had been. He followed Ashtoreth, the goddess of the Sidonions, and Molech, the detestable god of the Ammonites. So Solomon did evil in the eyes of the Lord; he did not follow the Lord completely, as David his father had done. (I Kings 11: 3-7). So bad news began trickling down. God had taken Solomon to the woodshed and given him quite a spanking.

We Jews were aware that God was not pissed-off at Solomon because he fucked hundreds of different women. They were his wives—his property. He could fuck them if and when he wanted to, and that was cool with YHWH. So why was the Almighty so mad at him then? Well, Solomon did the one thing you just cannot do as a Jew: he fucked around with other *gods*! Simple as that. Our god can handle a lot of dubious behavior from us, but we have to worship him exclusively and that is our prime directive. Funny, we all know the rules, and have for centuries, but I guess Solomon figured that just because he is king, he could get away with it. Not a chance.

The Lord became angry with Solomon because his heart had turned away from the Lord, the God of Israel, who had appeared to him

twice. Although he had forbidden Solomon to follow other gods, Solomon did not keep the Lord's command. So the Lord said to Solomon, "Since this is your attitude, and you have not kept my covenant and my decrees, which I commanded you, I will most certainly tear the kingdom away from you and give it to one of your subordinates." (I Kings 11: 9-11).

"But for the sake of David your father, I will not do it during your lifetime. I will tear it out of the hands of your son." (I Kings 11: 12). I was still putting some decorative flourishes on the temple when Solomon, the old guy, croaked. He was kind of in a funk in the end, as he had failed YHWH and still had a thing for Molech and some of those other "detestable" gods. But, true enough, once his son, Rehoboam, took office things began to slide perceptibly.

You know, you'd think us Jews would finally get the picture. Our god is a jealous god and he told us that right from the get-go. But those weird other gods with their strange orders and fetishes are just so interesting and appealing. Oh well, we all knew trouble was coming our way. We just didn't know when. But we *just* knew.

Chapter 20

Teensee and Weensee

The angelic twins retell the whole story of Job

Hey-ho, everybody! Me again, Teensee, and my twin brother, Weensee. Remember us? We are matching A-509 series angels in the service of our Lord. Most of the time we are up here with God singing his praises 10,000 years at a time, but now and then we get to go down to Earth and check stuff out for YHWH, who (although he is omniscient and knows everything already) needs confirmation of various cryings-out that we hear up here from various Earthlings.

Those are mostly called "prayers." They are constantly floating up here on the wind, and we just ignore most of them. Oh, yes, a flood here, a plague there. A mother losing a child to a fever in the night. Ho-hum. We get prayers like that all the time, so it is more important to keep up the praise cycle than to deal with them. Our prime directive is praise. We just are programmed to praise . . . praise . . . praise. Very dull, but what else is there to do up here? Think, create, innovate, imagine? Ha. That'll be the day.

We are up here in Heaven with God and the rest of the heavenly host. We're taking a break from all these Bible stories that you're reading about the Jews beating up on the Amalekites, the Amorites and the Ammonites, etc. So we want to tell you a story 'bout a man named Job. He was one of these guys who was born on third base but thought he hit a home run. He had it all. Land, cattle, camels, and donkeys. You know —the kind of stuff that indicates that you are in good with God. He was a true devotee of the *prosperity doctrine*. You know the one: if you praise God enough he gives you stuff.

Anyway, Weensee and I were hanging out near the Mercy Seat (that's God's golden throne where he sits to hear all the praises all day). God was digging the sounds of a new Christian rock group from Tuscaloosa when Satan walked right in unannounced and came right up to the M.S. and announced that he had returned from his trip down to planet Earth. Like, so what? Well, **the Lord said to Satan, "Where have you come from?" Satan answered the Lord, "From roaming through the earth and going back and forth on it."** (Job 1: 6,7). We gasped. "Wow, that was kinda cheeky, huh?" I whispered to Weensee—who was likewise a bit taken-a-back that Satan had the audacity to speak so casually and flippantly to the creator of the Universe. He almost treats the Almighty as an equal; sort of like he was as good as the Lord himself! Well, apparently, that didn't bother God who just said: **"Have you considered my servant, Job? There is no one on Earth like him; he is blameless and upright, a man who fears God and shuns evil."** (Job 1: 8).

Well, Weensee and I had actually been down there in the Land of Uz (not to be confused with Oz, which isn't really an actual place). Uz is where Job lives, and he is a big enchilada 'round those parts. He is a wealthy guy just dripping with "family values." He has wives and kids, servants and slaves (and he pays better than the minimum wage). Everybody loves Job. But not Satan. Lucifer can see right through him. He is only acting all righteous and gentile because he is in fat city. Hey, you would be praising God all the time too if you had all the shit Job does—and he knows it. He gives God all the glory-glory, so God loves him right back.

"Does Job fear God for nothing?" Satan slyly inquires. **"Have you not put a hedge around him and his household and everything he has? You have blessed the work of his hands, so that his flocks and herds are spread throughout the land."** (Job 1: 9,10). Satan states the obvious. God is coddling Job. Like other of his *Earth-pets* (for example: Abraham, Moses, and David), God likes Job better than other people around him. So he does special stuff for him (as he did for them) and ignores the rest. Satan can see that clearly, so he simply taunts God (right in front of the heavenly host). **"Stretch out your hand and strike everything he has, and he will surely curse you to your face."** (Job 1: 12). *Scommettiamo?* (Wanna bet?)

"You're on!" God roared enthusiastically. "You're gonna lose! Watch this! . . ." Then in a flash God withdrew his blessing from Job. He sent the death angel back down to Earth (like he did to Pharaoh back in

Egypt) and killed all his family—wife, kids, and babies. All dead. Poof. Then he sent a quick-acting plague and all his animals died . . .the camels, the cattle and sheep, the goats, the horses and mules. All snuffed in short order by the hand of the Lord. He didn't waste any time or mess around. In no time Job was standing all alone in a sea of dead bodies. Sniff sniff . . . poor Ol' Job, that righteous fellow full of praise for the Lord. Now what?

Then came the hemorrhoids. That was just the beginning. He broke out in hives, shingles, boils, and all manner of other rather unattractive pustules. "You look like hell!" exclaimed his friends, Eliphaz the Temanite, Bilbad the Shuhite, and Zophar the Naamathite. "Wow," they tisked, looking at all the dead livestock, "What did you ever do to piss God off so royally?" With friends like those who needs enemies, right? But since he didn't have any others left, he began to listen to what they had to say. OMG, were those guys ever blowhards! They went on and on about how it simply had to be Job's fault. "Surely you must have said or done something to make the Almighty dump on you like this!" **Now trouble comes to you, and you are discouraged; it strikes you, and you are dismayed. Should not your piety be your confidence and your blameless ways your hope? As I have observed, those who plow evil and those who sow trouble reap it. At the breath of God they are destroyed; at the blast of his anger they perish.** (Job 4: 5-9). "If you're so righteous and blameless, why are you suffering? Why?"

Job was really rankled by this. He told the friends that he was righteous and that he did nothing at all to offend God—implying that if it was a mere minor infraction, it was surely not deserving all this death and destruction. **"Although I am blameless, I have no concern for myself; I despise my own life. It is all the same; this is why I say, 'He destroys both the blameless and the wicked.' When a scourge brings sudden death, he mocks the despair of the innocent."** (Job 10: 21-23). What a downer.

While Weensee and I watched Job and his friends go back and forth in quiet despair, one thing was sure: Job had no idea what lesson was to be learned from all this carnage. Of course, we knew it was all about a bet in Heaven, and that there was no actual reason at all for Job's suffering. He was right that it was nothing that he *did* to offend God. God was just using him to prove a point to Satan (and to win a bet, of course :-) But, oddly enough, as God tuned in to what Job was whining and bitching about, you could see that he was getting annoyed with him. Job was coming to the conclusion that God was simply unfair and acting arbitrarily (which he was). Hell, it was just a bet after all. "How dare he question me? Goddammit, I'm God. That ingrate has no right to question me like this!" His dander was up. He was fuming and pacing around the Mercy Seat, muttering. "I ought to just go right down there and give him a piece of my mind!" I glanced at Weensee and winked. "I'll bet that's exactly what he's about to do," I said *sottovoce*. At that very moment he stormed out and was gone! (Down to Earth, that is.)

He encountered Job face-to-face and began his rant. The whole heavenly host was watching from our in-the-round theater up in the sky. (We're going to get to watch the *tribulation* from those seats one of these days as well.) God got himself all puffed up and let loose . . . **"Where were you when I laid the earth's foundations? Tell me if you understand! Who shut up the sea behind doors when it burst forth from the womb? Have you ever given orders to the morning, or shown the dawn its place, that it might take the earth by the edges and shake the wicked out of it?** (Job 38: 4,8,12-13).

Have you entered the storehouses of the snow or seen the storehouses of the hail? From whose womb comes the ice? Who gives birth to the frost from the heavens when the waters become hard as stone, when the surface of the deep is frozen? Do you send lightning bolts on their way? Do they report to you, 'here we are'?" (Job 38: 22,29,35). Well, do they, do they?

Well, that did it. Poor Ol' Job passed out! He just keeled over in a dead faint and hit the floor with a thud. God was a bit nonplussed. He just stopped, bent over, and said, "Job? Are you okay? Like, I didn't mean to scare you or anything." He was not out for long and when he started coming to, choirs of cherubim and seraphim began singing *Amazing Grace*. It was touching. Then Job sat up and began singing: **"I know that my redeemer liveth!"** (Job 19: 25). We were all so moved! Isn't that sweet?

Anyway, God had made his point. He is still in charge. He is the top dog . . . the big mean mothafukka in the sky, so don't mess with him. He flew back up to Heaven and plopped down on the Mercy Seat with much satisfaction. "Well, I guess I told him, huh?" he said triumphantly to all around. Some of the upper-echelon angels (like Michael the archangel) quietly asked if he planned to leave Job down there in such a state. "Don't you think you could help him out a bit?" they coaxed.

"Oh, yeah, I guess you're right. It wouldn't be cool to just leave him down there in a heap." So God restored his lands and fields, his cattle and his donkeys, his servants and slaves. Oh, and yes, some gold and silver. That is important. Then he gave him a new wife. **And he also had several sons and three daughters. His first daughter he named Jemima** (who made it big in pancakes later on). **The second, Kezieh and the third Keren-Happuch** (with a name like that you've got to be good). (Job 42: 13,14). We were all jazzed. **After this, Job lived a hundred forty years; he saw his children and their children to the fourth generation. And so he died, old and full of years.** (Job 42: 16,17). Hallelujah!

So existence in Heaven resumed as before . . . praising and praising. Then finally Satan showed up kind of dour-looking. He admitted that he lost the bet and was coming around to pay up. God held out his "mighty hand" and Satan gave him ten shekels of silver (grudgingly) and walked away. God turned back and resumed enjoying the choir of angels, chuckling to himself. "I told him he was going to lose. Like, duh, I knew it all along. I am God, after all, and I am *omniscient*!" Smile.

Chapter 21 (Part 1)

Shadrack

Oh no, not the fiery furnace!

Greetings from the court of King Nebuchadnezzar, ruler of Babylon. I am Shadrack, a friend of Meshack and Abednego. We are friends of Daniel, the chief of all the magicians in the kingdom. Our story begins back in Jerusalem in 597 BCE. For years prophets like Isaiah, Ezekiel, and Jeremiah warned us Jews to stop fucking around and to get our act together or face utter extinction. Ever since Solomon croaked the whole kingdom was on a downhill slide for years. God kept sending warnings by way of his holy prophets like Jeremiah who spookily proclaimed stuff like: **"The sovereign Lord says: My anger will be poured out on this place, on man and beast, on the trees of the field and of the fruit of the ground, and it will burn and not be quenched."** (Jeremiah 7: 20).

Finally, the kingdom of Israel split in half, and the people kept doing stuff that was "evil in the eyes of the Lord." So he quit blessing us, and King Neb finally invaded from the north and sacked Jerusalem. Mass deportations followed. In 586 BCE we three amigos (and Daniel) were rounded up and began our long slog to Baghdad . . . I mean Babylon. Now, the Babylonians were not like us Jews under David and Solomon and the sort. When we conquered a territory or a neighboring tribe, we simply went in and killed everybody in the place. Our God, Yahweh, told us to do it that way, so we did. But King Neb gave his generals different orders. "Why kill perfectly good slaves?" was his thinking. So they rounded up everybody in the whole country and enslaved us, marching us hundreds of miles away to work at various tasks suitable to our abilities. Yup, you heard me right. They gave us IQ tests, and some of us passed with high enough scores and got to do specialized training to become civil servants in the vast Babylonian bureaucracy. Works for me. But Daniel scored off-the-chart, and they singled him out for a postgrad level assignment in the government. We didn't see him for a while.

Dan got to work right in the king's court. But he never forgot his friends. While he was doing his thing as one of the king's "wise" men, the king had a dream and Dan interpreted it for him. Neb was wowed so he elevated Dan to top spot as "Chief of the Magicians." Of course, we all knew how much YHWH hated sorcerers of any kind (like warlocks and witches—like Endora). But Dan totally got into being a magician, and God let it slide. After all, I guess, like, we were in captivity, so we had to toe the line. After the dream thing and now that Dan was top dog in the palace, he requisitioned me and Meshack and Abednego to work with him, thus freeing us from the drudgery of working as paper-pushers for the Babylonian IRS. That was a drag, that was! We loved working for Daniel and things were groovy (like an old time movie) :-)

Then trouble started. The king decided to have the royal foundry produce a statue of gold. It was hideous. **King Nebuchadnezzar made an image of gold, ninety feet high and nine feet wide. Then the herald loudly proclaimed, "This is what you are commanded to do, O peoples, nations and men of every language: as soon as you hear the sound of the horn and all kinds of music, you must fall down and worship the image of god that the king has set up. Whoever does not fall down and worship will immediately be thrown into the blazing furnace."** (Daniel 1: 3,4-6). Well, Daniel—good Jew that he was—refused to bow down to that monstrosity. We followed suit. The king was spittin' mad.

Then Nebuchadnezzar was furious with Shadrack, Meshack and Abednego, and his attitude toward them changed. He ordered the furnace heated seven times hotter than usual. (Dan. 3: 19).The guards took Daniel away, and we were on our own—waiting to be thrown into the flames. As we were waiting, we overheard the guards and the firemen discussing the king's order. "How are we going to stoke the oven to be seven times hotter than usual?" they wailed. "The hottest we can get wood to burn is around 1,100 degrees. So seven times that would be approaching the temperature of the surface of the sun. And you just can't get that kind of heat out of wood!" the first fireman pointed out. "What if we use coal?" asked the second, trying to be helpful. "Too bad there are no coal deposits around these parts," sadly explained the third. "How about oil?" asked the first again anxiously. "Well, that hasn't been discovered around here yet," explained the third. Oh shit, what to do?

Well, they just told the king that is was indeed seven times hotter than normal, though that is impossible; and Neb bought it, upon which we were tied up ready to go in, clothes and all. **So these men, wearing their**

robes, trousers, turbans and other clothes, were bound and thrown into the blazing furnace. (Dan. 3: 21). Well, you know the story, we didn't burn. Neither did our turbans and trousers! It was totally radical; and the king couldn't believe his eyes. **Then King Nebuchadnezzar leaped to his feet in amazement and asked his advisers, "Wasn't it three men that we tied up and threw into the fire?" They replied, "Certainly, O King." He said, "Look! I see four men walking around in the fire, unbound and unharmed, and the fourth looks like a son of the gods."** (Dan. 3: 25).

Well, the fourth guy in the furnace introduced himself as Yeshua bar Yoseph, and told us that he was coming to Earth in the future to save all mankind. Then he disappeared and we were taken out of the furnace and stood before King Neb again. Only this time the king was visibly shaken. He called us by our first names and proclaimed that our God, Yahweh, the God of Israel, was henceforth to be the top deity in all of Babylon. And that we Jews and our super god were to have a special place in the realm of Babylonian mysticism. He went on and on. **"Therefore I declare that the people of any nation or language who say anything against the god of Shadrack, Meshack, and Abednego be cut into pieces and their homes be turned into piles of rubble, for no other god can save in this way."** (Dan. 3: 29). Wow, nothing like *privilege* is there? We three got promotions and elevated status in and around the imperial compound after that. Not too shabby, huh?

Well, Daniel was likewise forgiven for not bowing to the statue, which Nebuchadnezzar admitted later was a lame example of Babylonian artistic expression. It was an ugly statue in the first place, so they put it away in a warehouse somewhere and never put it on display again.

Chapter 21 (Part 2)

Arbondigas (brother of Abednego)

It all started with a dream . . .

The king was very openminded. His kingdom included people from many tribes and clans, and he was proud of his multiracial and multiethnic kingdom. Shortly after the fiery furnace incident, King Neb gave Daniel a new name—a Babylonian name: *Belteshazzar*. And he was promoted right up to the top of the Babylonian hierarchy. Daniel was right in the center of all the action and decision-making for the whole kingdom. But although the king faked along that he was totally into Yahweh and all that, he really was still a secret worshiper of Murdek, the top god of the Babylonians all along. We told Daniel, but he was so high on his new power trip that he just said: "Yeah, yeah, I know. But my being up here in this exalted place is good for *all* the Jews—really. It's high visibility."

So Daniel was at the king's beck and call. Then the king had a dream that totally befuzzelated him. None of the seers or enchanters or magicians could interpret it. But Daniel did. He told the king that he was going to have a psychotic break and imagine himself as a cow, eat grass, and trip out for, like, seven years. Well, it happened. The king must have eaten some magic mushrooms or got his hands on some real powerful hashish. He went out into la-la land and was out there while Daniel and others of the ruling elite ran the kingdom from the palace.

Well, finally the king came back down to Earth, but he decided that he rather enjoyed being a recluse. So he let his son, Belshazzar, take over; and Daniel went with the flow. The new king had been born and raised in the palace, and was totally familiar with the political and spiritual goings -on in that realm. He was a total playboy and gave lavish parties. Well, the Lord on high was watching all this, and got increasingly steamed. Then at one super-shindig the new king went too far. **While Belshazzar**

was drinking wine, he gave orders to bring in the gold and silver goblets that Nebuchadnezzar his father had taken from the temple in Jerusalem, so that the king and his nobles, his wives and his concubines might drink from them. So as they drink the wine, they praised the gods of gold and silver, of bronze, iron, wood and stone. (Dan. 5: 3,4). Daniel was pissed that those clods were drinking from Yahweh's special holy goblets. You could see it on his face. The other servants and I just watched in awe when the next thing happened . . .

Suddenly the fingers of a human hand appeared and wrote on the plaster of the wall. The king watched the hand as it wrote. His face turned pale and he was so frightened that his knees knocked together and his legs gave way. (Dan. 5: 5,6). **This is the inscription that was written: MEME, MENE, TEKEL, PARSIN** (Dan. 5: 25), which means: *You have been put in the scales and found wanting*. Bad news. I could have told him not to use those goblets. They were ripped off from God's temple, and Yahweh doesn't want any mere mortals drinking from them—especially those Murdek-worshipping Babylonians.

The jig was up and we knew it, but the king didn't. So he called Daniel over to interpret the meaning. Daniel walked all around the room, then went out on the balcony (everybody in the room could see him, and was watching with rapt attention as he looked up directly into the sky). Then he came back into the room, and announced that due to his misuse of Yahweh's sacred cups, the kingdom would fall immediately. "How do you know?" the king asked incredulously. "Did you see it in the stars?"

"No," Daniel answered emphatically. "There are 100 Persian soldiers on the roof!" **That very night Belshazzar, the king of the Babylonians, was slain, and Darius the Mede took over the kingdom, at the age of sixty-two.** (Dan. 5: 30). We held our breath as King Darius set up his cabinet. Daniel was picked right away, and, since he was an old friend of my brother Abednego, he picked me to be his secretary. So we began adjusting to the new regime.

I should have seen it coming. The other satraps and nobles, seers and magicians, all were jealous that Daniel was put in such an elevated position. After all, they reasoned, he is a mere Jew! OMG. So they put their heads together to conspire against him. They were dishing out all this false praise upon King Darius . . . and the king loved it. *Praise me more, praise me more.* Kind of like Yahweh, that, but this guy is a mere mortal, and YHWH is the creator of the Universe so he deserves all that praise forever and ever. Finally, the house of representatives drafted a bill that stated the month of April would henceforth be declared "The month of Darius," and nobody would be allowed to worship any god or man other than him. Darius loved it. Daniel didn't. He knew that he could not in his good Jewish conscience worship anybody but Yahweh, so he refused; and the king was totally bummed out since he had already signed the bill.

"Well, guess we're going to have to throw him into the den of lions," the conspirators all intoned gleefully. The king was in a bad place. He really liked Daniel, but, hey, he had signed the thing and couldn't rescind it. Of course, he could have offered an amendment—a religious exception for the Jews, for example. But his pride got the best of , and he went along with the punishment of Daniel, even giving his ring to seal the entrance to the den for twenty-four hours. He appeared totally distraught as he genuinely loved Daniel and needed him in his administration. The magicians were gloating.

Then the king called me over. I was shaking. He gave me a sack of coins and quietly whispered in my ear to use it to make sure that the zookeepers overfed the lions tonight so they would not be the least bit hungry when let loose on Daniel. They did well. The lions waddled out into their enclosure, plopped down, and went to sleep. Daniel kept up a prayer vigil throughout the night, praising Yahweh for saving him. He never knew that I, Arbodnigas, the brother of Abednego, had arranged his good fortune.

The next morning the king oversaw the removal of the seal on the stone door at the lion exhibit at Babylon Zoo. Daniel came out triumphantly, leaping and praising God. Everyone was happy. The king just quietly glanced my way, giving me a knowing wink.

So Daniel prospered during the reign of Darius and the reign of Cyrus the Persian. (Dan. 6: 28). Things went swimmingly after that . . . until a while later when Daniel began having his own dreams and visions. But that is another story!

Chapter 22

Scribner-Jai

*He wrote down Jonah's poetry and accompanied
him on his epic journey to Nineveh*

I met Jonah on a boat in the Mediterranean en route to Tarshish (which is in Spain). Later, he told me that he accidentally got on the wrong boat to start with as he really was intending to go to *Tarsus*, which is in Turkey. But, anyway, that isn't a big deal since most people you talk to don't know the difference themselves. LOL. Anyway, he was escaping an assignment from Yahweh, his Lord.

It all started like this: **The word of the Lord came to Jonah son of Amittai: "Go to the great city of Nineveh and preach against it, because its wickedness has come up before me."** Well, according to him, he was totally freaked at the challenge. So, what did he do? **But Jonah ran away from the Lord and headed for Tarshish. He went down to Joppa, where he found a ship bound for that port. After paying the fare, he went aboard and sailed for Tarshish to flee from the Lord.** (Jonah 1: 1-3).

Well, what was the backstory on all that? You see, Jonah was a Jew, and he wasn't all that fond of Gentiles of any kind. He never rubbed shoulders with those slobs whom Yahweh had ignored for centuries— just coddling the Jews and giving his favor to them *only*. I mean, he is their exclusive God, and Jonah was outraged that YHWH would actually send *him* to preach to those swine. He didn't want to warn them that Yahweh was totally pissed at them and was intending to dump on the place like he did to Sodom back in the day. He was shocked that the Lord would actually give those pigs a warning. He never gave Sodom a warning. He just bombed the place with fire from the sky and killed the whole lot of them. But now he was really going to send Jonah to *warn* them. Why the hell should he? He wanted them to fry. He explained all this to me later, of course, because when we first met we were in a rather dire circumstance. It happened like this:

Then the Lord sent a great wind on the sea, and such a violent storm across that the ship threatened to break up. All the sailors were afraid and each cried out to his own god. And they threw the cargo into the sea to lighten the ship. (Jonah 1: 4,5). You wouldn't believe the mayhem! Those guys were running around like crazy while Jonah was sleeping away down below deck. The captain was furious and yelled at him. Meanwhile, the crew—in despair—decided to cast lots to figure out whose fault it was that we were in such peril. But Jonah came up on deck and confessed that it was he who was responsible. **He said: "I am a Hebrew and I worship the Lord, the God of heaven, who made the sea and the land." This terrified them and they asked, "What have you done?" (They knew that he was running away from the Lord, because he had already told them so).** (Jonah 1: 9,10). Well, the sea was about to overwhelm the boat, sink it, and drown all of us in the process. They shouted to Jonah: "What the hell are we supposed to do now?" Then, shockingly enough, he told us to throw him overboard. He actually told us to drown him. I was nonplussed that he would do that.

Well, they wasted no time. They grabbed him and tossed him into the sea. Just then a huge wave hit the boat, and I fell overboard as well! I don't remember much, but suddenly I saw this huge mouth coming at me and was swallowed up by a giant fish. I ended up in the fish's stomach, and, lo and behold, there was Jonah—already there! He was surprised to see me. Well, it was really weird down there. There was light from somewhere, as I could see that the fish had also swallowed a desk and some writing supplies. Obviously, his God wanted me to take dictation.

From the inside of the fish Jonah prayed to the Lord his God. He said: "In my distress I called to the Lord, and he answered me. From the depths of the grave I called for help and you listened to my cry. The engulfing waters threatened me, the deep surrounded me; seaweed was wrapped around my head." (Jonah 2: 5). He dictated all that, and I just wrote it down. Very eloquent coming from a guy in the innards of a fish, huh? Well, he went on and on. So, I just kept up with my high school shorthand. **"When my life was ebbing away, I remembered you, Lord, and my prayer rose to you, to your holy temple."** (Jonah 2: 7). Jonah was making peace with his God, and, obviously, he was having a change of heart there inside the fish. We were on about day two at this time, and I was running short of paper. But he went on. **"With a song of thanksgiving, will I sacrifice to you. What I have vowed I will make good. Salvation comes from the Lord."** (Jonah 2: 9). At last, Jonah admitted to the Lord that he was a coward to run away, and added that now he was going to do his assignment after all (if the Lord would just get us out of this fish-belly, that is). So, get this: **And the Lord commanded the fish, and it vomited Jonah onto dry land.** (Jonah 2: 10). I might add that the fish burped *me* up as well! And I managed to save the parchments. Yea!

So there we were lying on the beach, the Mediterranean to our backs and Nineveh 600 miles away to the East—across the desert, and with no means of transportation anywhere in sight! Shit. So we set out, and along the way we bonded. I learned a lot about the history of the Jews, their scary sky-god, and the way they had systematically slaughtered all the inhabitants of the lands that they conquered. But Jonah was going to kind of make amends for the way their god treated non-Jews in the past . . . starting with Sodom . . . and then there were the plagues on Egypt . . . the extermination of the population of Jericho . . . and later the total destruction of the Amalekites, the Amorites, and the Ammonites. God obviously had concluded that slaughtering people with such abandon was not really a good testimony. In fact it was rather bad PR for his brand.

So our job was to give the Ninevites a second chance—unlike those other hapless folks who were simply killed off in turn. Well, when we finally got to Nineveh Jonah began his preaching crusade. He really needed a tent and a good sound system, but somehow he managed to convince the king of the city that he and his people were facing imminent destruction unless they would repent and worship the one true god (his God). I had already accepted Yahweh as my personal Lord at that point, figuring after what I had been through in the fish-gut, I should hedge my bets. But what happened next totally floored me, to be sure!

The king bought Jonah's message, and ordered the whole town to rip their clothes and repent in sack cloth and ashes—which they did! I was joyful. Jonah was sour. He wanted to watch them all fry like the Sodomites of old. But no. They all repented and called upon the Lord of Israel. Jonah had withdrawn from the city to watch the fireworks, and I went with him in case he wanted me to write down some more thoughts. He waited for the mushroom cloud, but nothing happened. God spared the place, and then Jonah was pissed off at God for being such a namby-pamby god.

Up above the city, where we were camping out of bombing range, he fell asleep, and God caused a magic vine to grow overnight to shade him as he waited for the destruction that was not to come. Jonah had words for God, and he likewise told Jonah off. He said in parting: **"You have been concerned about this vine, though you did not tend it or make it grow. But Nineveh has one hundred twenty thousand people who cannot tell their right hand from their left, and many cattle** (That's important.). **Should I not be concerned about that great city?"** (Jonah 4: 11). Well, I guess Jonah took away something from the whole thing, but the last time I saw him, he was still fuming that God had failed to just nuke the hell out of them. That's what he would have done for sure.

Chapter 23

Zachariah

*The parents of John the Baptist do their parts
preparing the way of the Lord*

Greetings to all in the name of YHWH, the God of all the heavens and Earth, the stars and other heavenly bodies. My name is Zachariah, a priest in the line of Aaron. My lovely wife, Elisabeth, is likewise of noble birth and linage. It would have to be so, as we have been given an assignment from the Almighty that requires we be faultless and pure, polite, and refined—wellbred and mature (and out of our minds). But, when God first broached the subject of sacred chosen offspring, we kind of laughed (at least to ourselves). After all, we are elderly, and Liz has been barren all these years. So when an angel of the Lord (named Gabriel) told Liz that she was going to have a holy baby, she was ecstatic and sent out word to her cousin, Mary (wife of Joseph), that we were— after all these years—expecting! And that our newborn was going to be a special little guy, called by God for a yet-undetermined job. **And for five months Elizabeth remained in seclusion.** (Luke 1: 24).

Of course, we were thrilled, getting together a nursery with all kinds of cool stuff to entertain our son-to-be who would be named John. Although nobody in either of our families has that name, the angel made a point that we were to name him that. And who are we to argue? Well, we were shocked (pleasantly, of course) when Mary, cousin of Elizabeth, knocked on our door. She had heard the good news that Liz was now six months pregnant. **When Elizabeth heard Mary's greeting, the baby leaped in her womb, and Elizabeth was filled with the Holy Spirit.** (Luke 1: 41). But, just to rain on our parade a bit, she announced that, likewise, *she* was three months pregnant too! No shit?! And that she was going to give birth to the son of God himself! Oooh. She too had been visited by an angel, and was due in December. We were thrilled for her, of course. But, really, after waiting all these years for a son—and now that we were going to be blessed—Mary, that teenager with no specialized training in the priesthood or anything, was going to have a divine child of her own. I can't say that Liz was jealous or anything, but a bit skeptical. Well, we conceived in the conventional way (by fucking), but Joe and Mary were still virgins, and Mary she had been impregnated by the Holy Spirit—and not by Joseph at all. Wow, wow, wow . . . their miracle was better than our miracle. I tried to just let it slide, but, as I say, I was kind of skeptical too. But she had to tell us the whole story.

God sent the angel Gabriel to Nazareth, a town in Galilee, to a virgin pledged to be married to a man named Joseph, a descendant of David. The virgin's name was Mary. The angel said to her: "Greetings to you who are highly favored! The Lord is with you." (Luke 1: 27,28). Mary was totally twitter-pated and nearly fainted, but she got over it. Then she learned from Gabriel himself that Elizabeth was in that "family way" also! **"The Holy Spirit will come upon you in power. So the holy one to be born will be called the Son of God. Even Elizabeth your relative is going to have a child in her old age, and she who was said to be barren is in her sixth month. For nothing is impossible with God."** (Luke 1: 35-37). I'll say! It was a total lovefest, and they congratulated each other greatly. **Mary stayed with Elizabeth for about three months and then returned home.** (Luke 1: 56).

Well, on time, Elizabeth delivered and, sure enough, we named him John —despite the objections of the elders who pointed out that nobody in either family was named John. But Liz put her foot down and insisted on the name as the angel Gabriel himself had thusly instructed her. It was a done deal. **And the child grew and became strong in spirit; and he lived in the desert until he appeared publicly to Israel.** (Luke 1: 80).

John was a very good child, and his mom and I knew from the Lord that he was destined for ministry. But we figured that we were talking about a temple-ministry. We even had him trained from childhood to ritually slaughter animals like pigeons, sheep, and cattle for sacrifices. He learned all his Bible verses by heart, and knew how to lead in prayer by the time he was ten. But both Elizabeth and I were a bit taken aback when John began spending an inordinate amount of time alone in the wilderness. That was a novelty at first, but had become an obsession. We were okay with his love of nature and all that, but then he started dressing funny. At first we just thought of it as his "hippy phase," which he would grow out of. But when he started wearing really odd garments (if anything), we became quite concerned. **John's clothes were made of camel's hair, and he had a leather belt around his waist. His food was locust and wild honey.** (Matthew 3: 4).

We didn't see much of John after a while, as he went on the road with his new gig—baptizing (in water)! How weird. How unJewish, and how downright strange. What was that all about? Yet he began to gather a following. Both peasants and highborn began to flock to him, listening to his preaching and teaching—being baptized in the Jordan River as an indication of their repentance and cleansing from sin. There was nothing at all like this in the Scriptures. He was just making stuff up as he went along, but he had a kind of charismatic personality that attracted folks from all around—from the cities and the countryside. But his antics were not missed by the leadership of the Jewish community, the Pharisees and the Sadducees. They came to him and confronted him. But he just mocked them . . . **"You brood of vipers,"** he sneered. **"Who warned you to flee the coming wrath?"** (Mt. 3: 7). Well, John's message was basically about repentance. And the baptisms were symbolic, indicating that the baptizees were washing away their sins. Yet, John knew that he himself could not forgive sin. There was another on the way who could do that, and his name was Jesus. But that is his story and John (humble dude that he was) would leave that telling to another.

Even so, he really pissed off the hierarchy of the religious and political establishment. So, as usual, they reacted true to form, and arrested him and threw him into prison. Well, actually it was Herod Antipas, son of Herod the Great, who had him incarcerated (at the behest of the Jews). And while John was there he heard of the healing and preaching ministry of Jesus. That really psyched him out. He was stoked. But while he was languishing there in the dark, the king was throwing an elaborate birthday party for himself in the palace. There was in their midst a certain young woman with ambitions to get her filthy claws into the king. Her name was Salome, and, on the goading of her equally slutty mother, she danced for the king. Well, it was (hear tell) a very sexy and suggestive dance. The king loved it. He was so taken with her wild performance that he made her a promise. She could have a wish and he would fulfill it for her . . . even though it was *his* birthday! (Mark 6: 25).

Well, Salome dashed out and conspired with her mother as to what she should ask for. Money, jewelry, fancy cars? Hell no. Her mom wanted to get even with John for condemning her illegal marriage to Herod Antipas some time earlier. So she goaded her daughter into asking for the *head* of John! **"I want you to give me right now the head of John the Baptist on a platter!"** she demanded. (Mark 6: 25). Well, the king didn't want to lose face in front of everybody at the party, so he gave the order and John lost his head that day. But, sad as that story is, John had served his purpose. He had fulfilled his mission to prepare the way for the Lord, the savior of mankind. All in all, it really was a pretty good accomplishment in the end. His mother and I were bummed, as we really never quite understood what our son's weird ministry was all about anyway.

THE NEW TESTAMENT

Chapter 24

Natalia (Midwife to Mary)

O little town of Bethlehem . . . how still we see thee lie.

Happy Holidays all y'all out there in the great beyond. My name is Natalia or Natalie—I answer to both. I have been in the midwife biz for years here in the quiet little town of Bethlehem. I was just settling down one evening to watch TV, and go to bed early, when the phone rang. It was the Hausmeister of the local inn, Mr. Brumblebot. Apparently, a young pregnant couple from Galilee had tried to check in, but his establishment was full due to the large number of people traveling to their hometowns to take part in a mandatory census which had been decreed by the Roman emperor at the time.

In those days, Caesar Augustus issued a decree that a census should be taken of the entire Roman world. And everyone went down to his own town to register. So Joseph also went up from the town of Nazareth in Galilee to Judea, to Bethlehem, the town of David. (Luke 2: 4). Well, as we know, Mary was very pregnant at the time, and being unable to find hotel accommodations was a total bummer to be sure. But, goodhearted Mr. Brumblebot offered to let them stay in the stable with the animals. They really didn't have a choice. Well, when Mary's water broke they called for me. I came right over and helped with the delivery. It went well. The new child, a boy, they named Yeshua bar Yosef, and he was a healthy newborn. They had him circumcised on the eighth day as is customary for newborn Jews.

So it was time for Mary to make a sin offering at the temple. I was kind of freaked, to tell you the truth. Why? Well, Mary was without sin. She had been impregnated by the Holy Spirit. She had not fucked around with Joseph at all. They were both pure as the driven snow. But some have said that they drifted. Rumors were all around Galilee during her pregnancy. Some bought her story of the angel visitation and all, but a lot of townsfolk were skeptical. I mean, there she was—very pregnant— walking around town like nothing was the least bit odd. They had not yet been married (although they were betrothed). Hmmm . . . Likely story.

But Jewish law is adamant that the process of procreation and childbirth is sinful. Any woman who conceives and delivers does so under a cloud of sin. The coitus itself—even in marriage—is a sin. Giving birth to a child—boy or girl—requires a sin offering to wash away the sin of fucking in the first place. Very strange, that. The required sacrifice is a young sheep. But, as they were too poor, they would be able to substitute a young pigeon instead. Mind you, it must be a *young* pigeon; old pigeons will not do. And, even with that, she would still be ceremonially unclean for forty days. (It would have been 80 days if it had been a girl! Talk about sexist. But I just kept mum about that shit.)

The night before they were to go to the temple to do the sacrifice, they had quite a fight. Mary insisted that if she were to go through with the sin offering, it would just scream that her story was total bullshit. She had *not* sinned (with Joe) yet. So technically she was still the BVM (Blessed Virgin Mary). Joseph said that it would be way easier just to go along with the program—let the priests slaughter the pigeon and burn the damn thing, and let it be over. It was just a formality. Mary felt that her reputation would be shot if she gave in and went through with the sacrifice. Well, even though they were not yet married, she was still under his "covering," so she acquiesced . . . with prejudice.

The sacrifice went off without a hitch. They went into the temple, bought a (young) pigeon from a vendor at the entrance to the temple, and had a priest gut it, drip blood all over, and set the thing on fire. They were just glad to be past that uncomfortable experience. In the end I guess Joe was right—better not draw undue attention to themselves. That attention would come soon enough and in spades.

Well, we were having an unemployment problem around the whole Roman province of Palestina. And Bethlehem was really hard-hit. So I decided to hitch a ride with Joe and Mary and try floating my resume around in Nazareth of Galilee for a while. They were glad to have me join them as I promised to watch Jesus while they were out looking for work themselves. So I kind of took up being a nanny. Now Joe was a carpenter, and he began teaching Jesus the trade from an early age. I just hung with the family, doing odd chores around the house and caring for Jesus . . . and Mary too, who was pregnant with their second son, James, who was to be born in a more conventional way (by plain, old-fashioned sex). Of course, there were those around town who insisted that Mary (the BVM) was still sinless, but once she got pregnant with James that notion sort of flew out the window.

Well, some years passed, and Jesus was spending his time making tables and chairs that they sold around the towns in Galilee. When Jesus was about twelve they went up to Jerusalem to visit the temple. They did this junket every year at the Passover. But this time was different. J.C. was definitely growing up, and, wow, was he ever smart! He studied the Scriptures, but it was as if he knew them already. Anyway, during that trip Jesus spent a lot of time on his own dinging around Jerusalem and having a good time away from Mom and Dad. You know—like most young men would want to do. But, when they left to head back to Nazareth, they didn't even notice that he wasn't with them. I was dealing with James, who was quite a handful at the time, so I have to admit that I also didn't see that Jesus wasn't with us for the return journey. Then, three days into the trip home, Mary (pregnant again) began freaking out. "Where the hell is Jesus?" she demanded. Joseph didn't appear to be too upset. After all, Jesus was very mature for his age and could take care of himself. But Mary insisted that we all go back to Jerusalem to look for him. We searched high and low in the city, with no luck. Then Joseph had a brainstorm. "Maybe we should go up to the Temple Mount and see if, by chance, he is in the temple." *Now why didn't I think of that?* I asked myself. Well, sure enough, there he was sitting and talking with a gaggle of Jewish elders gathered around listening to him intently. Amazing! Mary was livid.

"Son, why have you treated us like this? Your father and I have been anxiously searching for you." (Luke 2: 49). Jesus gave her one of those looks like *Oh, come on, Woman.* **"Why were you searching for me? Didn't you know that I would have to be in my father's house?" But they did not understand what he was saying to them.** (Luke 2: 50). What? They didn't understand? OMG, what were those two bumpkins smoking? Come on. Didn't the BVM remember the visit from the angel —you know—the one who said: **"He will be great and will be called the son of the Most High. The Lord God will give him the throne of his father David, and he will reign over the House of Jacob forever; His kingdom will never end."** (Luke 1: 31-33). Like, didn't that make an impression?

Anyway, the whole region was abuzz some time later when Jesus was a young man. He had not yet indicated that he was imbued with magical powers. But I felt the vibes as he went from a smart-as-a-whip teenager into a brilliant, good-looking young man. He was a real dreamboat with his lovely bedroom blue eyes and his flowing blond locks. I predicted that some day he would become a model, and many artists would paint him. But the thing that was on everybody's lips was what was happening out in the Judean desert. John, a relative of Mary, Joe, Jesus, and James, was doing this totally new thing—baptizing folks down in the Jordan River! Baptism? What the hell was that? No mention of it was ever made before—either in Hebrew scripture or in Pagan rituals. Obviously, John *the Baptist* (as he was now called) simply made the whole procedure up. It was a symbol. If a person would confess his or her sins and repent, they could be baptized in water and symbolically wash their sins away.

Peasant folks from all over were flocking to hear John preach, and stand in line to get dunked. Jesus got the wild notion to go out there himself. He told the BVM and Joe that he was just going to say "Hi!" to his second cousin, John. They said to tell him *hello* as well, and greetings to Elizabeth and Zacharias. Well, Jesus did say hello and all that, but he was more interested in getting baptized himself. I heard all of this through the grapevine, but apparently it was quite a show. Jesus got into the river and waited his turn. When he came up to John, he (John, that is) kinda freaked out. After all, by this time he had figured out that his cousin was really the divine son of God and that he should defer to him. But Jesus insisted on being baptized. He obviously knew something more was going to happen! It did.

As Jesus was coming up out of the water, he saw heaven being torn open and the spirit descended upon him like a dove. And a voice came from heaven saying: "You are my son, whom I love; with you I am well pleased." (Mark 1: 10,11). OMG! That booming voice from the sky totally shocked and freaked the entire crowd. They began running in all directions like a dog hearing fireworks. They were in a total panic. Well, that's how I heard it.

After that, Jesus told Mary and Joe that he was going out into the desert to fast for forty days. His mom was a bit concerned about that, of course, as any mother would be. But he gave her another of his looks like saying: "Come on, Mom, I am the son of God—remember? Do I have to remind you again? Besides, I won't starve. There are plenty of rocks out there, and if I get hungry I can simply turn one into a loaf of bread. But I doubt that I will have to go that far. I can handle fasting." So he went out and camped with the wild animals. But there were angels out there to "attend to him." Their names were Teensee and Weensee :-)

Then Satan made the scene. He was at his best—his white robes flowing and his fake angel wings spread wide. He was gorgeous. He was obviously trying to impress Jesus. The cool thing about Lucifer is that he can take all sorts of forms. He chose to become an *angel of light* to fool Jesus. I couldn't imagine Jesus being tricked by a simple makeover like that. He knew who he was dealing with all along. But turning himself into a mock divine personage is one of the devil's best disguises. Most people would have been wowed, but not our J.C. No, but he was intrigued and wanted to hear Satan's pitch. **The Devil took him to a very high mountain and showed him all the kingdoms of the world and their splendor. "All this I will give you," he said, "if you will bow down and worship me."** (Matt. 4: 8-10).

Oh, for Pete's sake—Jesus was just SO not impressed. Heck, he owns the cattle on 1,000 hills. He owns the rivers and the rocks and rills. What does he want with a collection of earthly kingdoms? Who needs them? After all, he was totally aware by that time that Yahweh had big plans for him. And he had no intention of disappointing the Lord, his dad in the sky. The angels and the heavenly host were cheering Jesus on when Satan gave up. They hadn't seen such a putdown on the devil since God won the bet clear back in the Book of Job. The cherubim and seraphim were all applauding wildly as Jesus finished up his period of temptation. Hell, he didn't even need to turn a single stone into bread. He just toughed it out and headed back to town to start his ministry. What a guy!

Chapter 25 (Part 1)

Schweinchen Dick (The Swineherd)

Herding pigs is hard work. A few pigs, maybe, but 2000? Oh sure!

Hello, my name is Schweinchen Dick. You can call me Dick. I work for a very wealthy guy named Mr. Solomon Geldfarb. He lives on a farm north of Capernium, which is on the west side (the Jewish side) of Lake Gennesaret. The Romans call it Lake Tiberias. Though I am a Jew, I live across the lake on the Gentile side. Why would I do that, you ask? Well, Mr. Geldfarb owns property on the east side of the lake as well where he raises pigs. I know, I know, what is a rich Jewish guy doing raising swine when it is 100% against all of our religious traditions and rules? Well, hey, he makes a lot of money raising pigs. Not only can he sell them to the Gentiles, but (get this) most Jews like pork chops as much as the next guy, and they really dig bacon. So we sell to them quietly on the side. Hey, biz is biz. He wanted me to run his herd of swine on his "farm" over across the lake.

I tried to explain to him that pigs can't be "herded" like sheep or even cattle. Pigs are rather independent-minded animals, and they tend to wander. They are scavengers and root all over the place, tearing up the ground, leaving it totally trashed. Unless they are confined with the likes of an electric fence, they will simply wander in all directions eating anything in sight. They are *so* messy. But he wanted us to run 2,000 pigs on his rather poor rocky land that goes right down to the lake. Well, I told him that was a totally impractical idea. So he suggested we hire a couple of Gentiles to stand around with canes and bomp any pigs that were wandering off. I had my doubts, but we gave it a whirl.

Oddly enough, Mr. G's property backed up against the cemetery for the town of Gadarenes. The place was kind of poorly kept-up (but for good reason). There was a goofy guy living in the place—a total schizoid who terrorized anybody who even came close. He lived among the tombs, and wore no clothes, and ran around the place screaming and yelling—frightening even the pigs. They wouldn't go even close to the place. Now this guy was desperately in need of psychological help. He was totally whacked out and delusional. The townspeople had tried to tie him down many times, and even used chains once to try to subdue him. But he was possessed of great powers, like a vampire. He had the strength of twenty men, so he just broke the chains and ran around cutting himself with sharp rocks. A real basketcase, that one.

Then one day a strange thing happened. The Gentile guys and I were eating lunch while watching the porkers. And, let me tell you, *2,000* independent-minded mammals require a lot of attention. We rarely got a chance to sit down while watching them. But this day they were being good, as we noticed something going on over there in the graveyard. The demoniac was yelling at some guy with a long robe and a staff. He had some other guys in tow, but he was conversing with the naked guy. I couldn't hear exactly what he was saying, but I heard later that he was actually talking to the great Jesus Christ, the son of God, and savior of mankind. Apparently, Jesus was not actually talking to the guy at all, but to the demons inside of him! **"What do you want with us, Son of God?" they shouted. "Have you come here to torture us before the appointed time?"** (Matthew 8: 29). We could hear that for sure. Those demons were very loud. "What appointed time?" we wondered.

Well, the interaction between Jesus and the demons inside the guy heated up. Then we could hear them all clearly. **"What is your name?" Jesus asked him. "My name is Legion," he replied, "for we are many." And he begged Jesus again and again not to send him out of the area.** (Mark 5: 9,10). **"Send us among the pigs; allow us go into them!" He gave them permission, and the evil spirits came out and went into the pigs. The herd, about two thousand in number, rushed down the steep bank into the lake and were drowned.** (Mark 5: 11-13).

Well, Mr. Geldfarb was furious about losing all his pigs in one fell swoop like that. The two Gentile guys ran off immediately, so I was left holding the bag. He blamed me for the whole thing. Well, I thought that was grossly unfair, but the other guys ran throughout the town telling everybody the whole story. So they all went out and found the guy sitting on a grave stone . . . fully clothed and in his right mind. They were happy, but scared. This was just too much weirdness for such a small town. **Then the people began to plead with Jesus to leave their region.** (Mark 5: 17). So Jesus gave them a sad look, as if saying "You dummies, if you only knew how great I am!" But he figured they were too dense to understand anything. He just got in a boat and sailed away.

Some time later, he walked on water and fed 5,000 people who came to hear him preach. Too bad those clodhoppers back in Gadarenes didn't see *that*! They might have changed their tune, huh? Well, eventually Jesus found himself and his disciples on the far side of Lake Tiberius (the Sea of Galilee) again . . .

Chapter 25 (Part 2)

Zephania (Jesus follower)

A follower at the Olivet Discourse

Well, hey there. My name is Schäflich, and I first heard Jesus preach back on the shores of the Sea of Galilee. He had preached all day, healing the sick and telling all sorts of marvelous stuff about the coming of his kingdom. I was totally jazzed, and, as it was getting late in the afternoon, we in the crowd were getting hungry. Jesus told his disciples to feed us. They freaked out. "How can we possibly feed this mob?" they asked Jesus. I mean there wasn't even a *Safeway* or a 7-11 in sight. And, besides, they didn't have much money between them. All they could rustle up was five loaves of bread and two wimpy fishes in a wrinkly brown paper bag. Like, how was that going to make a difference?

But Jesus said: "Watch this one! ;-)" Well, he just kept pulling more bread and fish out of the paper bag. And the astonished disciples just kept handing it out to us. We were impressed, and when we were full, he preached some more. We sang choruses and praised the Lord until way after dark. I went forward for the altar call. (Well, there wasn't a real altar there, but we imagined one.) I accepted Jesus that night as my personal savior. Hallelujah! Glory!

Now I have been kind of following the Lord around from venue to venue in and around Jerusalem, Samaria, and, hopefully, someday to the uttermost parts of the Earth. But for now I have become a JC-Groupie and was with him today on the Mount of Olives—not far out of Downtown J'ville. It was a wonderful day. Jesus talked about his coming kingdom and how us "saved" folk are going to get to go up in the sky with him someday soon! I am so thrilled :-)

As Jesus was sitting on the Mount of Olives, the disciples came to him. "Tell us," they said, "when will this happen, and what will be the sign of your coming and of the end of the age?" (Mt. 24: 3). Well, this was heavy shit, so we were all straining to hear his answer. He told us that there were bad times coming, and that we should look out for false prophets and teachers with strange-sounding foreign names such as Falwellio, Robberson, Doberson. We took note, but didn't understand. Then he got real specific . . . **"You will hear of wars and rumors of wars."** Wow, how much more clear can you get? **"Nation will rise against nation, and kingdom against kingdom."** That scared the shit out of me. Like, that has never happened in human history ever before! And there was more! **"There will be famines and earthquakes in various places."** (Mt. 24: 6-8). OMG! Earthquakes in diverse places! What could be more prophetic? These will surely be signs of the end! I am so glad I accepted Christ back there by the Lake of Galilee. But then he began getting kind of personal. I paid close attention.

The Lord was really leading us in praise. He was teaching us to sing and dance and clap to the tune of: **"Blessed are the poor, for theirs is the kingdom of heaven. Blessed are the meek, for they shall inherit the Earth. Blessed are the pure in heart, for they shall see God."** (Mt. 5: 1,5,9). Oooh, I was really getting goosebumps. That was like kind of the warmup, but then he got into the actual message, saying: **"Do not think I have come to abolish the Law or the prophets; I have not come to abolish them but to fulfill them."** (Mt. 5: 17). Okay, I could dig it. But then he took to preaching about stuff like adultery and lying and fightin' and stuff. Now, as a recent convert, I could be forgiven for being a bit dull-witted and taken with the singing and shouting and all. But once he got down to serious preaching to the believers, I began getting just a wee bit uncomfortable.

Now I'm a pretty mellow kinda guy, so when he got off to talkin' about murder, I just figured that he was talking to someone else. But then he said: **"Anyone who is angry with his brother is subject to judgment."** And **"Anyone who says 'you fool!' is in danger of the fire of hell."** (Mt. 5: 22,23). Yikes!

And then he said something weird (at least to me): **"You have heard it said, 'Eye for eye, and tooth for tooth.' But I tell you, if someone strikes you on the right cheek, turn to him the other also. And if someone wants to sue you and take your tunic, let him have your cloak as well. If someone forces you to go one mile, go with him two**

miles. (Mt. 5: 38-40). What? Oh, come on, nobody can do that! If somebody hits me on the right cheek, I'll blast his cheeks off with my NRA shotgun! And I don't mean maybe. And what a pile of crap all that talk of letting people sue you. No way, Jose. You have to countersue. I began thinking that maybe this guy Jesus was kind of a fringie.

But, finally, when he started talking about sex, I began to pay close attention. I began wondering if he was talking to me! Then he got going on my favorite subject . . . dames! I'm a married guy, as it is more or less expected or required. I mean, single guys over a certain age might be mistaken for something that we don't talk about. But I do admit that I enjoy girl-watching around the Temple Mount where the buyers and sellers do their thing. Lots of eye candy there. But Jesus put the nix on that! No kidding.

"You have heard it said, 'Do not commit adultery.' But I tell you that anyone who looks at a woman lustfully has already committed adultery with her in his heart." (Mt. 5: 27). What? Even if I just innocently look at a woman (even a slave), I have committed adultery in my heart? Oh, now that's a bit much. I mean, I am really not doing anything—just fantasizing. Like, what's wrong with that? Jesus says that even our thoughts are monitored by God. He must be very busy recording all our thoughts and schemes all the time. But finally he really said it . . .

"If your right eye causes you to sin, gouge it out and throw it away. It is better for you to lose one part of your body than for your whole body to be thrown into hell. And if your right hand causes you to sin, cut it off and throw it away. It is better for you to lose one part of your body than for your whole body to go into hell." (Mt. 4: 29,30). Oh shit! This is getting kinda hard, huh? I will have to think about this. Maybe following this guy, Jesus, is something for strong people who have deep commitment and a heavy-duty religious background, and not for a simple guy like me who is tempted and is in danger of looking at stuff I shouldn't or using my right hand as I should not. Hmmm.

Well, I think I will go home now and think all this over. I have a feeling I was a bit too hasty while the taste of those loaves and fishes was still in my mouth. But after hearing all this about cutting off my hand and all, I will definitely have to reconsider this decision. I mean, Jesus is cool and all that. But following him, it seems, is such a commitment—a sacrifice. Maybe I will just give it some more thought tomorrow.

Chapter 26

Jen Ke-lien (The old cripple)

The Pool of Siloam

I am the happiest man alive. I was recently healed by Jesus, the savior of the world. And how he came to heal *me* is anybody's guess. My name was Jen Ke-lien, which means *Really Pitiful*. But after receiving my divine healing, I have changed my name to Jen Quai-Lue, which means *Really Happy*! Thirty-eight years ago I developed rheumatoid arthritis, gout, and various other sundry ailments. I couldn't work anymore for the phone company as a result, so I retired early. My wife had to keep working as a typist at the local law firm of Bernstein and Bernstein to support the family. I was forty at the time, but I was so stove-up and gimpy that I had to quit. I took ibuprofen, acetaminophen, and various drugs, but that didn't really alleviate the pain. It was a bummer, and all these years later, at seventy-eight-years-old, I have a new lease on life (thanks to Jesus, that is).

Mildred, my dear wife, had heard that in downtown Jerusalem there is a magic pool called Bethesda. It is near the Sheep Gate. It is referred to as the *Pool of Siloam*. Now, the pool has curative powers, and hundreds of people like me go there and sit by the poolside waiting for a miracle. Apparently, you can't just go there, plunge in, and be healed. It is a waiting game. On any given day, unannounced, an angel of the Lord appears and "troubles" the waters. At that instant the first gimp into the pool gets healed!

I was jazzed. My first few visits I was hopeful as I waited as close to the edge of the water as I could get. I was shocked at how many others had arrived before me. It looked like they must have gotten up at, like, 4 a.m. to get to the pool ahead of the rest. I learned to do likewise, getting there before dawn on most days. So I have been limping daily down to Siloam to wait for the angel. My problem is that I have no one to help me get to the pool when the angel appears and begins to *trouble* the waters. Some guys there have their wives or kids or servants or slaves to help them scamper into the pool for healing. I couldn't ask Mildred as she had to continue working at the law firm to support the family. The kids were in school for the first decade and a half or so, so they couldn't help. And then they started having their own families, and their time was taken up with the grandkids. I was just shit out of luck in that department. But one day as I was just sitting there wallowing in my misery, this cool dude in a spotlessly clean, shiny robe walked over, squatted down, and began talking to me.

He introduced himself as Jesus, the Christ, Son of the Living God. He had come down to Earth to save humanity from its sins and to provide a way to Heaven when we die. And, he added, he also did miracles. He told of a few, like the feeding of the five thousand, and indicated that he could walk on water. Likely story, I thought, but I surmised he wasn't used to being doubted. He simply asked me a question: **"Do you want to be healed?"** (John 5: 6). What? What kind of a dingbat question is that? Of course I wanted to be healed. Like, duh, I had been hanging around that pool every day for thirty-eight years. I assure you it wasn't for the entertainment or so that I could work on my tan. I definitely wanted to get better.

Then Jesus said to him, **"Get up! Pick up your mat and walk."** (Jn. 5: 8). So, I did just that! I got up (pain-free) and began hopping and leaping and praising God. It was totally awesome. So I went home and told Mildred. She was flabbergasted and also began running and skipping and praising God. Together we sang: "In the name of Jesus Christ of Nazareth, rise up and walk!"

"You should go up to the Temple Mount and testify," she encouraged. "Hell, with a story like that, we might be able to put together a traveling road show and raise some bucks." She pointed out that she wasn't getting any younger, and working as a typist all those years hadn't done much for her carpal tunnel. So the next day, instead of going down to the gimp pool, I went up to the Temple and began sharing my testimony of healing. I gathered quite a crowd, and some folks appeared genuinely interested. So I made a little sign and put out an offering plate to see if I had any knack for fundraising. Then, suddenly, right there at the entrance to the Temple was Jesus himself, staring at me with a kind of strange look on his radiant face. I couldn't quite tell if he was happy or disappointed. He said:

"See, you are well again. Stop sinning or something worse may happen to you." (Jn. 5: 14). Wow, was I sinning by just giving my testimony for the random "love offering?" Apparently Jesus was a bit ticked-off at me about that, so I decided to go back home and discuss it with Mildred. But, before I could make my way down from the Temple Mount, I was stopped by some Jewish authorities. You know those guys —the black robes and tall hats guys. They grilled me about my healing: who did it and when? Well, I was kind of intimidated by those guys, but I told the truth. I had been healed on the Sabbath. They went ballistic. "When?" they shouted at me. I repeated that Jesus had healed me at the Pool of Siloam . . . on the Sabbath. Obviously, they were pissed. They whirled around and pushed the crowd aside as they strode purposefully into the temple. I ditched and went back to Mildred. The boys were coming over for dinner anyway, but I did manage to gather my offerings. That could be used to good purpose surely. Well, then it happened . . .

The next morning, I decided to go back to Bethesda to testify to a couple of old friends still hanging out there. I fully intended to witness to them, explaining that they didn't need to wait for the angel to come down and stir up the waters. Jesus could just heal them by remote control. All they would have to do is call upon his name in power, and they would be healed. But when I got to the place, there was an eviction notice there. NO JEWS ALLOWED it read. What? We have been hanging out there for years. And some of us had actually been healed there. So what is this all about? I read further: *By order of Maximilian Maximus Aurelius, Military Commander of the Sheep Gate Sector of Jerusalem. This facility is henceforth confiscated for exclusive use of the occupation forces of the Empire of Rome.* Nobody was around outside, but I heard Roman soldiers laughing and slapping each other around playfully inside. "What the hell?" I thought. "They are turning our sacred pool into an NCO club for the SPQR. How sick is that? How did that happen? And so fast!" Well, I hung around the shadows and eavesdropped on the soldiers' conversations as they came out refreshed and frisky. There were some young Jewish "attendants" who had been recruited to see to the bathing needs of the Romans, so I talked to them as well. I sort of pieced the story together.

Once the Jewish High Council caught wind of the story that Jesus had been hanging around the pool and healing people on the Sabbath, they ran right off and tattled to the Romans. The High Priest, Caiaphas, told the alderman for that district of Jerusalem that a certain Galilean named Yeshua bar Yosef was using the pool as an evangelistic backdrop for his new religion. Like the Romans gave a shit about that. "But he's doing *unauthorized* healings there!" they whined. "And, most likely, those newfangled baptisms as well." Again, the Romans shrugged. Big deal. The Romans never really gave a damn about what the Jews did . . . as long as they kept the rabble in the streets under control. Obviously, their objective was to get the Romans to shut the place down. But how?

I didn't hear this with my own two ears, but I have a friend on staff at the Office of the Military Affairs Command in downtown Jerusalem. He serves wine and other beverages to the bigwigs who come to talk to Max (as he was called by the troops). Well, the Jews (the Sanhedrin) went to Max for the second time with a complaint about this guy, Jesus. He had really upset them with all his rabble-rousing around Jerusalem and environs. Klaipedia, the spokesman for the Jews, related to Max with deference, but with urgency in his voice: "Sir, this troublemaker, Jesus, is causing a lot of civil unrest among the peasants. He is claiming to be God, which is frightfully against our religious traditions. There is only one God, and YHWH is his unspeakable name."

To which Max replied: "Well, you guys say there is only one god. Seems rather limiting to me."

"But sir," Klaipedia continued, "It should not matter who is claiming to be a deity here. How would you like it if some nobody from the sticks started claiming that he was Zeus?"

"Well, I would think he is a kook and needed to have his head examined," Max went on. "Like, why is that such a big deal to you people?" He looked at the collection of Jewish holy men standing before him. "I am here as head of the occupation. I am not needing to get embroiled in the petty religious squabbles of people in this or that occupied territory. My job is to keep the peace. But it appears that y'all are the ones disturbing it. This guy Jesus is a bumpkin from Nazareth and nothing more. Why don't you just ignore him?"

They all shouted at once: "We can't ignore him! He is contravening our ancient laws."

"Okay, let me ask the question this way," the commander continued.

"Tell me exactly what he has done wrong, how it is a crime, and what his penalty should be. There, how's that? Now answer it."

"He healed a crippled guy at the Pool of Siloam." They pushed forward.

"Really? Are you sure? Healing? What proof do you have of that?"

"We interviewed the guy who was healed ourselves, and he is walking quite well—without a cane, a walker, or any other device."

"Sounds to me like a miracle. Why aren't you guys rejoicing?" If I knew someone who had been healed as you say, I would be praising Zeus, Apollo, or somebody up there!" He seemed perplexed.

They shrieked, "But he did it on the Sabbath!" The Sabbath—like that was supposed to mean something to Max. It didn't.

"Look, I am trying here . . . I really am. I am to enforce laws—Roman Laws, not your ridiculous mumbo-jumbo Hebrew laws. I actually don't give a damn *when* he did it. I am impressed that he could, and think we should just leave it at that." The Jews were furious but tried not to show it. So they pulled out their final trump card.

"Do you know that place—that pool—is actually a hotbed of homosexual activity?" they seethed. "There are hundreds of men who hang out there all day, ostensibly waiting for an angel of the Lord to come down periodically and rile up the waters. Supposedly, the first one who "goes down" in the pool is cured? But that's just a front. It is really a gay bathhouse, and all sorts of licentious activities are going on there all the time right under your nose!" They slapped themselves in mock outrage.

Whether or not the Jews actually believed any of that was questionable, but since their law calls for the death penalty for male-to-male sex, surely, they felt, this would likewise similarly offend the military commander of such high repute. "Oh my god" Maximilian drawled. "Such a terrible thing as that? And right here in downtown J-town?" he added with obvious sarcasm. "My, my, what should we ever do?"

"You should shut the place down!" the Jews exclaimed, thinking they were finally making headway. "Have your soldiers drive those wicked sodomites right out of there once and for all."

"Well, you know that pool has been a public bath since the Greeks built it years ago. And we all know about those Greek guys, don't we?" the commander toyed with them. "There is no Roman law against people having a little fun at the baths. Hell, you should see the baths at Caracala in Rome. It is massively entertaining. But if you want me to close it to prevent the Jews from pleasuring themselves and others, I will!"

"Do it, do it!" they all urged. So he did. And now the Roman Regular Army guys are using it—but no Jews. I sadly went back home to Mildred thinking . . . hmmm. I wonder what that angel is going to do when he visits the pool now.

Chapter 27

Sorpresso (Observer at the Transfiguration)

Holy shit, what the hell is that?

I am named Sorpresso. I am the nephew of John the Apostle. My dad, Martichai, is John's brother. And since John has taken up following this guy, Jesus, he has been out of work. So my dad is working overtime at the tire factory near Jerusalem to feed the family. But John is totally oblivious. My dad is trying to save up enough to start his own tire biz in or around Galilee some day. I have absolutely no interest in the tire operation, so I like to hang out with Uncle John a lot as he tells us all about his big-time friend, Yeshua, the son of God.

He never gets tired of telling us about all the miracles he has witnessed. Heck, Jesus fed 5,000 of us with only a couple of fish and two loaves of stale bread. And, he can walk on water, and has even raised the dead (although I missed that one). Well, Jesus was preaching one day, and—unlike his usual uplifting fare—he began talking about sacrificing and suffering. That was kind of a downer. He predicted that the Romans would arrest him sometime soon at the behest of the Jewish authorities. He said that he would be brought to trial and found guilty of crimes against the state, and would be crucified shortly thereafter. Well, Uncle John was beside himself with grief about this news. He cried and whined and grabbed Peter (his weird-ass friend), and they both flopped themselves down at the feet of Jesus, carrying on like fools. Jesus told them to get up—stand up straight and act dignified. But I could tell that they were mightily distressed. I kind of hung back not knowing what to do. Then Jesus called out to Peter and Uncle John, "Hey you two, go get James. We're going on a field trip."

Once they got back with James in tow, the four of them began climbing up a rather steep hill just outside Jerusalem out in the desert. I tagged along, but although they didn't mind me being there, they ignored me, since they were totally tuned-in to what Jesus was going on about and what he might do next. "You boys are really in for a treat!" the Lord said enthusiastically as they reached the summit. Then an amazing thing happened. Right up in the sky above our heads appeared the most magnificent spacecraft you ever did see! It was right out of "Close Encounters." It hovered about fifty stories up and was kicking up a load of dust. And like a "mighty wind" it hovered and was spinning with lights like eyes all around. There were four wheels inside the outer ring. And they were all spinning independently. I felt just like the Prophet Ezekiel, when he wrote of a quite similar experience: **I looked, and I saw a windstorm—an immense cloud with flashing lightning and surrounded by brilliant light. The center of the fire looked like glowing metal, and in the fire was what looked like four living creatures.** (Ezekiel 1: 4,5).

Actually, I could see that there were four domes, and inside each was what looked like an angel. And a big dome at the top, which appeared to be the command center of the craft. Well, it went around sort of drunkenly, and banged into a cliffside and bounced off. **The creatures sped back and forth like flashes of lightning.** (Ez. 1: 14). Four creatures were inside the domes and they looked like angels to me. I mean, they were dressed in white and had real cool wings.

This was the appearance and structure of the wheels. They sparkled like chrysolite, and all four looked alike. (Ez. 1: 16). Their rims were high and awesome, and all four rims were full of eyes all around. When the living creatures moved, the wheels beside them moved; and when the living creatures rose from the ground, the wheels also rose. (Ez. 1: 18,19). I heard the sound like the roar of rushing waters, like the voice of the Almighty. (Ez. 1: 24). There was like a hole in the clouds and I could look straight up into Heaven. I almost wet my pants, it was so cool.

Above the expanse over their heads was what looked like a throne of sapphire, and high above on the throne was a figure like that of a man. Like the appearance of a rainbow, so was the radiance around him. (Ez. 1: 26-28). I strained to see who it was up there on that sapphire throne. OMG, it was Jesus! He was up there sitting as pretty as you please looking down on this whole show. Obviously, the angels didn't have much experience piloting the spaceship. After they finally landed the thing, Jesus looked down from his heavenly throne and chuckled: "You guys better practice your landings." James, Peter, and John were totally freaked-out. They were all lying flat, facedown, on the dusty ground. The wind finally calmed down as the engine slowed and stopped. The four domes opened, and the four angels hopped out and stood beside the shining saucer. They looked at the three disciples on the ground, but neither Uncle John, Peter, nor James looked up. Then the angels looked at me.

"Hello Earthling!" One of the angels spoke to me with a voice as sweet as honey. "My name is Teensee. What is yours?" Well, I had never been addressed so politely before. I was used to my dad yelling instructions at me about tire repair. And Uncle John—he is kind enough, but sort of gruff. He has never quite realized that I am eighteen-years-old now and a man (for the most part). He still kind of treats me like a kid. But this angel was ever so nice.

"My name is Sorpresso," I said in a manly voice. "Welcome to Earth!"

"Oh, thank you," said Teensee politely. "But we have been here quite frequently over the past few thousand years or so."

"Wow, really?" I stuttered. "Well, welcome back then!" I greeted them sincerely. "I'll bet you guys saw a lot of neat stuff down here in the olden days, huh?"

"Oh, yes!" Teensee exclaimed knowingly. "In fact, we are here to bring two old friends down from Heaven to meet Jesus!" he explained. "Take a look over there!" he pointed. OMG, right there, standing next to Jesus, were two old guys with white beards and robes. Old-fashioned looking, but quite well-groomed, they were talking to the Lord casually.

"Who are they?" I asked cautiously. "They are radiant!"

"Oh, that is Moses there on the right, and Elijah is on the left," he said proudly. "We were asked by God Almighty himself this very morning to bring them down here to Earth. They know Jesus from way back. You see—he is part of the "godhead" so he has been with the Father from the beginning. He has been down here to this planet many times . . . sometimes with God, and a few times on his own. He is down here this trip to redeem mankind." Teensee went on: "He is sorry that he bummed the disciples out when he informed them of his impending death, as he told his dad, the Heavenly Father. God suggested that we bring Moses and Elijah down to cheer him up and to help participate in a demonstration for the three most beloved of his twelve "friends." I think I understood. I had wondered why Jesus only hung out with twelve guys all the time. But I had my suppositions. *Wink*

Anyway, as we were speaking, the three disciples pulled themselves up from the ground, and, rubbing their eyes, they gazed at Jesus and then they looked with astonishment at Moses and Elijah. **Peter and his companions were very sleepy, but when they became fully awake, they saw his glory and the two men standing with him.** (Luke 9: 32). They began bowing in a most Japanese sort of way. "Lord, Lord, who are these guys?" they asked—panting.

"Oh . . . " Jesus muttered offhandedly, "This is Moses and this is Elijah. I've known them for centuries. They have been sent down today to encourage me. As I told you, I am going to be crucified soon, and I've been a bit depressed about it lately. The Heavenly Father obviously thought it would be nice to send down some reinforcements."

Then, all three of them (Jesus and his two heavenly friends) began to glow. Their robes went super white and looked like floodlights at a football stadium. We couldn't look directly at them, lest we do permanent damage to our corneas. But we squinted. It was wonderful. In fact, I think I could even hear some of the heavenly host up there singing praises . . . or maybe that was the doxology or *Amazing Grace*. (Boy, I'll bet the cherubim and seraphim get really sick of that song—ten thousand years at a time). Anyway, it was a very blessed experience. Then . . .

While he was speaking, a cloud appeared and enveloped them, and they were afraid as they entered the cloud. A voice came from the cloud, saying, "This is my Son, whom I have chosen; listen to him." (Luke 9: 34). When it cleared, Peter ran up and said: **"Master, it is good for us to be here. Let us put up three shelters—one for you, one for Moses and one for Elijah."** (Luke 9: 33). But the Lord just smiled at him and waved goodbye as the two Patriarchs of Old got back onto the space ship, walking regally.

Then there was the rush of a mighty wind, and the sound of bagpipes. The four little wheels began to spin. They gained some momentum. Then the big wheel began to turn . . . ever so slowly. The bagpipes died away, and the music of a merry-go-round calliope began to sound. It was so wonderful! The outer ring spun faster and faster, and you could imagine the images of winged horses running around and around. It was ever so festive. Then I looked at the top dome. There were two heavenly beings inside. One was gold and had big eyes that shone brightly. The other was rather short and round, and spoke in beeps and whistles. Obviously, they were piloting the ship. I heard them talk. "Well, another nice mess you've gotten us into, Artoo," the golden angel said with an upperclass British accent. "Maybe you should let Teensee or Weensee take over!" Well, the ship began to rise off the ground, and it sort of lumbered one way, then the other. It banged into the cliff again, but bounced off unscathed.

I watched as Teensee and Weensee each took positions in the smaller domes. The other angels waved, but I didn't catch their names. I waved enthusiastically. Then Teensee looked right at me and began to speak. I could not hear his words, as he was inside the transparent dome. But I understood his speech clearly. He was sending me thought waves. I had heard about telepathy, but was never sure until this very moment that such things are true. "Don't mind the way they drive," he said apologetically. "They are not very good drivers. We don't usually take an old tub like this when God himself comes down. He just teleports us down without any devices. But he thinks it is a good thing to have drivers around in case we have to answer a prayer or have to make a delivery of food or something to flood victims."

"That is thoughtful," I said inside my head. "At least I know that all those prayers from down here on Earth are actually heard up there in Heaven." Then I sighed. "But with a delivery system like that I can see why most go unanswered."

Chapter 28

Xin Loi

Jesus and a divorcee have a serious chat

Well, isn't that a bummer? I've been listening to this new guy, Jesus, who is preaching around Jerusalem and the suburbs of Samaria and Galilee. He has been getting quite a reputation as a revolutionary teacher. I came to him with my unique situation. I had married this woman named Veronika from Gad. She was quite nice—attractive and sexy. But once we were married, I discovered that she could be a full-fledged bitch. Although she was informally diagnosed with ADD *and* bipolar. There is no medication yet to treat those disorders. Well, I just couldn't put up with that rollercoaster all the time, so I decided to divorce her. Of course, I knew full-well that I was within my rights as a male to just write her a certificate and send her packing. But, since I can't read or write, I had to go to the Temple and have a scribe do the actual writing for me.

Once I got to the Temple, I was informed that I had to take *not only* a sensitivity class, but a divorce class as well. And it wasn't cheap. Just another way for those scoundrels to wring some more shekels out of us middle-class saps. The sensitivity training was okay, I guess. I did it over one weekend, so I didn't miss work. Of course, part of the class took place over the Sabbath, but as long as the classes were not held in the Temple itself, it was okay. And the facilitator of the class was not really a "practicing" Jew anyway. I just wanted to get on with it, and finish my required classes, and look for a new wife. I passed with an 87 on the test, which was good enough for me. Well, the divorce class was kind of more challenging. It began with the writings of Moses and his take on the subject, which, we were told, was dictated directly to him by Yahweh, the Great and Powerful.

If a man marries a woman who becomes displeasing to him because he finds something indecent about her, and he writes her a certificate of divorce, gives it to her and sends her from his house, and if after she leaves his house she becomes the wife of another man, and her second husband dislikes her and writes her a certificate of divorce, gives it to her and sends her from his house, or if he dies, then her first husband, who divorced her, is not allowed to marry her again after she has been defiled. That would be detestable in the eyes of the LORD. (Deuteronomy 24: 1,2).

Well, I was cool with that. After all, us guys have to hang together. If women don't suit our fancy, we should be allowed to just send them away with a certificate. It makes sense. Women can be so difficult, you know. Lord knows, even the Scriptures declare: **A quarrelsome wife is like a constant dripping on a rainy day: restraining her is like restraining the wind or grasping oil in the hand.** (Proverbs 27: 16). Is that right or what? Up to that point I hadn't considered that I couldn't just go back and retrieve her whenever I might want to. That would be detestable in the eyes of the Lord! OMG. But after I got over that, I decided to go ahead with the divorce. I went to the temple to get the divorce certificate when I happened upon a gaggle of middle-aged men listening to that preacher, Jesus. The Pharisees were questioning him about—guess what—divorce! So I listened in:

"Is it lawful for a man to divorce his wife?" "What did Moses command you?"he replied. They said, "Moses permitted a man to write a certificate of divorce and send her away." "It was because your hearts were hard that Moses wrote you this law,"Jesus replied. "But at the beginning of creation God 'made them male and female.' 'For this reason a man will leave his father and mother and be united to his wife and the two will become one flesh.' So they are no longer two, but one flesh. Therefore what God has joined together, let no one separate." When they were in the house again, the disciples asked Jesus about this. He answered, "Anyone who divorces his wife and marries another woman commits adultery against her. And if she divorces her husband and marries another man, she commits adultery." (Matthew 19: 3-9). Well, I had just learned in my Moses Divorce class that I could divorce my wife if she displeased me. (But I could not marry her again.) And now this guy Jesus is saying even if I remarry a *different* woman, I am committing adultery. Huh? Is that weird or what? A lot of the guys there were getting kind of pissed at Jesus over that, and the Pharisees were plainly upset too.

But then he really dropped a bombshell on all of us, saying: **"You have heard it said, do not commit adultery. But I tell you that anyone who looks at a woman lustfully has already committed adultery with her in his heart."** (Mt. 5: 28). What? Adultery in the heart? What's that all about? I mean, I love to hang around the market, and watch the servant (and slave) girls buying radishes. Gawd, that's hot. I get all excited sometimes, and, Lord knows, I have my fantasies. So, now I am an adulterer? Does that seem fair? Then that rabble-rouser really sent shock waves through the crowd: **"If your right eye causes you to sin, gouge it out and throw it away. It is better for you to lose one part of your body than for your whole body to be thrown into hell. And if your right hand causes you to sin, cut it off and throw it away. It is better for you to lose one part of your body than to go into hell."** (Mt. 5: 29,30). Holy shit. What is that all about? I mean I have never heard of this thing called "Hell" before, but Jesus talks about it like it is a real place, and that I may be a candidate to go there.

To be frank, I have never much thought about these matters before. Yikes. All I did was come up to the Temple Mount to find a scribe to write a divorce decree for me, as I (as a male in good standing) am fully within my rights to do. Then I ran into that preacher, Jesus, again. Somehow I am wondering if this is just a coincidence, or if the big man in the sky is trying to tell me something. I went home after that, minus the certificate. I can put up with Veronika a few more days if I have to, but I want to think through this notion that something actually happens after we die. Jesus is the first to really delve into the subject in this way.

I talked to my rabbi, who is a conservative. He told me to ignore that blabbermouth, Jesus, preaching at the temple. "He is full of shit," Rabbi Gutenburg assured me, "He is just pulling all that Heaven and Hell stuff right out of his ass. Just read the words of our famous King Solomon. What did he say?" So we did a little Bible study right there in the rabbi's house. It was most enlightening. We turned to the words of Solomon the wise. **As it is with a good man, so with the sinner, those who take oaths, so with those who are afraid to take them. This is the evil in everything that happens under the sun; the same destiny overtakes all. For the living know they are going to die, but the dead know nothing; they have no further reward, and even the memory of them is forgotten.** (Ecclesiastes 9: 2-5).

This is the longstanding Jewish position on death and dying. Now this Jesus comes along and throws all that tradition in the dumpster. But I still had that remark about gouging my eye out ringing in my ears. If I am a sinner and, lo, an adulterer by just fantasizing about the women I see on the street, and if, as a sinner, I am doomed to burn eternally in a "literal" burning hell, should I not then seriously consider Jesus' admonition to poke my eye out to avoid the alternative? Is that real or figurative? "Well, analytically speaking," the Rabbi went on, "we have to determine when Scripture is literal and when it is just being metaphoric."

"That helps not at all," I whined. "You are the clergyman. You tell me. When is Jesus being serious and when is he just joshing?" I was also concerned about cutting off my right hand, one of my favorite appendages. "What in the devil was he talking about with this hand-cutting thing? After all, the only place I remember in Scripture where hand-cutting is required was in the case of two men fighting when one guy's wife gets in the middle of it . . . and, like, how often does that really happen, I ask you."

"Oh, you mean: **If two men are fighting and the wife of one of them comes to rescue her husband from his assailant, and she reaches out and seizes him by his private parts, you shall cut off her hand. Show her no pity.**" (Deut. 25: 11,12). Obviously, the Rabbi was familiar with that verse.

"Well, do you buy that, Rabbi," I queried. "Is that not a bit farfetched?"

"Hell, no, that's not farfetched at all," gasped the Rabbi in shock. "You can't let women go around grabbing men by the balls—now can you?"

"Well, that wouldn't bother me really," I snickered. "But, tell me, should I cut off my hand or not?"

"Don't do it is my advice," he replied. "Jesus is just a flash in the pan. I predict that by this time next year you will be saying: 'Jesus *who*?'" So we parted ways and I went home to Veronika, who was being overly nice to me. Maybe she figured out that I was entertaining the notion of divorcing her, and she was not relishing the idea of having to crawl back home to Gad and move back in with Mom and Dad. She even made me Cherries Jubilee—my fave. Maybe I'll stick with her a bit longer. Can't really hurt—much :-)

Chapter 29

Drumpfie (The Rich Young Ruler)

Two rich guys meet Jesus

Pip Pip Cheerio. They call me Chickie. Got that nickname back in prep school. I was a member of the Jewish Glee Club, the Zion rowing team, and the Ben Bernaise Republican Party Debating Team. My good friend, Drumpfie (Baron Von Drumpf)—whom I met in military school—ran into a traveling evangelist named Yeshua bar Yosef (Jesus Son of Joseph) at the Temple Mount not long ago, and had a most interesting chat with him. I was listening in, but out of deference to my rich friend (whose dad is running for some high political office in the Sanhedrin), I just kept quiet. But Drumpfie was genuinely interested in what this guy was all about. He was polite. He asked:

"Good teacher, what must I do to inherit eternal life?" (Luke 18: 18). Jesus looked him up and down, and, likely ascertaining his wealth and status, sort of profiled him on the spot. I am sure he figured that Drumpfie is a good guy down deep inside, but, being young and rich, he is likely one to take advantage of his position now and then. But, he just wanted to find out about this eternal life stuff that has been going around since Jesus made the scene a year or so ago, doing all sorts of miracles that have become the talk of the town.

"You know the commandments: do not commit adultery, do not murder, do not steal, do not give false testimony, honor your father and mother," Jesus replied knowingly. (Luke 18: 20). Well, Drumpfie had been raised well, and I have met his parents. He certainly respected them (and their money). Not one to rock the boat in that way, he replied: **"All these I have kept since I was a boy."** (Luke 18: 21). I knew that was true. Sure, he was a bit of a tease and went a bit too far flirting with the girls and all that. But basically he was a good Jewish lad, and didn't get into serious trouble. He never killed anybody or had need to steal stuff. He didn't commit adultery per se, since he was not married. But he did fuck around with wild women now and then; but that was just blowing off steam . . . youthful indiscretions—you know. And besides, his dad paid to make those little infractions "go away." All in all I would call him a good kid. Of course, at eighteen he wasn't really a kid anymore. He was a young adult.

Then Jesus dug a bit deeper into his true self—his persona. Jesus could tell that he was rich enough alright. But *why*, he asked, was everybody referring to him as a "Rich Young Ruler?" What exactly was he a ruler of? Young Jewish guys like Drumpfie liked to call themselves stuff like "ruler" even though they actually didn't rule over anything. He was named Baron, but was not really a baron either. His dad was a bigwig in the Jewish community, and was in bed with the Roman authorities (we all knew that). But Drumpfie was not really a ruler at all. He just liked the sound of it. Kind of like his Uncle Saul who called himself "Doctor" even though he didn't have any medical training or a Ph.D. in any field of study. He just called himself that and everybody went along with it, not wanting to upset his father, who had connections with the Roman occupying forces in Jerusalem. Well, Jesus saw through him in a moment and replied:

"Sell everything you have and give to the poor, and you will have treasure in heaven." (Luke 18: 22). OMG, Baron was stunned. He actually looked shocked. I could tell what he was thinking: "Wow, how can I do that? I can give to some worthy charities, of course. But give *everything*? No way. I mean, sure, the poor need help. But, you know, if you just give poor people handouts it makes them lazy and dependent. They will expect it after a while." I could read his mind. He was channeling his dad. All those arguments float around constantly in conservative circles—both political and religious. Giving to the poor is a good thing. We all should do it. But here is this Galilean, a carpenter in a tatty robe and worn-out sandals telling Baron that if he would give up all his earthly wealth he would inherit eternal life. Still, I could see the wheels turning. He was in no way inclined to believe this bumpkin from Bethlehem. I mean, if he is so great, why isn't he rich?

Baron always thought like that. He was brought up to think that way. My family was sort of upper middle class, so I wasn't as flippant about class differences as Baron. He really felt himself "to the manor born." Jesus was making most of his headway with his preaching in the population at large with poorer classes of people. His message of sacrifice just didn't resonate with guys like Drumpfie. But then Jesus really dropped the bombshell on him: **"Then come, follow me."** (Luke 18: 22).

Well, that did it. Baron turned ashen. He was sweating. I thought he might drop over in a dead faint at that remark. Jesus was not only telling him that he had to give up his life and wealth, but that he had to become like this clodhopper from Nazareth. I could just see the ire rise up in him. There was simply no way that he would trade a good thing—his wealth and status—for such an unknown . . . eternal life. He was clearly not going to follow Jesus, and that was final. But I was kind of interested in what the preacher was going to say next. I decided to stay a while longer.

"Hey, I am going over across the courtyard," he said regaining his composure. "There is another preacher over there named Joel-something. He is preaching just the opposite message. They are calling it the "Prosperity Doctrine." It sounds interesting. I'm going to mosey over there for a while and chill. Interested?"

"No," I replied. "I'm going to stick around here just a bit longer to hear what Jesus is going to say next. But I will be over in like ten or fifteen minutes. Don't leave. Just hang there and I'll catch up. Okay?" He agreed and left. I tuned back into what Jesus was saying to his disciples. **"How hard is it for the rich to enter the kingdom of God. Indeed it is easier for a camel to go through the eye of a needle than for a rich man to enter the Kingdom of God."** (Luke 18: 24,25). Well, the disciples were perplexed. "How can anybody be saved at that rate?" they asked incredulously. "Come on. This is impossible. Everybody is wealthy relative to someone else. So in a way we are all rich if we have food, clothing, a bed to sleep in, and friends and family. How much richer are we than the beggar in the street who has none of that? Or what about the lepers? Hell, they are up shit creek no matter what.

So Jesus replied that although things seem impossible, with God all things are possible. Well, I had heard that line all my life, and have found it to be kind of lame. Sure, I guess, it's true if you believe it. But just a stroll across town to the Pool of Siloam will prove otherwise. How come most of those gimps who used to hang out there never got healed? And now that it has been shut down, what's the point of waiting on God? Like he really listens to the prayers of Earthlings? No way. He just heals who he wants to and says "screw you" to the rest. I decided to leave at that point and find Baron. I was ready to try something new. That "Prosperity Doctrine" sounded intriguing. Let's give that a whirl.

Dr. Joel O. Steinway was a kind of Jesus wannabee. I had heard him before at the Temple Mount, preaching a "feel good" message. I liked it. Obviously, Baron was digging it too. "Hey," he said enthusiastically, slapping me on the back, "this guy has a much more uplifting message than that Jesus back there. That bloke is a total downer. This guy has his act together. He is really in-tune with "the people." Besides, he isn't homeless like Jesus. He has a mega-temple across town, and they have all sorts of activities for young people, and their own dating service as well. You never know who we might hook up with there, hehe."

I was okay with that because I really liked Baron, and hanging with him was never a dull moment. Guys like me need to get in with the rich crowd if we can. A rising tide lifts all boats, right? So we sat on the stone pavement of the Temple Mount, and listened to Dr. Steinway. He liked to be called Dr. O. I never knew if he was a real doctor either. He was young, trim, and full of energy. He had a million-dollar smile and a personality to match. I could see why people would follow him. Unlike Jesus, that itinerant vagabond from Nazareth, this guy had class—style. He definitely dressed for success.

His operation, called "Victory Temple," was big. It had been built by the Greeks as a sports arena, but the Romans wanted something grander, so the Roman authorities leased it out to Dr. O. for his ministry. When we arrived at his outdoor rally, Dr. O was just wrapping up his presentation with an invitation. "Y'all come on over with us to Victory Temple. Come on down for a miracle service," he encouraged. "You will see healings, faith restored. The blind will see, and the cripples will walk!" I was interested. So we kind of fell in behind the throng and followed the cheering crowd all the way to the "Temple."

As we entered the stadium, we were greeted with all manner of noise— praise, that is. People were carrying on in total abandon—each singing his favorite golden oldie. I recognized some of the tunes, but others were quite new. I took to praising, and it was fun. Baron was quite taken with the whole production as well. The choir, which was located onstage behind the speaker's podium (which I learned is called a pulpit), was singing and clapping and swaying in unison. I felt dizzy. Then, as I looked around the audience (which they were calling a congregation), I noticed a lot of the same people who used to hang out at the Pool of

Siloam before the Romans re-appropriated it. There was no pool for the angel to come to and trouble the waters, but they did—hear tell—have a baptismal tank behind the pulpit, covered with nice curtains that can be drawn back for dunkings. Actually, that seemed so much more civilized than those weird baptisms done by John out there in the Jordan River. This was clearly a more upscale audience for the most part. Well, the gimps from the pool were hanging back toward the rear. Probably embarrassed about their shabby raiment. They should definitely learn how to "dress for church."

The service began. Dr. O. lead out in prayer. He prayed for guidance and a blessing on the sermon. He prayed for the Pharisees and Sadducees, that the Lord would bless them in their office. And then he prayed for Herod, leader of all the Jews, and Caiaphas, the Grand Poobah of the Roman Occupying Forces in the Levant. "We must pray for our earthly leaders," he indicated, "as God has installed them in positions above ours, and they need divine guidance."

Then he took to preaching. The crowd loved it. He said that "poverty is for chumps . . . losers." I agreed. We should all be rich. "If you want a blessing from the Lord," he continued, "Just ask! No, don't just ask, tell God that you *deserve* it. You are a King's Kid, and you deserve all good things that flow from the hand of God." I felt empowered and secretly sent up my own little prayer. (I have always wanted one of those real cool chariots that the rich kids drive.) I guess my faith wasn't strong enough yet, as nothing happened. But I was undeterred. I just went on listening to the sermon.

You have not because you ask not. (James 4: 2). Dr. O. quoted and continued: "We all must learn to be unafraid to ask of the Lord. We must come boldly before God and ask freely! The Lord will never hold back blessings from his chosen ones. We are so blessed here in Jerusalem. We have so much to be thankful for. We are living in the greatest empire the world has even known. Hallelujah. To quote my old friend and fellow minister, Creflo Dolor: 'When we pray, believing that we have *already received* what we are praying for, God has no choice but to make our prayers come to pass.' Now those is powerful words!"

"Did you hear that, my friends? God has no choice! He is powerless to do otherwise than to grant the requests of his followers." He began getting excited. "Simply said, God is *obligated* to answer your prayers. He can do no less because he is God!" Wow, I had never heard such a powerful sermon before. This was way cooler than that whiny hangdog preaching of Jesus, talking about sacrifice, giving to the poor, and following him! Ha. What a crock! Now, this guy has it right. I listened more intently.

"Though he was rich, yet for your sake he became poor, so that you through his poverty might become rich." (2 Corinthians 8:9). Yeah! That through him we can become rich. That's for me. I was already thinking of the stuff I will be able to afford when God opens the windows of Heaven and rains down material blessings on me. Any moment now.

Then Dr. O. really hit me with a new and glorious idea. "If you serve God, you need not suffer pain and misery in your temporal bodies!" he shouted enthusiastically. "Claim your healing. Claim it now!" The whole gaggle of gimps from the back ran, walked, hobbled, and crawled forward, carrying on down at the altar rail like a tribe of macaque monkeys. "Praise the Lord!" shouted Brother O. as he held up one poor fellow with incontinence. Well, that didn't go too well so he bellowed forth: "I perceive in the Spirit that someone among you has liver trouble! Let us know that you are healed right now. Come forward for your healing!" Nobody moved. I guess they didn't even know that they might have cirrhosis. But so what? They were healed. Dr. O. said so. "Does anybody have a cold? God wants to heal you right now." Several folks came forward, sniffling and sneezing all the way. They were cured on the spot. Hallelujah.

"Well, we have seen many miracles of the Lord here tonight," the preacher shouted, thumping his Torah. "Now it is time to show your love and appreciation to the Lord God and his servants. If you can give one talent or even one shekel, give it now. God will reward you tenfold. **Bring the whole tithe into the storehouse . . . and see if I will not throw open the floodgates of heaven and pour out so much blessing that there will not be room enough to store it.** (Malachi 3:10). Yeah. Dig it. If I give, I'm going to get something . . . something bigger and better. I want it. I want it now.

So I emptied my pockets and waited. The gimps at the altar really didn't have anything to give, but that's okay with the Lord. He makes people the way they are. And if they are born blind or infirm, they have to just learn to "Praise the Lord anyway." Well, the service went on into the night. I needed to get home, and Baron was approaching curfew. So we made our way out into the Jerusalem night. We had to walk, as all the buses had quit running. But that was okay as well. We didn't have any money left, but we felt blessed. I know God is going to remember my giving tonight. Sometime in the future he is going to bless me. It is all in his time. Besides, Brother O. promised that my ten shekels would definitely become a *hundred* at any time. I am so happy and blessed. So, I'm just watching and waiting, looking above . . . filled with his goodness, lost in his love. Glory!

Chapter 30

Bantay

A Roman soldier pulls guard duty at the Garden Tomb

My name is Bantay. I am a PFC in the Roman Legion—stationed in Jerusalem. I don't have any particular skills, so I was first assigned to the motor pool. But I wasn't very good with chariot repair. So they reassigned me to be an MP (military police). That was okay with me as it is a "dick job" (something easy—not requiring much brain strain or effort). Well, most of the time I just read the duty roster and showed up in full uniform to escort prisoners of the State to their audiences with various Jewish or Roman officials like Herod or Caiaphas or Pontius Pilate himself. One day last week, I was assigned to haul a young Jewish rabble-rouser from his holding cell to have a chat with Herod, leader of the Jews. He had been in front of the Romans already, and they just saw him as a pathetic lunatic. So they passed him on to Herod. "You're Herod's race . . . You're Herod's case," they deferred. "Get the hell out of here with your weird Hebrew doctrines and squabbles," they condescended. "We don't give a shit about your dumbass religion, so deal with your *own* issues."

So we dragged the guy to Herod, who just teased him. "So you are the Christ . . . the great Jesus Christ," Herod crooned. "Prove to me that you're no fool. Walk across my swimming pool. If you'll do that for me, then I'll let you go free. Come on, King of the Jews!" Nothing happened. Herod was unimpressed, so we dragged the dude back to the Romans. They were so bored with all this petty bickering among the *locals* by then. It was so beneath them. So, they did what any superpower would do. They sent him away to be flogged. That should fix him. But it didn't work. This clown really wanted to die. So the Romans (at the encouragement of the chanting crowd) sent him off to Golgotha to be executed. He was put in lockup for a few days awaiting the cross. Well, that was what you get for standing up to the government. So they crucified him and that was it. Our detail was to take the body away (along with two other petty criminals). Then this total unknown guy intervened. His name was Joseph of Arimathea (or some weird place that nobody had ever heard of before). He volunteered to take the body of Christ and put it into his own family crypt. He said that he was a Chreestian (a follower of Christ) and that he would take responsibility for the bod.

Our Captain, Maximus Qualcosa, instructed us to go with the small burial party and make sure they didn't steal the body. Like, why would they want a moldering corpse anyway? But for some reason, his "followers" were delusional and believed that he would come back to life. The Roman authorities just wanted this little episode over, so assigned me (and my friend PFC Minimus Lexius) to escort the party to the Garden of Gethsemane for interment. Piece of cake. But the hitch was that we had to stand guard for three days. Never knew why. Heck, the guy was dead. But orders are orders, so we lit up a joint and began our guard duty assignment. I really hate guard duty (boring). But we decided to just park it near the tomb and wait. Nothing happened. In fact, we both fell asleep. That hash was good stuff and made us relaxed and well . . . you get it. We were definitely stoned, so what we saw next just might be a bit fuzzy. It all started with the earthquake (the big one that rocked Jerusalem, Samaria, and the whole seismic region). I'm sure you have heard about in the press by now.

There was a violent earthquake, for an angel of the Lord came down from heaven, and, going to the tomb, rolled back the stone and sat on it. His appearance was like lightening and his clothes were white as snow. The guards were so afraid of him that they shook and became like dead men. (Matthew 28: 2-4). Well, I have to say that *something* big happened for sure. This glowing extraterrestrial guy showed up right there on the spot and rolled the stone away. I was so scared that I passed out! When Minimus and I came to, we immediately poked our heads inside the crypt. The body was definitely gone and the tomb was empty.

"Oh, shit!" exclaimed Minimus. "What are we going to do? What are we going to say to the captain? If we tell the authorities about the ET guy, I doubt that anybody would believe us. And we were smoking weed. Yet if we just say that we fell asleep, we will be court-marshaled for sure, as sleeping on duty—especially guard duty—is a big no-no."

"Well, I am sure that everybody in town felt the earthquake," I surmised.

"But can we just say that the quake moved the rock?"

"Sure but then we are definitely still minus one body."

"Hang on, I think I'm remembering something that Qualcosa mentioned. He said that the Jewish leaders had asked Pilate to put us on guard in the first place because they were afraid the cultists would indeed steal the body and claim that the guy inside had actually been raised from the dead. If we *just* say that the earthquake knocked us out and moved the stone cover at the same time—well—we didn't know how long we were unconscious,; so those Chreestians could have surely come into the garden and ripped off the body in the meantime. Heck, it wasn't our fault we were out-cold at the time."

So we got our story straight and when we reported the incident to the Captain, he told us to cool it until the higher powers got together to make a report. "We all have to keep mum until the Jewish leaders get their act together," he cautioned. "Then we and they can tell the Roman authorities. We can include the earthquake in our report for flair!" He grinned. **When the chief priests had met with the elders and devised a plan, they gave the soldiers a large sum of money, telling them, "You are to say, 'His disciples came in the night and stole him away while we were asleep.' If this report gets to the governor, we will satisfy him and keep you out of trouble."** (Mt. 28: 12-14).

So we ditched the whole ET incident. After all, we were still kind of high even then (and the captain could likely tell). So we swore out a statement that indeed his body had been stolen by the cultists. We were then actually paid by the Jewish hierarchy to spread that story around. They would publish it in their weekly newsletter and disseminate it around town and in the Temple. But then, the scuttlebutt around the barracks (and the whole legion) was that the Romans had crucified the wrong guy in the first place. He had a very common name, Yeshua bar Yosef (Jesus son of Joseph) . . . *Joe Jr.* And there were thousands of guys with the same name throughout the Province . . . a totally common Jew-name at that. So what was the big deal? Somewhere in the penal system they got hold of the wrong guy with the same name and executed him instead. Big deal. The Roman occupying force crucified common criminals like those troublemakers all the time. No biggie.

But there was another problem. The other guy—the real Yeshua bar Yosef—began appearing all over town! And beyond! Stories were swirling all around the suburbs of Jerusalem and as far away as the Sea of Tiberius in Galilee, where he went fishing with his friends (John 21: 1-14). And then there was a sighting on the road to Emmaus, where he had taken a hike with some other disciples of his group. (Luke 24: 13-32). Then, of course, there were countless stories being told by uneducated illiterate women around town. He had been appearing to them here and there as well. Hell, he was kind of like Chicken Man! (He's everywhere. He's everywhere.) **After his suffering, he showed himself to these men and gave them many convincing proofs that he was alive. He appeared to them over a period of forty days and spoke about the kingdom of God.** (Acts 1: 3,4).

Well, during these forty days after the earthquake and all, the whole city of Jerusalem was a mess. I mean, there was significant damage to buildings all over town and a predictable amount of chaos. Minimus and I spent much of this time on cleanup crews and still finding bodies buried under the rubble. But talk of that Jesus fellow just didn't go away. We heard of his interaction with all kinds of folks, and that his disciples were all hanging around Jerusalem. Apparently their leader, Yeshua, had instructed them to wait around because another big thing was about to happen. Funny, despite all the devastation and destruction caused by the earthquake that rocked the region and moved the stone in the garden and all, nothing was ever mentioned in the papers about it. Very strange, that. We Romans are meticulous record-keepers. But nobody bothered to tell Rome. When a boatload of new recruits arrived to replace us, they were shocked at the incredible devastation in the city and surrounding environs. "Why haven't we heard about any of this?" they queried. "Nothing in the papers in Rome. Is there some kind of a coverup—a conspiracy? We keep hearing of earthquakes in "diverse" places, but why was this one never mentioned by anybody in authority?" Beats me.

Well, as Minimus and I got our gear together to board a ship in Joppa bound for Rome, we noticed that a large number of refugees fleeing the earthquake ravages were heading that way as well. In fact, we were told that we would not be sailing back home on military vessels, which were all full. Instead we would have to share our passage with a host of civilian types from around the Province of Palestine; among them were a hefty number of Jews! What? Why would the Romans transport those filthy rabble around our "Lake," the Mediterranean?

I talked to the ship's captain. "Oh, they just call themselves refugees," he confided. "But they have all paid full fare, so we give them a lift. Many will get off in Crete, or Greece, or Malta. Many will transfer there to points further west like Spain and Gaul. Only a few will actually end up in Rome itself." That was reassuring. Rome had enough weird foreigners living within the city as it was. We simply needed no more illegal immigrants. Slaves were another matter. We can always use more of those. Of course, there is always the rumor floating around of a possible slave uprising. But with strict enforcement of existing laws, or better controls, hopefully we can keep more of those dark people out.

The rest of the trip was uneventful. The full-paying passengers were allowed up on the sun deck with us real Romans (even us soldiers). There I met a Galilean—a most amazing man. He had his pregnant wife in tow, but I didn't talk to her. He just mentioned her name in passing, Mary of Magdalene. Never heard of it but I was sure I had seen her before. He was from Nazareth—a Jew. I rarely spoke with any Jews all the time I was stationed in Jerusalem (like most military guys, we didn't much mix with the locals—except for the occasional prostitute, of course). There was something about this guy that kind of weirded me out. But I just couldn't put my finger on it. He told me that they would be disembarking in Cypress and then catching a connection to Gaul where he and this woman were going to establish a new bloodline called the *Merovingian*. "What's that?" I asked.

"Well, it is a kind of new kingdom on Earth," he explained. "We are a royal line of Jews descended directly from our ancient King David." Of course, that all sounded dumb and foreign to me. But since there was nothing else to do, I let him go on. "You see, mankind originated from a single couple and theirs was, like, the original bloodline, which separated and scattered in every direction years ago. The Jews had been occupied for centuries, so the bloodline had been polluted by interbreeding with the various tribes of old, and later with the Babylonians, the Persians, the Greeks, and now the Romans. We are moving to Gaul to establish a new and pure line—free from Gentile contamination."

I didn't have a clue as to what he was talking about, but figured he was basically harmless—a weird kind of wacko religious freak. But still, there was something undefined . . . like a haunting of the mind. *But I just couldn't put my finger on it.*

Chapter 31

Ano-ba-Ito (A waiter)

Serving the Brunch Special at the Upper Room Bar and Grill

Good evening, Sir. My name is Ano, and I will be your waiter this evening. May I get you something from the bar while I bring menus for your consideration? Thank you for visiting us here at the *Upper Room Bar and Grill* in the Jerusalem Downtown Hilton. You just can't imagine what has been going on here and all around town lately! . . . oh, you are from out of town. Are you here to celebrate Pentecost? How wonderful! Well then—when I get back with the drinks I will tell you what has been happening around here in the last few days. The whole amazing thing started right here in this very restaurant!

I was serving champagne at the Pentecost Brunch Special in this very facility the other day. I might add that Peter and the other disciples booked this place specially for the occasion, as they had been here for the famous *Last Supper* of Christ and just loved it. Our service is the best in all Jerusalem—if I do say so myself. Well . . . so they were waiting around town as the Lord Jesus had commanded them before he went up into the sky a couple of months or so ago. We all knew that something big was going to happen. After all, he had commanded them: **"Do not leave Jerusalem, but wait for the gift my Father promised, which you have heard me speak about. For John baptized with water, but in a few days you will be baptized with the Holy Spirit."** (Acts 1: 4,5).

Everybody was really jazzed, as they knew deep down that something big was about to happen—and most likely on the day of Pentecost itself when out-of-towners (such as yourselves) would all be here. So the disciples booked this place in advance "on faith" that the promise was going to be fulfilled on that very special occasion. It was big time!

Well, they all got here early on the big day. They grazed a bit at the buffet and began with the champagne. I was instructed to keep the bubbly flowing freely. I did. It's my job. They were having a wonderful time "in the spirit" when someone left one of those big windows over there open. We have always been instructed never to do that, as when the opposing double doors are open as well there is a terrific cross-draft caused and the wind really races through here, knocking things down and causing total havoc. But someone (not me for sure) forgot and at about nine a.m. there was a huge sucking sound and the mighty wind began to race into the room and out into the hallway over there.

When the day of Pentecost came, they were all together in one place. Suddenly a sound like the blowing of a violent wind came from heaven and filled the whole place where they were sitting. (Acts 2: 1,2). I mean, it was awesome! It sucked those two doors shut with a bang. Everyone began shouting and praising God! "Hallelujah!" they all yelled with joy. "The Lord's promise is being fulfilled!" Peter jumped right up, raised his champagne glass to Heaven, and held forth: "A toast to Jesus, the redeemer of the world!" They all agreed enthusiastically, "All hail Jesus, king of the Jews!" It was so exciting.

Then the mighty wind blew over a candle from one of the chaffing dishes near where Peter and Bartholomew were standing. They were so ecstatic about the rushing wind and all that they barely noticed that their robes had caught on fire! **They saw what seemed to be tongues of fire that separated and came to rest on each of them.** (Acts 2: 3). Actually, the fire began to spread, and the other disciples' garments began to burn as well. It was amazing how quickly the flames spread! I was horrified, and ran behind the bar to get the fire extinguisher. Meanwhile, my serving partner, Ewan-Ko, ran to try to shut those windows. But, apparently, the wind was so strong that he was having trouble getting them latched since they had been blown off their hinges.

The disciples began dancing in the spirit. Their clothing was on fire, but they were still shouting uncontrollably and in weird languages that I had not heard before. Of course, they seemed rather drunk and were "feeling no pain." Good thing, that, as the fire was getting quite out of hand at this point. **All of them were filled with the Holy Spirit and began to speak in other tongues as the spirit gave them utterance.** (Acts 2: 4). I'll say. It was quite a spectacle! But before I could get the fire extinguisher operational (it hadn't been checked in ages), they all ran outside—still shouting and praising God.

Ewan-Ko grabbed the extinguisher and yelled to me to follow them. They had not paid their bill. And, besides, there was a certain amount of fire damage around the head table to account for. I didn't want to take the fall for that, so I ran out into the street to follow them. They were really being filled with the spirit (or spirits) :-) Fortunately, when we got to the square called Quadrangalus Maximus, a huge crowd was standing there waiting for something. There was a stage already set up and a covered awning which was a bit askew due to the mighty wind that had just roared through Jerusalem moments earlier. Onstage were some microphones, a couple guitars at the ready, and a lavish drum set. But what was everybody waiting for? It appeared as if they were anticipating entertainment. Well, the disciples ran up and onto the stage (clothes still ablaze). The crowd went wild. What an entrance! No one had ever seen anything like it. They began jumping and leaping and praising God. By then, Ewan-Ko arrived at a full run with the fire extinguisher, which was now operational. He dashed up on stage and shot white foam all over the twelve apostles, including Matthias, the newest member of the group, who had only been with the band for a few days. Dazed, he looked kinda shocked and bewildered as if to say: "Do these guys always act like this?" The crowd was loving it, and Ewan, assuming that they were cheering for him who had just saved the apostles, took a bow.

Then Peter, so newly filled with the spirit, began to preach. **And when they heard this sound, the crowd came together in bewilderment, because each heard them speaking in his own language. Amazed and perplexed, they asked one another, "What does this mean?"** (Acts 2: 6,12). To tell you the truth, I wasn't quite sure myself. **Some, however, made fun of them and said, "They have drunk too much wine."** (Acts 2: 13). No, no! I declared loudly and emphatically. It was champagne!

Then Peter stood up with the Eleven, raised his voice, and addressed the crowd: "Fellow Jews and all of you who are in Jerusalem, let me explain this to you; listen carefully to what I say. These men are not drunk as you suppose. It's only nine in the morning." (Acts 2: 14,15).

"Good one!" the crowd cheered. "How are you by eleven?" At first Peter didn't get it, but, realizing that the crowd was in a festive mood, began a standup routine that he and John had been working on. Andrew and James picked up the guitars (that had been conveniently left onstage) and Phillip took to the drums. They had been working on a great opening tune for their upcoming road show—should they need to take to the road, that is. Someone offstage produced a trombone, which James grabbed so he could begin the tune, entitled: "Jesus Called Us, This I Know." The rest of the disciples formed a choral ensemble and began to sing in a most spirit-filled manner:

Jesus called us—one by one.
Peter, Andrew, James, and John.
Next came Phillip, Thomas too,
Matthew and Bartholomew.

Yes, Jesus called us, 3X
He called us one by one.
James, the one we called a mess,
Simon P. and Thaddeus.
Yes, Jesus called us, 3X
He called us one by one.

The crowd was on its feet, cheering and begging for more. So Phillip taught them a few new choruses and the band played on. Then Peter took to preaching. **"In the last days, God says, I will pour out my spirit on all flesh. Your sons and daughters will prophesy, your young men shall see visions, your old men will dream dreams."** (Acts 2: 17). How cool is that? The crowd was really getting into it.

Peter told the crowd about the plan of salvation and how they all needed to get saved. After preaching a real stemwinder sermon upon which the crowd (clearly moved by Peter's fabulous oratory) cried out: **"Brothers, what shall we do?" Peter replied, "Repent and be baptized, every one of you, in the name of Jesus Christ, so that your sins may be forgiven. And you will receive the gift of the Holy Spirit. Save yourselves from this corrupt generation!"** (Acts 2: 38-40). The crowd was electrified.

Those who accepted his message were baptized, and about three thousand were added to their number that day. (Acts 2: 41). But this presented a logistical problem. "Where are we going to baptize all these thousands?" asked Thomas thoughtfully.

"How about the Pool of Siloam?" suggested Thaddeus.

"Nah, the Romans took that over and turned it into a branch of the Continental Baths," informed Andrew. "Looks like we are going to have to march everybody out to the Jordan River."

"Well, if it was good enough for Jesus, it is good enough for these guys!" sighed Phillip. So they began making their way out of the city, over the Mount of Olives, and out into the Judean Desert. "What are we going to feed all these people?" queried Matthew in wonderment. "It is like thirty miles from here to the river, and it is already getting late in the afternoon! And, as it is, it will take this mob a couple of days to walk thirty miles." He was being practical. "Come on, think about it. There are women, children, and old people to think of. Hey, they need to get baptized too. So I repeat: what are they going to eat on the way?"

"Well," Peter suggested, "maybe we could just bring along a couple of fish and some loaves of bread!" He was still high from his success in preaching the Gospel for the first time. "After all, our Lord fed the 5,000 that way. Maybe we could practice on this 3,000!"

"Or we could stop at the Denny's in Jericho. That's on the way!" Thomas said doubtfully.

"Oh, come on, we are filled with the *Spirit* now. Surely we can turn a couple of loaves and fishes into a total feast!" encouraged Peter enthusiastically. So they began to sing as they set out. Ewan-Ko and I decided to join in and get baptized as well. Hey, can't hurt. They made up new choruses en route as there were no choruses or hymns yet invented at that point. Everything was new and oh so fun! They taught us *Marching to Jordan, On Jordan's Stormy Banks,* and *Somewhere Over Jordan.* It was very uplifting. But my favorite was when all the Apostles got together at a rest stop along the way and sang acapella:

We're the Apostles, my friend.
And we'll keep fighting til the end.
Cuz we're the Apostles . . .
We're the Apostles of the world!

Wow, so inspirational! I just wanted to get saved all over again!

Chapter 32

Ragionieri (Accountant of the Apostles)

He recounts the tragic story of Ananias and Sapphira

I hate to be the one to have to tell you this tale. My name is Jacob Ragionieri. I am an accountant here in Jerusalem. I used to work for Matthew when he was still working for the IRS as a tax collector for the Romans. He was a real bitch to work for back then. But then he met Jesus and got saved, and he is now filled with the Holy Spirit. The transformation is remarkable. Heck, he even got me this new gig as accountant to the disciples (now known as the *Apostles*). The situation was shocking. Let me tell you about it and about the death of two of the original members of the church here in J-town. It starts like this:

All the believers were one in heart and mind. No one claimed that any of his possessions was his own, but they shared everything they had. There were no needy persons among them. From time to time those who owned lands or houses sold them, brought the money from the sales and put it at the apostles' feet, and it was distributed to anyone as he had need. (Acts 4: 32,34,35). What a cool system, huh? Well, of course all that money had to be accounted for, right? So I was hired on to make sure that nobody was cheating. After all, we were all aware that we were in on the ground floor of this new scheme—this founding of a new religion—a "church." Well, corporations such as this need organization and rules and regulations. So the Apostles had regular prayer meetings followed by normal business meetings. I kept notes, typed up the minutes, and distributed them to the key members of the growing congregation.

One central element of the new corporation was that it was intended to be a total communist endeavor from the get-go. There was to be no private ownership of property or the means of production. Everybody was to be equal in the sight of the Lord, the Apostles, and the congregation. I loved it. The various members would come out to our regular worship services, hear the preaching of the Word, and get saved. Then they would get baptized and take out church membership. Thereupon they would sell everything they had, including all real estate, and give the proceeds to us!

They would bring the cash and deposit it—not in a bank, but at the Apostles' feet. Cool, huh? Afterward, I would take the haul, count it, write it down in a ledger, and put it in the company safe. This worked swell, and whenever the church elders needed petty cash, they would simply come to me; I would give them what they needed, have them sign a receipt, and call it good.

Well, that system worked well, but then a bad thing happened. Now, a man named Ananias, together with his wife Sapphira, also sold a piece of property. With his wife's full knowledge he kept back part of the money for himself, but brought the rest and put it at the apostles' feet. (Acts 5: 1,2). Well, someone tattled on them. I wasn't sure who, but I think it was a guy named Joseph (a Levite from Cyprus) who had made a big show of giving all his money to the church, laying a huge wad of cash and some gold and silver coins at the feet of Peter and the elders.

Obviously, Peter caught wind of the rumors that Ananias and Sapphira were withholding some of their profits for themselves, thus cheating not only the church and the apostles, but God himself! Bad move, that. Well, Peter called him out for it right in front of the whole congregation. **"Ananias, how is it that Satan has so filled your heart that you have lied to the Holy Spirit and have kept for yourself some of the money you received for the land?"** Busted! Obviously, Peter planned to make an example out of him, as he drilled right down on him in front of everybody. He continued . . . **"Didn't it belong to you before it was sold? After it was sold, wasn't the money at your disposal? What made you think of doing such a thing? You have not lied to men but to God."** (Acts 5: 3,4). The poor guy was really sweating bullets. Clearly, the "lying to God" part really got to him. **When Ananias heard this, he fell down and died.** (Acts 5: 5).

I had never actually seen somebody just keel over like that. At first I thought he had just fainted. But when Peter began shouting a message in tongues, I knew for sure that the Lord had taken him. Ananias was dead as a doornail right there on the floor in front of the altar rail, and Peter was holding forth in a heavenly language for effect. Thomas gave the interpretation. It was like: "Yea, I say, I say, Yea! I am the Lord your God, and harken unto my voice all ye people! If you fail to give full measure, if you fail to bring your full tithes and offerings into the Lord's storehouse, this same fate will befall you!" **And great fear seized all who heard what had happened.** (Acts 5: 5). No shit! Everybody was in a total state of apoplexy. Some shouted and prayed. Some sang and danced, some cried out in tongues, and some even fell to the floor, rolling around and convulsing. It was quite a spectacle. I have to admit, I was freaked as well.

Then the young men came forward, wrapped up his body, and carried him out and buried him. (Acts 5: 5,6). Well, the whole service changed tone at that point. After removing the body, we sang and prayed in a somber way as we anticipated what was coming next. **About three hours later his wife came in, not knowing what had happened.** This situation was most uncomfortable.

Peter asked her, "Tell me, is this the price you and Ananias got for the land?" I mean, we could all see that he was setting a trap for her. And she walked right into it.

"Yes," she said, "that is the price." Game, set, match!

Peter said to her, "How could you agree to test the Spirit of the Lord? Look! The feet of the men who buried your husband are at the door, and they will carry you out also." I felt sorry for the poor woman. I mean, Peter didn't even give her a chance to explain, to change her account, or to repent. He simply pronounced a death sentence.

At that moment she fell down at his feet and died. Then the young men came in and, finding her dead, carried her out and buried her beside her husband. We were all totally bummed out.

Great fear seized the whole church and all who heard about these events. (Acts 5: 7-10). Well, events like that rarely go unnoticed. In fact, word got out about it immediately and many puzzling questions followed. Like, who said that this whole operation had to be *communist* in nature? Where did God tell us anywhere to give *all* our money? We all knew of tithing, of course—but that is ten percent. It is true that Jesus challenged the "rich young ruler" Baron von Drumpf to give his all. And yet the Baron didn't. And the apostles had indeed been preaching a doctrine of sacrifice, but wasn't this a bit over the top?

Of course, as the resident bean counter, I noticed an immediate drop off in church attendance after the Ananias and Sapphira incidents. Funny how people dropping dead in church can dissuade people from attending —especially if the death threats were based on whether they gave enough money. Matthew (a former tax man himself) expressed concern at our next weekly board meeting. "Guys," he said carefully, "I think we may have a problem here. Maybe we better back off a bit on this communism. It could be that some of the new converts are a bit skittish about emptying their entire bank accounts for us. I mean, I think it is cool that they bring gold and silver and paper to lay at our feet. That's hot. But maybe we had better think of a limit. I mean, after all, they do have to eat, pay rent, and take care of their kids. And you all know that the price of charter schools isn't cheap these days!"

"Well, yeah," grumbled Peter, "But if we are to have a pure communist society here, everybody has to give up self, and join the group, and get with the program. And if we have a bunch of namby-pamby Christians hanging around who won't contribute to the cause of Christ—and give everything to us—how is that going to work in the end?"

"True enough," intoned Bartholomew. "But maybe we wouldn't have to have an actual kibbutz—a commune. Perhaps we could find a middle ground somehow."

"Yeah, I agree," said Phillip, thinking aloud. "Perhaps we could make giving optional. You know—kind of like an *offering*—not mandatory."

"Right," threw in Thaddeus. "We could still have them bring their money and throw it at our feet. I do like that part. It makes the experience of giving more real to the masses. And, besides, it is a good opportunity for them to show their generosity in public. An example for others to follow, you know."

You could tell that Peter wasn't buying these suggestions of compromise. "I threw in 100 percent with Jesus," he boasted. "I gave 100 percent for the Lord, and—by God—these newcomers should be required to do the same in order to gain the blessings that we are now enjoying!" Outside I could hear a cock crow :-)

Chapter 33

Katulung (Paul's Valet)

He witnessed Saul's conversion on the road to Damascus

My boss was a monster. His name was Saul. He is way better now. Let me tell you our story. My name is Katulung, and I took care of his horse and managed his affairs. He had other servants that did the cooking, cleaning, and household chores. I did the "manly stuff" like carrying important documents and packages, delivering stuff, and taking messages for him. He was a bigwig Jewish Pharisee. That is, he was a very high-ranking clergyman in Roman-occupied Jerusalem. He had wealth and power, but under the Roman administration the Jews had to be very careful to walk a thin line lest they rock the boat with the occupation forces, bringing disaster down on the Jewish community here in Jerusalem. The job of the Sanhedrin was to keep the lid on the local Jewish population, which was prone to resist the Roman domination of our very old and traditional homeland. Like the Greeks before them, the Romans ran the place with an iron fist. But not wanting to get entangled with day-to-day squabbles and religious conflicts, they let the Sanhedrin administer the general population for the most part.

Well, in the last year or so a lot of bubbling, gurgling fomenting has been going on right under the surface, not only in J-town but throughout all Palestine as well. The Romans have been uncool about the whole thing. You see—this itinerant preacher from Galilee was wandering all around the whole province of Roman Palestine preaching a new doctrine of salvation, baptizing in the Jordan River, and giving all the Jewish leadership massive headaches. Finally, they (including my boss, Saul) got together with the Romans, and, with the help of one of the rebels, captured the guy and executed him summarily.

Well, we thought that was that. But his followers didn't give up so easily. They actually got organized and started a rival movement that they called a "church," which is not really just a building like the temple, but a "body of believers" that can meet up and congregate just about anywhere . . . in houses, barns, or even caves and other off-the-wall places. Their numbers kept growing, and the elders were worried that the Romans might just step in and take away our "religious freedom" completely. Saul was one of the true rightwing conservative members of the council, and, OMG, did he hate that "church." He railed against them at every opportunity. BTW, I can say this now, but, when all this was happening, I was a "secret" Jesus follower myself. If Saul had known then . . . well, I shudder to think.

Anyway, Saul's fury began in earnest when he heard a certain young guy named Steven preach to the new believers. He was convinced that Steven was the source of the problem. He said: **"We have heard him say that this Jesus of Nazareth will destroy this place and change the customs that Moses handed down to us."** (Acts 6: 14). Actually, over years of foreign occupation by the Greeks and the Romans, many of the old customs of Moses had been fading anyway. But Saul was alarmed at the "erosion" and longed to restore the "good old days." I heard him say to the honchos in the temple that if they could eliminate Steven they could eliminate the church movement. Likely story. Yet he succeeded in getting them to arrest, try, and execute the guy. But guess what? It didn't change a thing. The movement continued to grow, and Saul was even more pissed-off about the whole thing. So . . .

Saul began to destroy the church. Going from house to house, he dragged off men and women and put them in prison. (Acts 8: 3). Actually, he didn't do the dragging personally. Since the Romans didn't give a shit about any of this inter-Jewish bickering and some whoop-de-do new sect, Saul had to hire local thugs to do the dragging. Of course, if you hire "muscle" they have to be paid, lest they turn on you. Saul knew that, and paid well and promptly for their services. They broke up most of the larger groups and even a lot of the smaller house churches as well. The believers were scattered all over the region as a result.

Those who had been scattered preached the word wherever they went. (Acts 8: 4). Gawd, how that infuriated Saul. He was in a foul mood all the time. He threw stuff around and cursed at the other servants and me all the time. He was insufferable, but what could I do? I had to take it as there was really no choice for a guy like me. I didn't have any real job security, nor other realistic possibilities. So I took the abuse. But the movement kept spreading. He couldn't even see that his actions were actually contributing to the growth of it all. Heck, even I could see it. But he was just pissed that this new trend was in some way threatening his old-fashioned traditions.

Meanwhile, Saul was still breathing out murderous threats against the Lord's disciples. (Acts 9: 1). He caught wind of a big "outpouring" of the Spirit up in Damascus and decided right away to go there personally to put a stop to it! **He went to the high priest and asked for letters to the synagogues in Damascus, so that if he found any there who belonged to the Way, whether men or women, he might take them as prisoners to Jerusalem.** (Acts 9: 2). Just between you and me . . . he was making such a pest of himself that the HP and the Gang of Four (Sanhedrin top dogs) issued the documents to get rid of him. I heard them talking and realized that Damascus was not even in their area of jurisdiction! Although they had no right to send a goon squad from Jerusalem up to D'ville to round up Christians, they gave him their blessings, thus foisting off their problem onto the hapless leadership of the synagogue in what was the province of Syria. Haha. LOL . . . You can have him—good luck—have fun.

Saul was elated. He rounded up his "enforcers" and hit the road to Damascus. I was along, of course, to make sure he got his lunch and that his horse was fed and all that stuff. Well, this is what happened next . . . **As he neared Damascus on his journey, suddenly a light from heaven flashed around him. He fell to the ground and heard a voice say to him, "Saul, Saul, why do you persecute me?"** (Acts 9: 4). Well, there he was flat on his back on the ground. Bizarro, huh? Nobody else (including me) saw a light. **The men traveling with Saul stood there speechless. They heard the sound but did not see anything.** (Acts 9: 7). Like, all of a sudden he was on the ground flailing around like a fish on the dock.

"Who are you, Lord?" Saul asked. "I am Jesus whom you are persecuting," he replied. "Now get up and go into the city, and you will be told what you must do." (Acts 9: 5,6). Of course, we all thought he was having a seizure or something. But when he came around and tried to stand up, he couldn't. He was totally blind. Apparently he had been blinded by the light, but we did not see it. He had been having his own private vision, and told us that God had directed him to seek out a man in town named Ananias. Meanwhile, God was telling Ananias to be ready to receive Saul. **This man is my chosen instrument to carry my name before the Gentiles.** (Acts 9: 15). Oooh, how great is that?

So then I led him by the hand all the way into town and found Ananias, who, knowing Saul's reputation in advance, was a bit trepidatious to be sure. But when he touched Saul he regained his sight immediately. Praise the Lord. You have to give that guy a lot of credit. He said: **"Brother Saul, the Lord—Jesus, who appeared to you on the road as you were coming here—he has sent me so that you may see again and be filled with the Holy Spirit."** (Acts 9: 17). Well, he definitely got the "spirit"— like right away after getting baptized. Then he took to preaching. Now, one thing is for sure: this guy was a cut above Peter and all those rummies who hung out with Jesus in the beginning. Heck, they (except Matthew) were a bunch of fishermen and farmer types. This guy was clergy, with the education and credentials to prove it. He could preach up a storm from the beginning, and everybody was totally wowed.

We hung around Damascus together after I finally found the courage to confess that I was a Christian all along. He more or less proved to the skeptics at the church in Damascus that he was the real deal, and that he had indeed been converted. Well, the local Jews—the power structure directly under the Romans—were royally pissed, and hired the very thugs that Saul had brought up from Jerusalem to kill him. They staked out the joint where Saul was preaching, but the locals caught wind of their plans and warned us. **His followers took him by night and lowered him in a basket through an opening in the wall.** (Acts 9: 25). They lowered me too, but that is rarely mentioned as we found our way back to Jerusalem on our own (minus the thugs, who were left in Damascus unpaid—haha).

When we got back to J-town nobody wanted anything to do with Saul. They were scared shitless of him, lest he be faking and spying for the Sanhedrin. I told them that he was legit, but only a guy named Barnabas would take him in. So we stayed with Barn for a while until Saul really won over the skeptics. **He talked and debated with the Grecian Jews, but they tried to kill him. When the brothers learned of this, they took him down to Caesarea and sent him off to Tarsus.** (Acts 9: 29).

That was the last I saw of him. He was off on what he was calling his "missionary journey." I was jealous and wanted to go with him, but he thought it best I stay, find Peter, and hang out with him a while, as something big was about to happen to him and I'd really want to see it!

Chapter 34 (Part 1)

Sidewinder (Observer at Peter's vision)

If its back faces the sky!

Hello everybody, and greetings from Joppa in the year of our Lord 33 . . . or something. My nickname is Sidewinder, and I am a member of the new church—the one started by that guy, Jesus, and his now famous disciples. I really never met the guy, but was "led to the Lord" by Peter, the most wonderful of the disciples (now called apostles). He has sort of taken me under his wing and become my mentor. He is teaching me new things daily. But most of all he talks about Jesus, his master, who walked on water, healed the sick, and fed the 5,000.

Well, Peter and I arrived here in Joppa a few weeks ago, and are currently staying with **Simon the Tanner, whose house is by the sea. About noon, Peter went up to the roof to pray. He became hungry and wanted something to eat, and while the meal was being prepared, he fell into a trance. He saw heaven opened and something like a large sheet being let down to earth by its four corners.** (Acts 10: 9-11). I was praying (in tongues) with him on that bright day. I could hear the women and servants and slaves banging around downstairs in the kitchen as they prepared the food. Both my mentor, Peter, and I were kind of freaked-out eating together with non-Jews. We call them Gentiles, and we have heard that they eat all manner of totally hideous stuff that we Jews are forbidden to even touch, let alone put into our mouths. So, in our fear and trepidation as to what was going to be served to us, I kept thinking to myself, "Will I be able to keep lunch down? Will I avoid barfing?" I knew Peter was thinking likewise.

Then Peter began having a vision. I likewise saw the white sheet descending from the sky, and some angels were holding the edges. Along with them were two rather strange-looking angels—one tall, gold, and kind of effeminate—the other short, round, and making funny whirring and whistling sounds. Obviously, they were speaking in a heavenly language quite unlike our own glossolalia. Peter threw himself down on the flat tile roof and said: "Welcome, thee heavenly messengers. What do you have to tell me?" The gold fellow bowed slightly back and said:

"Greetings Earthling, nanoo nanoo. We have been sent from Jesus, the Christ, who is now sitting at the right hand of the Father in Heaven. He has a message for you!" Peter was so excited I thought he might wet himself. "Please speak, for your servant is listening!" Peter was very deferential. Then the golden angel spoke in a most formal stiff British accent and said primly:

"Here is the message . . . *If its back faces the sky!"*

I looked at Peter. "Huh?" he said with the most puzzled look on his face. "That's the message?"

"Yup," said the gold angel. And the short round angel with the domed top and lights said something in the heavenly language. "Yes, Artoo," the gold angel replied, "That's the message." And they just stood there. Peter was totally nonplussed. So was I, by the way. It was hot, and I felt heat from the sun. Then the sheet began to glow with a heavenly aura. The angels began very quietly humming the doxology.

Praise God from whom all blessings flow, praise him all creatures here below. Praise him above ye heavenly host. Praise Father, Son, and Holy Ghost. It was quite moving. Then the sheet turned into a hologram, and earthly creatures began appearing. They looked quite real and three-dimensional. Small mammals began scurrying around the sheet. Then larger ones, like cats and dogs, appeared. Horses and other ungulates trotted by—then cattle and other livestock. Peter was turning green . . . especially when the pigs ran by on screen. I think he was beginning to get the message. I sure was. *If its back faces the sky* I kept thinking over and over.

Then birds flew by on the shining screen, followed by fish swimming on the brilliant surface. Other strange sea creatures that I had never seen before swam into view—some with eight rubbery legs! Crocodiles (like those in the Nile) crawled by, followed by snakes. My nickname is Sidewinder, so I realized that this part of the vision involved me too.

Maybe God had noticed that day when I had tried a bit of snake on a toothpick at the Farmers Market in Joppa. I felt guilty about that at the time, but was beginning to get the meaning of Christ's heavenly vision for Peter. *If its back faces the sky.* Ah, yes.

Then a voice told him, "Get up, Peter. Kill and eat." (Acts 10: 13). The shocked look on the apostle's face was dumbfounding. He began to shake spastically. He fell on the hot, flat-tile roof, writhing and rolling around like he was having a seizure (or like he was receiving the baptism in the Holy Spirit again). He began frothing at the mouth and shouting in tongues. His arms were lifted skyward. He called forth as in pain: **"Surely not, Lord." Peter replied. "I have never eaten anything impure or unclean."** (Acts 10: 14). "I am a Jew, and have always followed all the ridiculous dietary laws that you gave us way back when. I can't imagine eating stuff like pork, reptiles, or those disgusting shellfish. Oh, the very thought of crabs, shrimp, and lobsters make me turn green." Actually, he was already rather green in appearance at this point. **Then the voice spoke to him a second time. "Do not call anything impure that God has made clean."** (Acts 10: 15). Well, Peter was freaked. He pleaded with God not to make him eat all those horrible unclean things. I could tell that he was genuinely appalled. Finally, after one more go, the angels rolled the hologram sheet up and it floated heavenward. The two angels who had been talking with Peter likewise drifted up up and away—back up into the sky to join the rest of the heavenly host.

Well, as we were contemplating the meaning of the vision, there came a knock on the door and a call came up to Peter that he had company downstairs. So we went down—rather shakily—to see who they were and what they wanted. There were three guys standing at the gate. Peter said to the men, **"I am the one you are looking for, why have you come?"** (Acts 10: 21). "What can I do for you?" Come to find out they were sent by a Roman centurion from Caesarea. Apparently, God had told their master, Cornelius, to come here to Joppa to fetch Peter. And meanwhile, up on the roof, the tall, golden angel had communicated to Peter that he was indeed to go with the three visitors. So the next day we all set out together to Caesarea to meet this Cornelius.

Chapter 34 (Part 2)

Cornelius and His Own

Suck it up and eat whatever is on your plate!

The following day we arrived in Caesarea and entered the house of Cornelius, an uncircumcised Roman. Normally, I would have just considered him one of the "occupiers," but on the day-trip from Joppa with a couple of his soldiers (called centurions) I got acquainted with a guy named Lavidico, who worked for Cornelius. He talked glowingly of his boss, a top-wop in Caesarea who had made it his policy to befriend us Jews. Well, we had been more or less trained from childhood to distrust the Romans. Like, duh, they were occupying our country. Apparently, according to Lavidico, not only was Cornelius friendly to the Jews, but he was also generous and kind to the poor in his jurisdiction. A couple of days earlier when Peter and I encountered the angels and the glowing sheet incident on the roof, Cornelius was having a vision of his own. **He distinctly saw an angel from God, who came to him and said, "Cornelius!" Cornelius stared at him in fear. "What is it, Lord?" he asked. The angel answered, "Your prayers and gifts to the poor have come up as a remembrance before God. Now send men to Joppa and bring back a man named Simon who is called Peter."** (Acts 10: 4-7).

So here we were standing together in this Roman's pad with a collection of "uncircumcised" Gentiles. It was weird as, although we Jews encounter various non-Jews from time to time, we rarely interact with them unless absolutely necessary. Cornelius' extended family was there, as well as some other strangers. They served us lunch. I had been dreading this meal, as had Peter. No way would any of this "food" be clean enough for us Jews. But we swallowed hard and chocked it down to be polite. I had heard the admonition of the angels up on the roof: "kill and eat!" I knew something like this was coming. Actually, the seafood wasn't half bad. Peter was doing well, and I was proud of him that day.

Cornelius got up and began to offer a toast. Then Peter addressed the group. The men were all sitting around as Romans do with the women clustered in the back, spilling into the kitchen. Peter began: **"You are well aware that it is against our law for a Jew to associate with a Gentile or visit him. But God has shown me that I should not call any man impure or unclean."** (Acts 10: 28). I don't think some of the men there were even aware that our just being in their midst was an Old Testament offense. But they listened politely.

Peter launched into a full-blown spirit-filled sermon interspersed with some speaking-in-tongues here and there. It was a stemwinder, and it was clear to me that the apostle was polishing his act as an itinerant preacher. He was actually getting pretty good at this; and in a way more dignified manner than the early days back in Jerusalem in the upper room. Of course, there was no mighty wind this time. But it was getting exciting, as some of those uncut Gentile men began raising their arms in praise of the Jewish god, complete with speaking in tongues. I was freaked. I had never seen anything like it. God was indeed pouring out his spirit on *all* flesh (including the pagans). I was happy. Peter was happy. But once the Jews outside caught wind of it, they were *not* happy. How dare those rowdy guys get filled with the spirit and speak in our heavenly language? Peter followed up his homily with an explanation . . . and an altar call.

Of course, there was no proper altar there in the house of Cornelius, but we were all definitely getting into the spirit of the thing. I knew that something really new was happening here. We were doing something that was very un-Jewish-like. We were not just preaching to the Gentiles, but we were actually worshiping with them. It was cool. Lavidico was really getting into the whole praise thing. Some of the servants brought out some musical instruments and began to play them with zeal. Some newcomers knocked at the gate, desiring to join us in prayer and praise. Before we took our leave, Peter wrapped up his sermon with a marvelous remark: **"John baptized with water, but you will be baptized with the Holy Spirit. So if God gave them the same gift that he gave us, who believed in the Lord Jesus Christ, who was I to think that I could oppose God?"** (Acts 11: 16,17). Peter went on to much acclaim after that, which ticked off King Herod. Finally, he just had enough of Peter preaching around the country, and had him arrested along with some others of the new movement. He had planned to bring him to a public trial the day after the Passover. But while Peter was incarcerated, another angel appeared to him and poked him in the ribs. "Get up and follow me," the heavenly being said. Peter was getting quite used to interacting with angels at this point; so he got up, and his chains fell off immediately, and he followed the angels right out to the gate of the city, which opened miraculously by itself.

Herod was not the least bit happy that the guards had let Peter escape, so he had all sixteen of them shot on the spot. Then he went to Caesarea to deal with yet another Jewish dispute. He was genuinely sick of all the squabbling among his people. **On the appointed day Herod sat on his throne and delivered a public address to his people. They shouted, "This is the voice of a god, not a man."** (Acts 12: 19,20). Well, this absolutely did not fly with God. Herod should have tried to be a bit more humble, but egotist that he was, he took the praise and adulation all on himself. And immediately an angel of the Lord appeared and smote him. Of course, I felt he deserved it, but you could tell that the crowd was shocked as the most peculiar thing happened at that point.

Immediately an angel of the Lord struck him down and he was eaten by worms and died. (Acts 12: 23). OMG, it was horrible. All of a sudden these hideous worms came slithering into the throne room and began devouring the king. He was dead in no time, and the worms just kept gobbling him up. Of course, that emptied the place out posthaste. Peter grabbed me by the hand and pulled me out of there. We decided not to stick around Caesarea, but to head for Antioch where Paul was preaching with Barnabas and a new young guy named Mark. Peter and Paul were never close, as they were from such diverse backgrounds. But, personally, I was looking forward to hearing Paul preach. He was already famous around these parts for his fabulous preaching. But I came to learn that he had some teachings that were really rankling the churches as far away as Ephesus, Colosse, and Laodicea.

Chapter 35

Sottomesso (Timothy's Tale)

Slaves, submit to your earthly masters with respect and fear

Hello, all our dear brothers and sisters in the Lord. My name is Timothy (but you can call me Tim). I have been hanging out with the Apostle Paul, his bud, Barnabas, and a few other apprentice preachers like me that Paul has taken under his wing over the last year or so when we began our second missionary journey. I have always loved to travel, so hanging with such a well-traveled fellow as Paul is quite a treat for me. Paul tends to be dictatorial at times, but I am learning submission. He must have picked up this concept back in Jewish school and in seminary as he is quite a stickler for this protocol.

As you know, Paul was once a very wicked character. I have talked to several folks who knew him back before his miraculous conversion on the road to Damascus. He had a classical education and was one who loved to argue. When he was saved, he became like a different person. Well, over time, that has begun to change a bit. He has been reverting to his old ways—at least as far as his legalism is concerned.

It kind of began last year when we were in Ephesus and Antioch, Lystra and Derby. Well, some women in the churches in Asia Mina were kind of jealous of the men getting to do all the preaching. One particular woman named Mi-Shell Balken began preaching all over the region. She was clearly not "under submission" to her husband, as is fittin'. Well, Paul called that guy (her hubby) a total wimp because he simply could not keep her in her place. Paul wrote to the church in Ephesus as a result: **Wives, submit to your husbands as to the Lord. For the husband is head of the wife as Christ is head of the church. Now as the church submits to Christ, so also should wives submit to their husbands in** *everything.* (Ephesians 5: 22-24). Well, Sister Mi-Shell was outraged when the church in Ephesus got that letter from the apostle.

"Who does he think he is?" she exclaimed dramatically. "Why, I was speaking to the Lord personally just last night, and he told me that Paul was wrong and that I was right. And it is my Christian duty to speak out against that religious chauvinist." Many women who follow "Sister Mi-Shell" have also spoken out on her behalf. "If Paul is going to make policy around here," they claimed, "we are going to have to start our own church." And that is where it stands at the moment. TV station KEPH sent a reporter to interview a spokeswoman for Ms. Balken yesterday. Rev. Sheeril Bettinger of the newly-founded "Reformed Church of Jesus Christ of Modern Day Saints" has joined with Mrs. Balken and her husband, Derwin, himself a minister of the Gospel.

"Our new movement has ordained my wife and me, as well as some of our elders, deacons, and choir members," he stated emphatically. "Why should Apostles be the only ones to ordain folks?" The new church has grown exponentially, deviating substantially from the original writings of Paul to the Ephesian Church, which he founded last year during his second missionary journey. "Although we think Paul is all wet that women should keep quiet in church, we agree with the part of his letter stating: **Slaves obey your earthly masters with respect and fear, and with sincerity of heart, just as you would obey Christ.**" (Eph. 6: 5).

Senior religion reporter for KEPH details that a staggering number of slaves have been turning to Christ in recent months since Paul's first visit to Ephesus last March. They have even been seeking the infilling of the Holy Spirit and the signs that follow (namely, the speaking in other tongues as the spirit gives them utterance.) Well, many slaveowners and church leaders have expressed concern that this slave movement could get out of hand, and that slaves may seek freedom as a result. "We simply cannot have slaves challenging the existing order," Rev. Ali Baddah proclaimed. "They are hardly in a position to seek their freedom and independence. Come on, they are slaves. They were born that way (or purchased with good money). And as such, they are *property* pure and simple. There is no provision in the law for them to be freed—even by the most beneficent master. Like, where would they go?"

Back to Timothy . . . From the time of Noah, it is claimed, slavery is a bedrock scriptural principal. Ever since Noah cursed his grandson, Canaan, into slavery for the sin of his father, Ham, we have had slaves and masters. Slaves have always been admonished to obey, be good, and do what they are told. How can they just decide to accept Jesus and be free? Unthinkable. Not only is this move to free slaves unprecedented, but it is dangerous. Consider those stories we are hearing about an actual "slave rebellion" taking place in Southern Italy and Sicily. That wicked and evil slave-leader, Spartacus has led thousands astray. We can expect that very thing if we don't nip this in the bud. Paul also reiterated this very instruction to the folks in Colosse and Galatia. Slaves are property and must obey their earthly masters and owners unswervingly. They will get rewards in Heaven if they are cooperative.

But some new problems have arisen for the churches in Asia Mina. The issue of mistreating slaves has become a Christian question. Many media outlets are calling for a referendum on this issue. Should Christians be allowed to beat their slaves, as is clearly explained in the Holy Scriptures? **"If a man beats a male or female slave with a rod and the slave dies as a direct result, he must be punished, but he is not to be punished if the slave gets up after a day or two, since the slave is his property."** (Exodus 21: 20, 21). The consensus seems to be that slave-beating *is* scriptural. **Jesus said: I have not come to abolish the law, but to fulfill it."** (Matthew 5: 17).

As the Apostle Paul has said, Jesus has come to fulfill the law, and since the law clearly states that it is okay to beat a recalcitrant slave, end of story. Well, not quite. The press all over Asia Mina has been asking: "Yes, but if the slave dies—is actually beaten to death by his master— what should the punishment be? In Exodus 21: 32, we read that the penalty for the death of a slave is **thirty shekels of silver.** (About $240 bucks.) But isn't that kind of steep a price for a mere slave? There have been some hard times around Ephesus, Galatia, and elsewhere like Cappadocia, and the slave trade has taken a severe hit. What should the Christian position be regarding the pricing of slaves these days?

Paul has been adamant that slaves are worth $240 no matter what, as it clearly states in scripture that that is the fair market value. So, what about slaves who want to live a free life in Christ? Should they be allowed to buy their own freedom? Well, this angle has not been much discussed in the press, as it would come down to another scripture that Paul cites frequently revolving around the question of the nationality of the slaves in question. The OT is very firm. If the slave is a Jew, he is to be treated a certain way (that is scriptural), but if the slave (male or female) is a foreigner, each may be bought, sold, or bartered for a different rate.

"**Your male and female slaves are to come from the nations around you; from them you may buy slaves. You may also buy some of the temporary residents living among you and members of their clans born in your country, and they will become your property. You can will them to your children as inherited property and can make them slaves for life, but you must not rule over your fellow Israelites ruthlessly.** "(Leviticus 25: 44). So, since Jews are allowed to own Colossian slaves, and some of those slaves want freedom in order to pursue a healing or teaching ministry for Christ, should not the owners of those slaves free them so they may follow their life callings? And what of those called into a music ministry? As slaves, they could likely become musicians. But who would be entitled to their royalties arising out of the sales of CDs and DVDs? It is a legal question at this point.

And there is the pressing issue of the sale of children—another biblical issue vexing the new churches in Asia Mina. Sister Mi-Shell weighed in: "**If a man sells his daughter as a servant, she is not to go free as men servants do.**" (Ex. 21: 7). Now, the Lord leaves little there for interpretation. "**If a man needs cash for a new cow or a car, he can sell his sons or daughters into servitude. However, the man child is only indentured for seven years, but the girl must remain in permanent service for her entire life.**" Some of the younger Christians in the congregations around Asia Mina are perplexed. How is that fair? "Well, **Jesus came to set us free from the law,**" stated Sister Mi-Shell, once again quoting from Matthew 5: 17. "There is no getting around it."

"It is a good thing that God is calling so many slaves into the ministry, but we have to take into account the economy. Heck, we need those slaves to keep everything afloat financially. What would we all do if we were to just say 'Okay, if you feel God is calling you into a ministry, go ahead, trust the Lord. Go out on your own "on faith" and see what happens.' Hey, you are *slaves* already. God created you that way. It is your lot in life—like being born women, Cretans, or fags. We realize that you can't help that you were born into a subordinate station in life, but don't blame us. God made y'all that way!"

So the controversy rages on in the new churches, as these converts to the faith proliferate. But there is a glimmer of hope. As I spent more time with Paul, and later received personal correspondence from him, he pointed out a fabulous "final solution" for this problem. He calls it the *rapture* of the church. And is it ever a cool fix to the whole issue of Christians owning each other. Basically, his answer for this dilemma is that we won't have to even deal with it much longer. It is moot. Jesus is coming soon, and we are all going to be whisked away out of this world of woe. In the twinkling of an eye, Jesus is going to appear in the clouds and we are going to be transformed. All the saved, sanctified, satisfied born-agains will be called home to Heaven to live with YHWH, Jesus, Mother Mary, and the angels forever and ever. Cool, huh? I am wetting myself with pure anticipation. Hallelujah.

Chapter 36

Meensee (Gabriel's assistant)

The trumpet of the Lord shall sound and time shall be no more.

Blow, Gabe, blow! All of heaven is atwitter. Earth's big surprise party is on tap. It is going to happen at any time. Up here in Heaven (God's home above the sky) we are all getting ready for the rapture. This is such a thrill for us, as it has been pending for centuries down there on Earth. Jesus mentioned that he would return to the planet the next time as a **"thief in the night"** (Matthew 24: 42) . . . unannounced and quickly. He warned everybody to be ever vigilant. Yet, he kind of faked everybody out, delaying his coming far beyond what anybody was expecting. Of course, those of us who live up here were onto his tricks. We knew that mankind would grow weary waiting and let their guard down. Then JC will strike! Yay.

Then Paul wrote a clear warning to the Thessalonians. **According to the Lord's own word, we tell you that we who are still alive, who are left till the coming of the Lord, will certainly not precede those who have fallen asleep.** (I Thessalonians 4: 15). Now we up here knew that Paul actually thought that he would still be alive personally when Jesus would return. Of course, we knew quite well that he would not be. But we just played along, all the time knowing that it was going to be sometime in the 21st C (Earth time) when the Son of God would reappear.

Well, there is this huge theater in the round up here in Heaven where we will all get to watch events as they transpire in the "end times." Lately, we have noticed some of the "Delta" angels working on sprucing the place up—sweeping stale popcorn from under the seats and doing general cleaning in anticipation of the great show ahead when Jesus descends on a cloud and calls his people home. We are looking forward to greeting them and welcoming them to their temporary home here in the heavenly realm with us, the "heavenly host." And good hosts we hope to be. This is *our* permanent home, but the Christians down there on Earth are actually going to get their *own* permanent home later after the Great Tribulation. But I will let the Gatekeeper tell you about that later. This is my assignment—to explain the rapture to you. So I don't want to steal his thunder (and lightning and hail) :-) Down on Earth, men and women are living their lives of sin and debauchery as if nothing is up. Well, we are sitting up here looking down through the hole in the ozone layer from the *Heavenly Theater in the Sky*. Oh, look, some of the performers are already tuning up their instruments and some of the "choirs of angels" are practicing their scales. I am so excited.

Oh, yes, back to Paul: **For the Lord himself will come down from heaven, with a loud command, with the voice of the archangel and with the trumpet call of God.** (I Thes. 4: 16). That's referring to my boss, Gabriel, the leader of the band. We do have a cool Gospel band up here in heaven, and get a lot of practice praising God in the highest and playing accompaniment for the many choirs from around the Heavens and the Earth. Any time a new group gets together to enter the Holy of Holies, the brass section is called upon to really get the place to rocking for our great leader, YHWH, the Almighty. Yea! Praise his holy name forever . . . and I do mean *forever*!

Of course, we have a woodwind section as well, but they don't get as much attention as the brass. I mean, come on. Have you ever heard a grand proclamation like: "And the oboe of the Lord shall sound?" Just doesn't have the same pizzazz does it? But there will be a command! Who will shout this command? And what will it be? None of us knows for sure, but it is assumed that it will be Michael, another archangel who was with the Father from the beginning of the Universe.

Anyway, **and the dead in Christ shall rise first.** (I Thes. 4: 16). This has been kind of weird for us up here, because we have never understood what this means. Well, the dead in Christ have been rising after their mortal earthly deaths for centuries, and have gradually filtered up here through the hole in the ozone layer since Jesus led the way back in 33 CE or so (Earth time). We really don't have a concept of time like y'all down on Earth do. We mostly just while away our "time" here based on a 10,000 year time frame. But that is just an estimate, as every moment, minute, day, and year on Earth has no clock up here. Based on that famous heavenly-inspired tune: *When we've been there 10,000 bright* *shining as the sun . . . We've no less days to sing God's praise than when we first begun.* (Way bad grammar, huh?) But, anyway, up to now if a Christian dies in the Lord, he gets to stick around the Earth long enough to watch his own funeral—to make sure that it is carried out according to his or her wishes.

Then, they gradually float up through the atmosphere and the stratosphere and the ionosphere. Then they glide silently up through the ozone layer and arrive here in Heaven. We are all singing—as we do incessantly. So when a newcomer arrives, he is greeted with Christ-centered music. They often think we are singing especially for them in welcome, but they learn pretty quickly that we are always singing praises anyway, so they need to learn the words quickly. Of course, most English-speaking folks just assume we sit around up here singing in English. But actually we sing mostly in Chinese because it will take eternity to learn it. :-) A little heavenly humor there.

But the actual rapture is going to be way different and far more exciting than the miscellaneous souls drifting up as they die. This is going to be a mass migration of millions of souls from America, Europe, and the "uttermost parts" all jamming their way through the ozone hole at the same time. It is going to be a blast as it will be such a welcome relief from our endless praising which most of us have long tired of tens of thousands of years ago.

So once the trumpet of the Lord sounds, all the "dead in Christ" will rise first (although most are here already). Those that will be raptured at that time are a few odd fellows from a few denominations that believe in "soul sleep." They don't believe that to be dead in Christ is to be alive with him (and all of us) in Heaven shortly after "passing on." So they hang out in Sheol, the place of the departed waiting. But better late than never—they will all make it up here finally by and by. The rest of the *living* Christians will hear the trumpet and will begin rising bodily into the air to meet the Lord in the clouds. As the Apostle wrote: **After that, we who are alive and are left will be caught up with them in the clouds to meet the Lord in the air. And so we will be with the Lord forever.** (I Thes. 4: 17). Doesn't that just make you quiver in pure anticipation? And there is more. We up here are not quite sure how that's going to happen, as some of the dead-in-Christ don't have any earthly bodies to resurrect. Some died in battle and were blown limb-from-limb, and some lost their lives and bodies in various plane crashes or terrorist bombings, etc. God hasn't even told us angels how he plans to reconstruct the bodies of believers who died in explosions or were eaten by sharks and have no bodies left. Of course, that will be revealed to us when this all happens in the 21st C. (Earth time). I can't wait for that.

And we are a bit unclear about the holy "glorified" bodies that they are going to wear when they get up here with us. Of course, we assume that glorified means perfect. Certain groups on Earth assume that everyone will just enter through the ozone hole and that their old, infirm, or crippled bodies will transform themselves en route. So everybody will have a replica of a twenty-year-old earth-body "without spot or wrinkle" when they get here. No one up here is quite sure about that either. Like, is a dead Christian six-year-old going to get a twenty-year-old perfect bod too? Or will he have to be a child for all eternity, sort of like a child vampire that never ages? And what of the elderly who once had great physiques? Will they get their younger body back? And will their relatives recognize them? Of course, all of that is moot, as the Lord will make it all good no matter what.

Once the neophytes get the drift that none of that matters they are not going to be sitting up here fellowshipping with their long dead relatives, but, rather, worshiping nonstop. There will be no time for frivolous fraternizing. And in addition to families, there are the children killed or dead of disease before reaching the "age of accountability" which Earthlings don't fathom either. They are all so wrapped up in just getting here themselves that they often fail to take into account the fates of babies who die young or even in childbirth who will all get to be up here too as they are blessed with a "childlike" faith all their own. They got to come up here very early on, not having to spin and toil on Earth, earn a living, pay the rent, or deal with nasty neighbors or bosses. They live in a kind of blissful grace.

All children at birth, they say, have a "potential" to sin because they were all born under "Adamic Sin" which dooms them to death and Hell the minute they come out of the womb. Well, years ago the various religious groups down on Earth petitioned the Almighty to make a "new rule" allowing infants and toddlers free access into Heaven to join with us angels and the cherubim and seraphim and the putti. Who, you ask, are the putti? Well, those are the souls of the *really* little Earthlings who died in childbirth or abortion. They are *so* special. Aren't they sweet? Of course, they don't know the words to the songs of praise that we all sing endlessly and forever. They just sort of flutter around the mercy seat of Christ, humming along with the saints and us angels (but definitely in the spirit). God loves them, but I find their constant buzzing around Heaven like flies rather annoying . . . and distracting to those of us who actually can carry a tune and know the lyrics.

But, as I told you, the newly incoming Christians' stay here is going to be temporary, as all the humans that were redeemed by the blood of the lamb will be sooner or later moved to their permanent home: a place called *The City Built Foursquare.* And that is really cool. We angels are not sure if we are going to be allowed to visit there, as it is designated for homo sapiens only. They will get to go there at some point after the *Great Tribulation,* which is coming on Earth right after they all get up here and are settled in. But it is not my place to tell you about those things myself. There are others coming who will explain all that soon after the rapture.

So I will take my leave and get back to my praising. Hallelujah, hallelujah, hallelujah! Ten thousand more years coming up. Sigh. Meanwhile, back down on Earth, life without Christians is bleak indeed. Whatever is it going to be like on that sinful planet without Christ's ambassadors telling everybody how to live exemplary lives as *they* do? Well, it ain't going to be fun or easy!

Chapter 37

Pretrib (John's scribe)

Shipwrecked with John on Patmos, he found the magic mushrooms!

Wow, this is strange. Do I ever have a story to tell you! My name is Pretrib and I was traveling some time ago with the Apostle John of Gospel fame. He also wrote some epistles here and there in his journeys. But what he wrote as his last *magnum opus,* entitled *The Revelation,* was too weird for words. He and I got exiled together on an island in the Mediterranean Sea. He was in a total state of distress, not knowing what to do with himself. I, too, felt that our days were numbered, as Patmos was less than welcoming. We did find water and some grubby plants and shrubs and things to nosh on. But, while I was out foraging for chow, I discovered something that made both of us forget all our worries—forget all our cares. I discovered the magic mushrooms, which we had for dinner. They were quite tasty and we really enjoyed them. After a while the fun started :-)

John began telling me the most wild and wacky story I had ever heard. He began going on and on in his "preacher voice," speaking of things to come when the world ends. I immediately began taking dictation, as he was too blitzed to write a word. I had given him the lion's share of the shrooms. (After all, he is an Apostle and I was—at the time—just a traveling partner and part-time scribe.) I knew right away that God was in it, because he miraculously provided a package of Bic pens, several yellow legal pads, and a convenient scroll, which I opened and began writing on . . . and we were off! John made it clear that he was exercising one of the *gifts of the spirit* given back in Jerusalem at Pentecost. He was prophesying! I knew this was going to be good.

John began: **Woe woe woe to the inhabitants of the earth.** (Revelation 8: 13). Oh, I knew this was going to be a horror story. But the cool part is that us Christians are going to be exempt from all the shit that is going to unfold. See, we will not be on Earth by the time this prophesy begins to take place. In fact, we who believe will be raptured up into Heaven to be with Jesus and the angels before this—the Great Tribulation—is to start. That's how I got my name, Pretrib, as I fully intend to be raptured right before the tribulation (therefore, pre-trib—get it?). Cool, huh? So, John said in a loud voice:

On the Lord's day I was in the spirit (or in his cups), **and I heard behind me a voice like a trumpet, which said: "Write on a scroll what you see and send it to the seven churches . . . Write what you have seen, what is now and what will take place later."** (Rev. 1: 10,11,19). Well, I was listening to the dictation, but John wasn't getting it quite right. Assuming I couldn't hear what the voice was saying, I noticed right away that he wasn't getting things straight. So I began to just ignore him now and then, writing down more accurately what we were hearing from on high. Come on—he's an old guy and his hearing isn't what it used to be. And that voice *like a trumpet* was annoying.

I looked before me and there was a door standing open in heaven. And a voice said: "Come up here, and I will show you what must take place after this." At once I was in the spirit, and there before me was a throne in heaven with someone sitting on it. (Rev. 4: 1,2). **In the center around the throne, were four living creatures, and they were covered with eyes, in front and in back. The first living creature was like a lion, the second was like an ox, the third had a face like a man, the fourth was like a flying eagle. Each of the four living creatures had six wings and was covered with eyes all around, even under his wings!** (Rev. 4: 6,7,8). Well, the mushrooms were really kicking in at this point. John was somewhere out there beyond the ozone layer in Heaven. Of course, he wasn't really there physically, as I could see him plainly there on Patmos, ranting and raving like a lunatic.

Then I saw in the right hand of him who sat on the throne a scroll with writing on both sides and sealed with seven seals. Then I saw a lamb looking as if it had been slain, standing in the center of the throne, encircled by four living creatures and elders. He had seven horns and seven eyes, which are the seven spirits of God sent out into all the earth. (Rev. 5: 1-6). Whew. Okay, let me skip ahead a bit. So the lamb opens the scroll. That is important, but we'll get back to that later.

Then John envisioned four horsemen on four horses, each of a different color. The first horse was white, and the rider rode onto the scene as a conqueror. The second, a fiery red one, carried a rider who had the power to take away peace on Earth and to make men slay each other. At this point I was screaming for John to slow down and explain. He was ranting, and I just couldn't keep up. Oh, for a Dictaphone!

I was shouting at the Apostle, "What's the big deal with that? There has never been any peace on the planet, and men have been slaying one another since Cain killed Abel. So why include this in your vision?" But he didn't hear me, or was ignoring me in his excitement. So he went on about the third horse, a black one whose rider carried scales in his hand. Symbolizing justice, I suppose. And the fourth horse (a pale steed) emerged. Its rider was named *Death,* and Hades was following close behind them. I thought this was supposed to be a prophesy, a vision of the future. So how did Hades, the Greek god of the underworld, get into the act? But John just kept going and I never got a suitable answer to that question. **They were given power over a fourth of the earth to kill with the sword famine and plague, and by the wild beasts of the earth.** (Rev. 6: 8). John was frothing at the mouth at this point, but the hits just kept on comin'. "Why only a quarter of the Earth?" I cried out. "And which fourth?" But the words continued to pour forth from his trembling lips.

There was a great earthquake. The sun turned black like sackcloth made of goat hair, and the whole moon turned to blood, and the stars in the sky fell to earth. (Rev. 6: 13). The moon turned to blood? Oh, come on, John, I thought. Those mushrooms were really zonking him at that point. But he just kept it up. **Then the kings of the earth, the princes, the generals, the rich, the mighty, and every slave and every free man hid in caves and in rocks in the mountains. They called to the mountains and rocks, "Fall on us and hide us from the wrath of the Lamb!"** (Rev. 6: 12-16). "OMG," I wailed, "Who is this lamb anyway, and why is he so pissed off?" John heard that question, and his whole countenance changed. He stopped prophesying, foaming, and frothing. He looked me in the eye as if he was in a Greek play, and answered my question (albeit in a rather huffy and condescending way). "The lamb is Jesus, you dummy. The Lamb of God. Duh. Come on, get with the program. You *do* remember Jesus don't you? Well, he is ticked-off at mankind for failing to recognize him adequately when he came the first time as the humble carpenter from Galilee." Then he paused.

"Now he is coming back as the righteous avenger and is unleashing the horsemen and the attendant plagues and earthquakes and astronomical mayhem that they bring with them." And then he went back into his trance and began nattering on again . . . this time about more about hail and fire mixed with blood. "How can blood be mixed with fire?" I shouted, but he was ignoring me again. He was fixated on all this destruction. **A third of the earth was burned up, a third of the trees were burned up, and all the green grass was burned up.** (Rev. 8: 6,7). Give me a break. How can a third of the Earth be burned up? Which third? Come on, John, I thought. Isn't your math off a bit? But he went on and on again about fire, blood, and burning stuff.

A third of the seas turned to blood, a third of the living creatures in the sea died and a third of the ships were destroyed. A great star, blazing like a torch, fell from the sky on a third of the rivers and on springs of water. And a third of the sun was struck, and a third of the moon (which had already been turned to blood) **and a third of the stars, so a third of them turned black.** "Hmmm . . . But wait, John," I lamented, "You just said that all the stars had fallen to Earth already." (Rev. 6: 13). **A third of the day was without sunlight, and a third of the night.** (Rev. 8: 12). "Isn't the whole night without sunlight anyway?" I asked lamely. But he went on to another subject altogether at that point.

He shuddered as he railed on about the appearance of locust as big as horses that sting like scorpions. And they stung the remaining earthlings for five months. Why not six? But weirdly enough, they were not allowed to sting those who had the mark of God on their foreheads. What? What mark of God? Who at this point would have such a mark, and where would they get it? All those folks went up in the rapture some time ago, remember? But he was ignoring me again.

A third of mankind was then killed by three plagues: one of fire, one of smoke, and one of sulfur. OMG, I thought, what a shitty mess! Why is Jesus doing all this to mankind? Why has he gotten so mean lately? Then, as if John was reading my mind, he continued: **The rest of mankind that were not killed by these plagues still did not repent of the works of their hands; they did not stop worshiping demons, and idols of gold, silver, bronze, stone and wood—idols that cannot see, hear or walk!** (Rev. 9: 20). Oh, for pity's sake, I mused. Why is God still so hung up on those idols that cannot speak, hear, or talk? For God's sake, he created the whole Universe, didn't he? Like, why is he still so fixated on statuary or totem poles? Well, he just is. He never liked them.

But could things get worse? Oh sure. Then enters "the Beast," and we're all supposed to be scared of him. John continued: **He forced everyone, small and great, rich and poor, free and slave, to receive a mark on his right hand or on his forehead, so that no one could buy or sell, unless he had the mark, which is the name of the beast or the number of his name. This calls for wisdom. If anyone has insight, let him calculate the number of the beast, for it is man's number. His number is 666.** (Rev. 13: 16-18). Be afraid. Be *very* afraid.

"Now, hold on a minute!" I exclaimed in exasperation. "After all these plagues, firebombings of sulfur, hailstorms, and blood; the annihilation of the entire agricultural base; the darkening of the sun and moon; and millions of stars impacting on Earth . . . what—pray tell—would there be left to buy or sell anyway?"

Chapter 38

Putazona and Puzzuola

*The story of two strong women as told by a
couple of friendly demons from Hell*

Hello everybody, hello. Hell is a place where you are bound to go! It is a literal place where most of y'all are going to end up, so you should probably get used to dealing with that fact. I am Little Diomede. And my elder brother, Big Diomede, and I are demons serving our cool master, Satan. This is an interesting story, and it involves two of the few women of any measure that you are likely to read about in God's book, the Holy Bible. But at least they get a mention, albeit a rather negative one.

It all started like this: **A great and wondrous sign appeared in the sky. A woman clothed with the sun, with the moon under her feet and a crown of twelve stars on her head. She was pregnant and cried out in pain as she was about to give birth. Then another sign appeared in heaven: an enormous red dragon with seven heads and ten horns and seven crowns on his heads. His tail swept a third of the stars out of the sky and flung them down to Earth.** (Revelation 12: 1-4). Like how many stars could could possibly be left at this point? Anyway, finally she gave birth and God snatched the baby (a male child, of course) up to his throne in Heaven. Meanwhile, the woman, named Puzzuola, ran full-tilt out into the desert (what desert?) for 1,260 days. What's that got to do with the story, you ask? Beats me. But anyway with the male child now in Heaven, war ensues. (In Heaven, that is!)

Are you following this? Well, keep trying. Anyway, the big battle in Heaven had something to do with the dragon, who ostensibly has something to do with our master, Satan, who was "flung down" to Earth. It has also been claimed that we of his denomination were likewise unceremoniously kicked out of Heaven by YHWH and the rest of the heavenly host. Now, I have to mention that we all left *voluntarily.* Satan, or Lucifer as he is sometimes called, was the most beautiful of all the angels, and was always preening and careening around Heaven in a most un-angelic fashion. He was way too cool for that dreary place where there was nothing to do but sing praise to Yahweh constantly and incessantly. What a drag! So when the big battle between God and Satan took place, we all "fell to Earth" *on purpose.* We did have a choice. We could stay and worship the big daddy in the sky for 10,000 Earth-years at a time, or follow Lucifer. Big Diomede and I jumped at the chance and leaped right out of Heaven through the hole in the ozone layer and landed down here on Earth, which is now going to be our domain for seven years during the *Great Tribulation.* The Earth by this time is totally fucked up. But who did the fucking? Not Satan or us. NO, it was God himself who sent all the plagues, floods, hailstorms, and the locusts as big as horses that sting like scorpions for five months.

Anyway, moving right along: We couldn't catch the woman in the desert, so Lucifer told us that we were going to make war on her *other* offspring instead. So we looked for them, but were out of luck as we couldn't find them either. Sigh. So we got to run wild all over the Earth. But that wasn't as fun as it sounds, as the whole planet was totally trashed by all those stars falling to Earth right after the rapture. All those potholes were very annoying. So Satan got into a disguise and dove into the ocean. Then . . . are you holding your breath?

And I saw a beast coming out of the sea. He had ten horns and seven heads, with ten crowns on his horns, and on each head was a blasphemous name. The beast resembled a leopard, but had feet like those of a bear and a mouth like that of a lion. (Rev. 13: 1,2). Well, the Earthlings were totally freaked. I commented to my big bro, "Cool costume, huh? Ol' Satan really fooled them with that beast outfit. LOL." But it scared them all shitless. So they worshiped him, saying: **Who is like the beast? Who can make war against him?** (Rev. 13: 4). Well, I thought, these Earthlings sure are dumb. Why would they worship such a hideous monster? We all knew it was our lord, Lucifer, who really is the most beautiful angel of all. So why the hell put on that hokey costume? I mean, the heads and horns and crowns don't even match (in number)! But we knew he had a plan, so we just went with it.

Then the beast began doing nifty tricks to impress the Earthlings who were totally wowed. So they worshiped him all the more. What a bunch of dummies! Then he suggested that they all take a mark on their right hands and foreheads! That sounded easy enough. Aha, but *we* saw what he was up to. **So that no one could buy or sell unless he had the mark, which is the name of the beast or the number of his name. This calls for wisdom. If anyone has insight, let him calculate the number of the beast, for it is man's number. His number is 666!** (Rev. 13: 17,18).

OMG! That is so spooky, huh? Even my big brother and I were scared. What could be more scary than a number? I hate numbers. Hell, even calendars scare me. . . . all those numbers. But the Earthlings were genuinely freaked out, so they took the mark in droves. Why would they do that? Apparently, they were scared about not being able to buy or sell stuff. Gawd are they ever dumb! The Earth had already been firebombed and the seas and rivers all turned to blood. A third of the ships had been sunk, so worldwide shipping was rather totally interrupted. A third of all the trees and plants and *all* the grass had already been burned up, so with that, the entire world economy was rendered inoperative for sure. So, what would there be to buy or sell? Not much. All the computers were down along with the Internet. Nothing was functioning. So what's the big freakout about the mark of the beast? Well, apparently, there were places on the planet "in the East" where things weren't so bad. Aha. There is more to the story! Enter Putazona, the Great Whore of the Earth. And was she ever a bitch!

She rode in from the desert on the beast with all those heads and horns (really Satan—wink, wink). **The woman was dressed in purple and scarlet.** OMG, that should have been a dead giveaway. What a totally hideous color combination! A total fashion victim, she was also **glittering with gold, precious stones and pearls. She held a golden cup in her hand, filled with abominable things.** Too bad we are never informed what those abominable things actually are. Damn, I wanted to know too.

She was drunk with the blood of the saints, the blood of those who bore testimony to Jesus. (Rev. 18: 4-6). "Oops, hold it right there," I said emphatically, "WTF? *What* saints? Weren't they all raptured in the last chapter? Aren't they up there in Himmel right now watching all this mayhem taking place down here on Earth? Where the hell did she get *their* blood from?" **This calls for a mind with wisdom. My god, I'll say! The seven heads are seven hills on which the woman sits. They are also seven kings.** (Rev. 18: 9). Now, these kings are kind of like the only semblance of government left on the planet at this time . . . and they are all beholden to Putazona, the great whore. They are fucking with her (symbolically, that is), and it is all quite a menage-a-mess. **The Kings of the Earth committed adultery with her, and the merchants of the Earth grew rich from her excessive luxuries. But her doom is sealed. She will be consumed by fire, for mighty is the Lord God who judges her.** (Rev. 18: 3,8). Well, just when the kings and merchants were establishing some order in a post-Christian world, a final round of plagues is announced: **I saw in heaven another great and marvelous sign: seven angels with the seven last plagues—last, because with them God's wrath is completed.** (Rev. 15: 1). Finally! **Go, pour out the seven bowls of God's wrath on the Earth."** (Rev. 16: 2).

Seven more angels appear, and each was carrying a bowl. The first angel pours out a bowl full of sores and other rashes and disgusting skin diseases. Yuk. The second angel dumps his bowl of divine sewage into the ocean and turns the *whole* thing into blood (unlike before when only a *third* of the ocean was polluted beyond measure). Then the third angel made the scene with its bowl of blood, contaminating all the *rivers* of the world. Then . . . **The fourth poured out its bowl on the sun, which scorched all the remaining peoples on Earth.** (Rev. 16: 4). Wow, I thought, what now? That fourth angel finished all mankind off by causing what is left of the blackened sun to toast every last soul left on Earth. It clearly says that *all* the remaining people on the entire planet were scorched. And that wasn't just second degree sunburns either. They were cremated for sure. And that would obviously take out all the animals as well, huh? "So what's next after that?" I asked Big Dio, "Now that all animal life on Earth has been toasted, what's left for the other angels to do to this lifeless rock anyway?" No need to guess . . .

The sixth angel poured out his bowl on the great river Euphrates, and its water was dried up. (Don't they mean *blood?* . . . as the third angel already turned all the rivers on Earth to blood, didn't it?) . . . **to prepare the way for the kings of the East.** (Rev. 16: 12). Oh, I see. Sort of. Where are these guys coming from, and they are kings of what? Wasn't the whole of mankind scorched by the fourth angel already? Come on, I thought, get your chronology right. I mean, if these angels were sent down here to finish off obliterating the Earth, at least they could do so in an organized way . . . in a logical fashion.

Anyway, what's the story about these kings of the East? Somehow they managed to escape the sun-scorching of the rest of the Earth—possibly with a super high sunblock. But as we waited for an explanation, **Then I** saw three evil spirits that looked like frogs; they came out of the mouth of the dragon, out of the mouth of the beast. They are the spirits of demons performing miraculous signs, and they go out to the kings of the whole world, to gather them for the battle on the great day of God Almighty. (Rev. 16: 13,14).

"Hey, gang, this is fucked!" Big Diomede shouted to the rest of us *fallen* angels, "How can there (all of a sudden) not only be kings of the East still standing, but now kings from all over the world?" He was obviously pissed off. "What the hell is this big battle coming up on the great day of God Almighty?" I looked at him blankly. "Beats me," I said lamely.

Then a booming voice from Heaven shook the scorched Earth, saying: "It's the announcement of the super-duper upcoming battle at Har Meggido, you idiots! Weren't you paying attention at all when you were up here in Heaven with the heavenly host and Moi? We talked about it all the time. It is when all the remaining peoples of the Earth are going to fight the cataclysmic battle of all time and eternity. You know, we have referred to it as the 'Battle of Armageddon' . . . gawd are you guys ever stupid. I am glad I kicked y'all out of Heaven. You were not only not paying attention in prophecy class, but you were faking singing praise to Moi as well. I can always tell when you really don't have your hearts in it. And I hope you enjoy your new life in the lake of fire with your la-la wa-wa master, Satan . . . that creep." YHWH was mad.

"But you already toasted the Earth, and the fourth angel poured out his bowl on the sun and it scorched all the people on Earth!" we noted in bewilderment. "Like, who is going to fight that battle that you are so keen on provoking?" We were genuinely mystified.

"Hmmm," the Deity mumbled to himself—but we could hear.

"If there are no people left on the planet (nor horses or other livestock), who, pray tell, is actually going to fight the war? Looks to us like you are just moving phantom armies around your war map up there in the sky," I snickered under my breath.

But he heard me and retorted: "Well, I have creative powers! If I want a battle, I can just speak the armies into existence. So there." Yeah, I knew he could do that.

"But you've already killed everybody (again, like in the flood)."

"Oh, that. I do remember that," he said wistfully. "That was sure fun. I loved drowning all those wicked assholes . . . and all the animals too." He was smiling, we were sure—even though we couldn't see him in all his glory. (We weren't allowed to look upon him, as we were *fallen* angels, you know).

"Well, fuck it then. I officially call off the Battle of Armageddon," he said sadly. "It appears that there will be no one left to fight it." So there we were, standing alone in a dark, bleak dead world with no sunlight or plant life or humans left in sight.

"So what are we supposed to do now?" we asked in bewilderment. We sure didn't want to stay here.

"How about you admit you were wrong for leaving Heaven so capriciously? If you promise to be good and worship me only forever and forever, maybe I will forgive you and take you back unto me :-)"

"Or you can come live with me in the Lake of Fire," a smooth voice crooned from out of the darkness. It was Satan. "I am done playing these silly games here on Earth. Let's blow this popstand and take a dip in the lake. The fire's fine. All the dead Earthlings are down there already, so you are welcome to join us. We can skinny dip. :-)

"Or you can choose to come back up here and be angels again and praise me endlessly," God promised.

Big Dio and I looked at each other for a moment and immediately took off our angel robes and fake wings. There, standing buck-naked as the Earth opened up, Big Dio shouted to me, "Last one in is a rotten egg!"

Chapter 39

Virgil (Still in Hell)

Dante's vision of the inferno revisited

Since the ancient poets Virgil and Dante Alighieri visited Hell together in 1300 CE, no *living* human being has been allowed in. But that is about to change. Time to get ready for a big influx of visitors and full-time residents. After the rapture is over, the realms of Heaven and Hell will be forever changed. Well, after the rapture and all the born-agains were gone, the Earth was, like, totally trashed by God, as he sent plague after plague and all manner of evil onto the planet. Most of the inhabitants of the place died and had to wait for the judgment. **And I saw a great white throne, and him that sat on it, from whose face the earth and the heaven fled away; and there was found no place for them. And I saw the dead, small and great, stand before God; and the books were opened; and another book was opened, which is the book of life; and the dead were judged out of those things which were written in the books, according to their works. And the sea gave up the dead which were in it; and death and hell delivered up the dead which were in them; and they were judged every man according to their works. And death and hell were cast into the lake of fire. This is the second death. And whosoever was not found written in the book of life was cast into the lake of fire.** (Revelation 20: 11-16).

"Well," explained the poet, Virgil, "see, I was born in 70 BCE (before Christ), so I wasn't really familiar with all of this condemnation and I had no real idea about the Christian Hell and judgment. When my friend Dante arrived years later and we took a visit to Hell, we learned a lot. That Jewish god was one mean mother. He was way worse than any of the Greek gods up in Olympus, and the Roman gods were way kinder and gentler than YHWH. He really was a maniacal egomaniac. He insisted that no one is allowed to worship any god but him. Years ago I was aware of the Jews, but they were to me a small, weird tribal people who had been for years under Greek—and later Roman—control. They were always at odds with our occupying forces. I mean, it really was for their own good. But long after my death in 21 BCE, I was shuffled off to Limbo, a cool place on the perimeters of the Christian God's special creation, the dreaded Lake of Fire. Those in Limbo had not been condemned to a place in the lake yet, as Christ had not yet been born. So, when we all died back then, we either went to Limbo or Hades, called Sheol by the Jews. We have been waiting here for centuries, anticipating the end of the Earth when Yahweh blows the place up and brings about the final Judgement. Guys like me who lived before Christ are all going to be judged, of course, and just not knowing about an unborn savior will be no excuse. So some day after the thousand years reign of Christ on a post-apocalyptic planet, we are all going to be judged and sentenced to spending eternity in the lake, aka, Hell or the "Inferno."

Dante was down here doing research for his upcoming book entitled *The Divine Comedy*. I understand it was a real hit, and I was glad that I could show him around this place. Now I have been in Limbo for centuries and enjoy it very much. It isn't bad at all. All sorts of cool artists, writers and poets hang out together here. The fellowship is great. Dante explained to me that after Christ was born, died and went back up into Heaven, an organization called "the church" took over the Roman Empire. It sounded dreadful to me. Dante was writing all about it, so I really appreciated the update of what was happening back on Earth during what he called the "Dark Ages," a time when the new religion, the Christian faith, would take over the western world.

It sounded hopelessly dreary to me. The Roman emperors were gradually replaced by rulers called popes. Of course, according to Dante, they were just as evil, wicked and corrupt as the emperors of old. Anyway, they ran the world for years while we all waited in Limbo for the final judgment when Jesus would send all of the non-Christians to Hell. To tell you the truth, last time I heard rumors of what was going on up topside on Earth, the rapture had taken place, all the Christians were up with Christ in Himmel, and the Earth was going through a worse than awful event called the Great Tribulation. So glad we down here were avoiding all of that. It sounded dreadful to me. We tend to lose track of Earth time here, as there is really no need to pay it much mind. But now and again we hear from some of the former inhabitants of Heaven called "Fallen Angels," who rebelled against the Jewish sky god and were "cast down" into the Lake of Fire with their leader, Lucifer. I have met him once or twice when he passed through Limbo. Nice guy. Very polite, thoughtful and quite beautiful in countenance. I can see why his minions followed him down here voluntarily. The only thing to do up in Heaven is praise YHWH all the time, forever and forever. So dull, that. So, as time passed, and the end of the earthly reign of Jesus (called the Millennium) was at hand, the great judgment was nigh.

Well, we knew big stuff was happening up on Earth, as the demons who could come and go to the place kept us informed. Their jobs were to scare the wits out of Earthlings, and to talk them out of wanting to worship Yahweh and Jesus. Kind of a dumb job, huh? But they did get a lot of travel miles out of the deal. The demons weren't as spooky as the Medieval church artists depicted them. That was all made up—kind of like Dante's story that he shared with me during his time writing it. I was sort of serving as a resource person for his writing, and my taking him on our tour of Hell was most enlightening to the both of us. Anyway, the demons were allowed to come and go up to what was left of the planet after the tribulation. Their reports were sad. All the stars had fallen to Earth, so the sky was totally black. The sun was gone, and the moon had turned to blood. God did all that. I wasn't particularly interested in going back up to the planet for a look-see, but maybe some day.

Whether we are in Limbo, Sheol or Hades, or just stuck buried back on Earth, all of us are going to have to finally face judgment sooner or later. We all know that we are condemned already, as only the born-agains get to live in the new place that God has created for his chosen Earthlings. It all seems so pointless to me, as I have no desire to spend eternity in the Christian heaven, or worse, the *City Built Foursquare*. What a drag place! Hell is fine with me. Limbo was nice while it lasted, but all my friends here are getting ready for the call to leave here and go up for our "show trial" in the sky. Since most of us never even had heard of Jesus before we died, ain't no way we could have trusted him for salvation, could we?

So, when the roll is called up yonder, we won't be there, will we? But that's okay, I guess. We were just predestined to spend eternity in Hell. Of course, in Heaven, there will be rewards for good behavior on Earth. But Yahweh really never figured out a way to quantify punishments in a similar way. Looks like we are all going to be called to take our turn before the Great White Throne, get condemned and end up back here anyway. Pointless, huh? Nevertheless, I have noticed that the judgments must have started already up there, as so many newcomers keep showing up. They are fun to talk to, as they lived long after the church age and through all manner of new things, which they call "modernity." I have noticed that the Lake of Fire has many lagoons radiating out in various directions, and artists and poets like me (and writers) tend to hang together as we have always done in Limbo. I met a real cool guy named Mark Twain recently. He had us all in stitches. There are some other writers and painters who lived centuries after my death. They have such interesting stories to tell. I met a guy named Thomas Jefferson some time ago when he first arrived. He was looking for me, as he had read my stuff in the 18th Century. I liked a lot of the folks from the 20th C. as well. They talk of flying to the moon and horseless vehicles that go very fast. I wonder if I would have rather lived during later times. But, it all sounds so strange and scary to me. Maybe not. But it is fun just hanging in our little lagoon and talking philosophy and comparative religions. I'm not sure how rewarding this will be eons from now, but for the moment it is better than the alternative. Heaven.

I was recently informed that my name has come up and that I will be summoned to stand before the Jewish sky god to hear my sentence. Presumably at that time I will at lease get a short glimpse into an eternity that I will never share. I am looking forward to the process, but since the outcome is pre-ordained, it isn't even going to be a surprise. Meanwhile the Lake of Fire is filling up with all manner of new souls from places I had only vaguely heard of like China, India and Japan. Well, like us who were born pre-Christ, they are all doomed to be in Hell here with us as well. I am also a bit shocked at all the babies and young people from all over the planet who died before they could "Choose Christ." Well, I do feel kind of sorry for them. Most never got much of a chance on Earth to live, love and be loved in their short lives. But rules are rules. They are all down here swimming around in the lake with the rest of us.

Oh, wait, I think I just heard my name called! "Publius Vergilius Maro! Come forth and be judged!" Oooh, this is it. Time to stand and learn my destiny in Hell. So, I call out to all my friends old and new, "I'll be back!" See you on the flip-flop.

Chapter 40

The Gatekeeper (Papers, please)

The guy in charge of who can enter the New Jerusalem,
the City Built Foursquare

I've got a mansion just over the hilltop in that bright land where we will never grow old. And somewhere yonder, we'll never more wander, but walk on streets of purest gold! Hallelujah :-) Hello, my name is The Gatekeeper and I live in the holy city, the "New Jerusalem," aka: The City Built Foursquare. I am also called the *Seventh Angel* model Nr. 007. And I was the one who gave John his first vision of this place. And what a totally groovy place it is! Entrance to the city is severely restricted, and my job is to make sure than only worthy souls can enter it.

When the Apostle John first envisaged this place during his sojourn on the island of Patmos years ago, he spoke with another angel who was responsible for laying out the measurements of the city of God, the New Jerusalem, where only the righteous will live forever. **The angel who spoke with me had a golden measuring rod to measure the city and its gates and its walls. The city lies foursquare, with its width the same as its length. And he measured the city with the rod, and all its dimensions were equal—twelve thousand stadia (cubits) in length and width and height. And he measured its wall to be one hundred four cubits, by the human measure the angel was using.** (Revelation 21: 15-17). Quick update for you of the 21st C. who are reading this: The measurements of the holy city are: 1400 miles (2,200 km.) cubed and the walls are 200 feet (65 m.) thick. Now that's thick!

My job is to check the papers—the credentials if you will—of all those seeking entry into the city. They have already been judged worthy of this wonderful place with all its glitz and glory. They are all born again

Evangelical *Protestant* Christians from the late great planet Earth. They have been through a lot in the past few years, and they are the only Earthlings allowed into this holy city of God, the giant cube floating in the starless sky. There was no longer a need for stars, which all plummeted to Earth during the immediate postrapture period when God poured out his wrath on the planet for rejecting Jesus, his boy, the Lamb of God. Likewise, the sun and moon had been evaporated, as there was no longer need for them to give light on Earth for the plants and trees and shrubs and things needing photosynthesis. There was no need any longer for those artificial lights in the sky. The glory of God the Almighty will henceforth provide all the light that the Universe will need forever.

Now, Heaven, the realm of angels, cherubim and seraphim and all the rest of the heavenly host, will still be out there surrounding the mercy seat of the Lord as always. But the redeemed by the blood of the lamb folks will get their *own* cool place to spend eternity—in the big cube. Let me tell you more about it! It is so marvie-poo! I said to John (in his mushroom vision): **"Come, I will show you the bride, the wife of the lamb."** Then I carried him (in the spirit) to a mountain great and high. And I showed him the Holy City, the New Jerusalem . . . **coming down out of heaven from God. It shone with the glory of God, and its brilliance was like that of a very precious jewel, like a jasper, clear as a crystal.** (Rev. 21: 9-11). I told you it was groovy, huh?

It had a great high wall with twelve gates, and with twelve angels at the gates. On the gates were written the names of the twelve tribes of Israel. (And you know how important that is!) **The wall of the city had twelve foundations, and on them were the names of the twelve apostles of the Lamb.** (Rev. 21: 12-14). Oooh, I was so excited showing it off to John that I began praising the Lamb (in tongues). **The twelve gates were twelve pearls, each gate made of a single pearl. The street of the city was of pure gold, like transparent glass.** (Rev. 21: 21).

The glass street was a cool feature as well, because the "saved" who get to look down through it can see down into Hell and watch all their friends and relatives who did not listen to them. They are down there in the Lake of Fire, frying away for time and eternity. And will the ransomed care? It is hard for me to know, as I rarely interact with the Earthlings, except to check their papers, and match them up against the record in "The Lamb's Book of Life" wherein are contained the names of all the born-again Christians, who are the only inhabitants of the big cube. None of those other folks are allowed. We all get to look down and pity them—especially those who never even heard of Jesus and his sacrifice on the cross for them. They are damned, as are the *true* baddies, like Hitler, Mao Tse Tung, Jerry Falwell and Pol Pot. It really doesn't matter much at this point for them, as they are all dumped into the lake based solely on whether or not they accepted Jesus into their heart during their lifetimes. All the popes, Catholics, Buddhists and Muslims are also floating in the lake. There are no rewards there—just punishments.

The Christians, however, in the city, get rewards commensurate with their deeds while on Earth. They get to live in better neighborhoods in the cube based on their "good works" while alive. Many of the lesser districts in the cube are populated by baby Christians, those who accepted Christ, but died too young to fulfill their earthly destinies to serve God and lead others to him. Their accomplishments on Earth were small, alas, so their rewards in the cube are likewise rather humble. But also, many Christians who lived "good lives" on Earth still end up living in more simple houses, because they never actually witnessed to others, leading them to a "saving knowledge" of Christ, which is the ultimate criterion for greatness in the heavenly cube. They are really not entitled to real "mansions." They do get bungalows, though, and for that they are grateful, though they will realize forever that they should have worked harder while on Earth.

Meanwhile, in Heaven itself where God lives with Jesus, Mother Mary and the heavenly host, the angels continue to timelessly chant: Holy, Holy, Holy and recite the Doxology. The endless prayer meeting goes on and on and on. God sits on his golden throne with Jesus at his right hand. Now and then they wander over to visit the cube (sometimes together and sometimes separately). The munchkins who inhabit the cube get all excited when either of them shows up unannounced. The little people, the munch-Christians, also get surprise visits from other angels as well, and they giggle and titter in delight when angels like Glenda, the Good Witch of the East, arrive in a bubble. That is so special as they know that she is not a witch at all, but an angel herself :-) God has his archangels as well who get to visit the cube from time to time to see the munch-Christians in their happy cubical home in the starless sky.

Often they are accompanied by flocks of flying putti—little winged souls of dead children who died before the age of accountability. They died as infants, so never developed a sense of self (and thus, sin). So they get to fly and flutter around the Mercy Seat forever and ever and visit the happy campers in the cube now and then.

And swimming around in the holy aura are the souls of the unbor
still-born and the aborted. Those little souls are tiny, but God loves
of them equally. No favorites there. Those little "babies" were never
born, so they never made it down to Earth in the first place. But they are
precious in his sight nonetheless. They spin around and around swirling
in a holy sea of love and light. Hallelujah.

So, as you see, the heavenly cube is a busy place. But there are no
sinners or unrighteous ones in the cube. **And there is no temple in the
city, because the Lord God Almighty and the Lamb are its temple.
The city does not need the sun or moon to shine on it, for the glory of
God gives it light, and the lamb is its lamp. Nothing impure will ever
enter it, nor anyone who does what is shameful or deceitful, but only
those whose names are written in the Lamb's Book of Life.** (Rev. 21:
22, 27). And how is God going to rest assured that none of those impure
souls will ever look upon or defile that book? He has put a flaming sword
(formerly guarding the Garden of Eden) flashing back and forth in front
of it so than no undeserving Earthlings will ever even get near it!

The End :-)

Proof

Made in the USA
Columbia, SC
04 November 2017